THE UNLEASHED

THE UNLEASHED

THE SEQUEL TO *THE HAUNTED*

DANIELLE VEGA

RAZORBILL

RAZORBILL

An imprint of Penguin Random House LLC, New York

alloyentertainment

Produced by Alloy Entertainment
30 Hudson Yards, 22nd fl.
New York, NY 10001

First published in the United States of America by Razorbill,
an imprint of Penguin Random House LLC, 2020

Copyright © 2020 by Alloy Entertainment

Visit us online at penguinrandomhouse.com

LIBRARY OF CONGRESS CATALOGING-IN-PUBLICATION DATA
Names: Vega, Danielle, author.
Title: The unleashed / Danielle Vega.
Description: New York : Razorbill, [2020] | Series: The haunted ; book 2 | Audience: Ages 14+.
Summary: "Hendricks discovers that even though Steele House is gone, the hauntings in Drearfield are far from over—and it's up to her to stop them"—Provided by publisher.
Identifiers: LCCN 2020002315 | ISBN 9780451481498 (hardcover)
ISBN 9780451481504 (ebook)
Subjects: CYAC: Ghosts—Fiction. | Demonology—Fiction. | Friendship—Fiction.
Dating (Social customs)—Fiction. | Family life—New York (State)—Fiction.
New York (State)—Fiction.
Classification: LCC PZ7.1.V43 Unl 2020 | DDC [Fic]—dc23
LC record available at https://lccn.loc.gov/2020002315

Printed in the United States of America

1 3 5 7 9 10 8 6 4 2

Design by Kristin Boyle
Text set in Adobe Jenson Pro

THE UNLEASHED

PROLOGUE

THE CLOCK BESIDE SAMANTHA DAVIDSON'S BED READ 3:17 A.M.
Then 3:18 a.m.

3:19 a.m. 3:20.

9:22.

Samantha blinked. The clock didn't read 9:22, of course. It read
3:21. She groaned. Her eyelids felt gluey. Heavy. Forty-nine was too
old for insomnia, she thought. Her body wouldn't be able to take
much more of this. But whenever she closed her eyes and tried to tell
her spinning brain to just *shut up* and go to sleep, the still, dark world
around her seemed to . . .

Change.

It was only small things. The little dorm room where she slept
was already small and stuffy, but when her eyes were closed, she could
swear that the walls inched a little closer, that the ceiling sunk lower,
that the floor beneath her narrow twin bed shifted in place. The air
felt heavy. It felt like someone was holding their breath, watching her.

Her heart beat hard against her chest. She opened her eyes again,
fumbling beneath the sheets until her fingers touched the handle of
the knife she kept tucked between her mattress and box spring.

It was only a butter knife. Longwood Farm didn't allow its residents
anything sharper than that. But still. It made her feel better, safer. A butter knife could do a lot of damage, if you put enough muscle behind it.

1

Samantha curled her fingers around the cool metal handle and, without realizing what she was doing, began to hum under her breath. The words to an old Prince song floated through her head.

The woman in the bunk next to her groaned and turned over in her sleep. She was new to the community, in for depression. Samantha was in for schizoaffective disorder. Technically. What she really had wasn't so easily diagnosed.

She pressed her lips together, heat rising in her cheeks. She'd had that song stuck in her head for more than thirty years. She hardly even noticed when she started humming it, anymore.

Stop it, she told herself. *Go to sleep.*

She closed her eyes.

Maybe I'm just too . . .

She opened her eyes. She'd definitely heard that. Had she started humming again? A glance at the next bunk told her no, she hadn't. Her roommate was now fast asleep, mouth slightly open, snoring softly, even as the music filled the room and grew louder, practically pulsing off the walls, and drifting down the hall.

Samantha sat up, looked toward the door. She squinted. Just there, in the inch of space between the bottom of the closed door and the scarred, wooden floorboards, she saw a kind of dizzy, shifting light. It danced across the floor outside her dorm, casting off rainbow shards of color.

Samantha felt a bead of sweat drip down her back to the base of her spine.

That light . . . It was like the light of a disco ball.

She put one foot on the floor, and then the other.

It's not real, she told herself. *It's the disease, it's all in your head.* Her doctors had spent thirty-two years drilling those lies into her, and she'd never once believed them, so it was hard to convince herself that they were true now.

She crept toward the door and pressed her ear to the wood.

The music was still out there. *Maybe I'm just like my father . . .*

All in your head, she told herself again. She tightened her grip on the little butter knife. *Or maybe you're dreaming. Maybe you finally fell asleep, and now you're dreaming of your senior prom . . .*

That would've been a logical thing to think, except that Samantha had barely slept in over three decades, and when she had, she'd never dreamed.

Something moved over her shoulder. It was light as a feather's brush, barely there at all. Samantha flinched and went to swat it away, thinking a bug must've gotten in through the window.

But it wasn't a bug. It was a single piece of confetti. Samantha held it on the tip of her finger and thought of *him*. His terrible face, his rasp of a voice.

I'll be back for you.

Acid rose in her throat. She pushed the door open and stepped into the hall.

Samantha Davidson had lived at Longwood Farm her entire adult life, and she knew every inch of its halls by heart. Tonight, they were different. Blue and purple streamers hung from the ceiling, and confetti blanketed the floor. It was the same shiny, silvery confetti that had landed on Samantha's shoulder back in her dorm. Empty plastic cups rolled along beside the walls, giving Samantha the feeling that other people had been here, that she'd just missed them, and now they were waiting for her somewhere deeper in the building. A disco ball spun above, sending light dancing around her.

Maybe I'm . . . Samantha's pulse thudded in her ears. She sensed movement and whirled around to look down the dark corridor behind her. There was nothing, and yet there was a strange twitch in the corner of her eye, like whatever was there had leapt back into the shadows the moment she'd turned.

Her right hand was sweating around the handle of her knife. She switched it to her left and went to wipe her palm against her cotton robe—then froze.

She was no longer wearing her robe. Instead, a white gown with tiered skirts floated around her feet, the hem dragging along the floor. Her arms and shoulders were bare, and when she went to touch her hair, she found that it'd been twisted into a complicated bun.

Her legs swayed with fear. She could hardly keep hold of her knife. Suddenly, she realized what was happening. After thirty-two years of waiting, it was finally time. The taste of dread filled her mouth, but there was nothing she could do. It was much too late.

She turned and he was there. It was as though he had appeared from the darkness, shadows still curling around his arms and legs, caressing him. His eyes were lit with a black, murderous glow, and his mouth was twisted in a familiar, garish grin.

He had his head bowed, and Samantha knew he was preparing to run full tilt toward her. She had a split second to decide what to do: either she could let him take her, or she could run, too.

Just as he took his first step, she turned and raced for the opposite end of the hall.

His voice echoed behind her, barely audible over the music. "I told you I'd be back."

She was running as fast as she could, but it still felt much too slow. It had been so long since she'd run. Her legs were like lead, her joints creaky from not being used.

The floor rumbled beneath her. He was getting closer.

Samantha pushed herself forward, chest bursting, and veered into another hallway. She saw a window: dead end.

No.

She didn't stop running but pumped her legs faster. She was only on the second floor. She could survive that jump. There was no time to struggle with the latch. She threw her arms over her face and barreled into the window.

A shriek escaped her as the sound of breaking glass filled the air. She was falling now, tumbling head over feet. The ground rushed toward her—

She still might've survived. The ceilings in the dorms weren't very high, and so the second floor wasn't that far above the ground. If she'd landed right, she might've gotten away with a broken wrist or a sprained ankle.

But Samantha was still holding the butter knife. As she spun toward the ground, she struggled to get her hands beneath her, to cushion the fall and, in doing so, she managed to arrange the knife so that it pointed directly beneath her ribs. When she landed, the ground pushed the blade right through skin and muscle, between two of her ribs and through her chest.

She released a single, dull *ah* as the knife cut into her. She opened and closed her mouth, blood oozing up between her teeth. She was surprised by the feeling that flooded through her: not horror but relief.

It had happened finally, and now she didn't have to dread it anymore. Now she didn't have to worry about anything. It was time to sleep.

Seconds later, she was gone.

Above, moonlight glinted off the broken glass still clinging to the window frame. But the hall inside was dark.

Three months later . . .

CHAPTER
1

HENDRICKS BECKER-O'MALLEY AND PORTIA RUSSELL HUDDLED inside Raven's bedroom, the entire Drearford High track team crowded around them, all of them singing in off-key, faltering voices.

"Happy birthday, dear Raven . . ."

Portia held out a giant cookie cake from Mae's Treats & Things, the words HAPPY SEVENTEENTH, RAVEN written across the chocolate chips in strawberry-pink frosting. This was the moment that the birthday girl herself should've leaned over the cake, one hand holding back her glossy black hair, the flickering candlelight making her skin all glowy and Instagram-perfect. They should've clapped and cheered as she blew out the candles, her eyes closed for a second longer than necessary as she made a wish for her seventeenth year.

But none of that was going to happen, because the birthday girl was in a coma.

Raven was lying in the middle of the room, in a hospital bed her mother had managed to rent from the Drearford Medical Center, where she worked as a nurse practitioner. Raven's skin was pale and gray, and her long black hair—hair that she had always taken so much pride in—was tied up in a messy knot on top of her head, out of the way of the tubes trailing into her mouth and nose. Raven wasn't wearing her octagon-shaped glasses, and her blue, paper-thin pajamas looked somber compared to the brightly colored vintage clothes and beaded jewelry Hendricks was used to seeing her in.

Hendricks shifted her stance as she stared down at her friend. It was hard to keep her fake smile fixed in place. Three months ago, Raven had been badly hurt at a party at Hendricks's old house, and she'd been in a coma ever since. It was impossible for Hendricks not to feel responsible.

"Happy birthday to *you*," they finished together.

Machines beeped around them, sounding ominous in the sudden silence that filled the room.

After a long, awkward beat, Portia cleared her throat. "O-*kay*," she said, her voice a touch too cheery. "Let's blow out the candles and make a wish for Raven! Hendricks? A little help?"

Hendricks felt a jolt move through her as every set of eyes in the room fixed on her face. Did her smile look okay? She didn't want to look too happy, but she didn't want to look as miserable as she felt, either. Her cheeks felt suddenly stiff, her smile comically wide.

She leaned forward with Portia, and the two of them blew out the candles together, plunging the room in darkness. People cheered and clapped, but it was that kind of fake cheering that was worse than if they'd just stayed silent.

Hendricks gritted her teeth to keep from shivering as Portia fumbled with the lamp by Raven's bed. She was *freezing*. It shouldn't even be this cold—they were inside, after all—but Raven's mom kept the window cracked open so Raven could get some fresh air, and Hendricks hadn't dressed appropriately for the forty-degree day.

It had been the kind of clear, sunny May morning that tricked you into thinking spring was finally here. Hendricks had taken one look outside, at the bright, beaming sun and Technicolor-blue sky, and pulled her favorite vintage jean jacket out of storage without bothering to check the weather. She'd even felt a brief lift of optimism as she'd tugged on a pair of red Converse sneakers without any socks. Her first horrible gray winter in Drearford was behind her.

Maybe today, *finally*, things would start to feel a little better.

Her good mood had lasted exactly as long as it had taken to walk the half block from her mom's car to Raven's house, shivering like crazy the whole time, because it might be *sunny*, but it was still *cold*.

Once inside, she found that the only people who'd shown up to Raven's big birthday party were Portia; Portia's girlfriend, Vi; Connor; and Connor's entire track team.

Looking around, her eyes ticking off the tight smiles and distant expressions of the rest of the track team, Hendricks had a horrible feeling that Connor had bribed them to come.

Which made sense. Raven had a lot of friends at Drearford High, but three months was a long time to stay positive, and Hendricks had noticed that most of those friends had stopped coming by Raven's house to check on her or bringing her up in conversation. Owen, the boy Raven had almost had a thing with, had started seeing someone else, a sophomore girl who wasn't nearly as cool as Raven, in Hendricks's opinion, and everyone else had taken to saying Raven's name in a whispered tone, like she was already dead. If they bothered mentioning her at all.

It was the reason Portia had wanted to throw a party in the first place.

"It'll be festive!" she'd said, her eyes getting that kind of manic gleam they sometimes did when she had an idea Hendricks knew she wasn't going to drop. "It's her seventeenth birthday, we have to do something. We can have streamers and cake and music. We need the party for—for *morale*!"

Whatever the party was doing, it definitely wasn't improving morale. Streamers drooped from the ceiling and spilled in piles onto the floor, along with half a dozen balloons. Hendricks figured Portia had meant for it to look arty, but it just looked sad, like they'd gotten bored of decorating the bedroom halfway through and hadn't bothered finishing. Portia had bought the brightest colors she could find at the Party Town in Hudson—lipstick pinks and neon greens and sunshiny yellows—but the light in here somehow turned it all drab.

Connor and his friends were all shuffling around awkwardly, and there was a ton of hospital equipment crowding Raven's beds, beeping machines and IVs with trailing tubes, and something drooping out from beneath Raven's sheets—something that looked a lot like a *catheter*—that was Hendricks was trying very hard to pretend she hadn't noticed.

Raven looked so much smaller lying there on that cot than she ever had in real life. Hendricks couldn't imagine that she would want any of them standing here, gawking at her, when she was like this.

"Who wants to play Truth or Dare?" Portia asked. Her voice was the same as it had been earlier: a touch too high and fake cheery, the same voice you'd use with a toddler. She alone had dressed up for the occasion, in a sparkly, sequined dress layered over a pair of black leggings and combat boots. She had a cone-shaped hat with the words PARTY PRINCESS written across it in glitter, and she was holding a kazoo.

"Or we could do Never Have I Ever?" Portia offered, when no one said anything. "We don't have any"—she lowered her voice, eyes darting around the room for Raven's mom, who'd been popping in and out all morning—"*booze*, but we could play with cookie cake? That could be cool."

Hendricks couldn't imagine anything sadder than playing Never Have I Ever with *cookie cake* while Raven lay unconscious a few feet away, her mom listening outside the door. She cleared her throat and said in a small voice, "I feel like maybe . . . we don't need games?"

10

She was careful to use the "I feel" language that the counselors at Catskills Therapeutic Expeditions had taught her. It was supposed to keep the other person from feeling attacked. Or something.

Portia's eyes flicked to her, and Hendricks knew she was thinking of camp, too. The two of them and Connor had gone together, at the suggestion of their school counselor, who'd been worried that the three of them hadn't "dealt with their trauma" appropriately. Apparently "wilderness therapy" was a thing. The counselor had sent them all home with brochures for CTE to give to their parents.

The brochures had convinced Hendricks's parents that a little time outdoors was all she needed to get over the death of her ex-boyfriend, whom *they* thought died in a freak fire at their old house. So, while everyone else went somewhere warm for spring break, Portia, Hendricks, and Connor spent a week hiking through the mountains with forty pounds of gear strapped to their backs, and chopping wood, and talking about their feelings around a fire. They weren't allowed to use their phones or the internet or electricity, and they slept on sleeping bags on the ground, not even a tent separating them from the stars.

Hendricks had been surprised to discover that she'd sort of loved it. And it had helped. She and Portia and Connor were all friends again, maybe even closer than they'd been before the accident. Hendricks wasn't *over* what had happened, obviously. But she felt stronger.

Now Portia clapped her hands, grinning like Hendricks had just offered up an amazing idea. "Oh my God! You're so right. We should do music instead. Raven would have wanted music. She *loves* to dance."

Portia whirled around and started digging through her backpack, quickly producing a Bluetooth speaker and her phone.

Hendricks worked a little harder to keep her smile firmly in place. At CTE, she'd learned that Portia tended to get bossier when she was feeling overwhelmed or freaked out. So, when ABBA filled the room a minute later, Hendricks tried very hard to look like she was having fun.

All around the room, people glanced at one another, wondering if they were supposed to dance. Hendricks had been staring off into space, and it was a moment before she realized she hadn't exactly been "staring off into space" so much as "staring directly at Connor's face." Awkward, considering their . . . history.

He was standing right across from her, one eyebrow cocked, waiting for her to notice him. Somehow, he managed to look even taller and blonder and more all-American surrounded by all this sadness.

Camp had been good for them, too. They'd agreed to be friends—just friends. So far, it had been working. They'd come a long way since the party. *The* party, the one where they'd broken things off once and for all, the one where Raven had gotten hurt, and the sky had rained blood, and the skeletons of three teenage boys had dug their way out of her backyard. And Eddie . . .

Hendricks closed her eyes, tears gathering along her lashes. It still hurt every time she thought about it. This was the one thing camp hadn't helped her work through. It had been three months since Eddie died and still she couldn't make herself believe he was really gone. She kept expecting to see him standing at some sidewalk corner, leather jacket thrown over his shoulder, eyes dark and hooded, watching her. She'd found herself flinching at the smallest noise, whipping her head around whenever she saw something in her periphery, sure that Eddie would be there.

But he wasn't there. Eddie had been buried in the Drearford Cemetery on a miserable, rainy Monday morning. Hendricks had stood on the frozen ground in her one black dress, watching Eddie's mother cry while his casket was lowered into the earth, his dad's arms wrapped loosely around her as he tried not to break down himself. Hendricks had looked from Eddie's gravestone to the two just beside them.

Eduardo Ruiz

Maribeth Ruiz

Kyle Ruiz

Three children. All of them dead.

Thinking about it now, Hendricks felt a lump forming in her throat. She pressed her knuckles to her lips and swallowed, her breath hitching. The boy next to her—Blake, she thought his name was—glanced over, frowning.

Time to go, she thought. Portia would just have to understand.

"Excuse me," she murmured, ducking past Blake, toward the door. The room didn't seem cold anymore. It was hot now, the air heavy and thick. She couldn't breathe.

She stepped into the hallway and was halfway to the door when she heard her name.

"Hendricks! Wait." *Connor*.

Hendricks swallowed, her eyes trained on Raven's front door. She wanted to be alone right now, so she could cry in peace, but Connor had been a real friend to her at camp. She couldn't just blow him off.

Slowly, she turned around. "Hey."

"Hey," Connor said. "I, uh, just wanted to see how your hands were feeling."

Hendricks smiled, despite herself, and rolled her eyes. Back at camp, Connor had taught her how to chop wood, but he'd forgotten to make her wear gloves, and she'd gotten these massive, gross blisters all over her palms and fingers. Of course, the blisters had healed weeks ago.

"They're good," she said. "No thanks to you."

"Hey, it's not my fault your city-girl hands aren't used to hard work," Connor shot back. His lips twitched from a smile to a frown and then back to a smile again, and Hendricks wondered if he was doing the same calculation that she'd done earlier: Was it okay to smile at a time like this?

She felt suddenly exhausted.

Connor shook his head, the grin falling from his face. He looked just as tired as she felt. "This is weird, isn't it? Being back."

Hendricks nodded. "Tell me about it."

"I keep waiting for it all to feel real," Connor added. "It's like every morning, I wake up and I have to remind myself that Raven's in a coma, and Eddie . . ." He trailed off, his cheeks blazing. "Sorry," he murmured. "I know it's not like that for you."

Hendricks bit her lip, saying nothing. They'd talked about this at CTE. This had all seemed "real" to Hendricks the moment it'd happened. Much, much too real.

She had a sudden flash of memory: standing in a long line of people wearing black, dropping a handful of dirt over Eddie's casket, rain drizzling around her. Once again, tears pricked the corners of her eyes, only she wasn't so sure she'd be able to stop them this time. She blinked. Time to go.

"I really should—" she started, at the same time that Connor said, "Listen, I just wanted to—"

They both stopped talking. Hendricks nodded at Connor. "You go," she said.

"This might sound kind of weird," Connor said, "but I, uh, I just wanted to say that I'm still here."

Hendricks stared at a freckle on Connor's forehead because she knew that if she looked him in the eye, she would break down. "Thanks."

"I know we aren't at camp anymore," he continued, "but ... we can still talk. Or chop wood, if you want. My parents have an old shed out back that they're always trying to get me and my brothers to bust up into firewood."

Hendricks felt her lip twitch. "Trying to get me to do your chores for you?"

Connor scoffed. "Like a city girl could even handle my chores," he teased, and Hendricks socked him on the shoulder.

Connor flinched, feigning pain as he rubbed the spot where she'd hit him. "Anyway," he added. "I'm still here. That's all I wanted to tell you. See you later, friend."

Hendricks stiffened. *Friend*, Connor had said. She suspected that he still had feelings for her, that being her friend was the last thing he wanted. And yet, he was willing anyway, without her even having to ask. For the first time all morning, something like warmth spread through her chest. It reminded her of how she'd felt when she'd looked outside and saw the sun shining. *Maybe things will be okay.*

"Thanks," she said, reaching for the door. "That means a lot."

Her mom's old Subaru was parked at the corner. Hendricks ducked her head against the early spring wind, huddling down in her jacket as she speed-walked toward it. Tears streamed down her face—for Eddie, for Raven, for everything—but at least the wind did a good job of blowing them away. By the time she reached the car, she was dry-eyed, and she felt almost normal. Almost.

Through the trees, she could just make out the roof of the hospital where, a few months ago, her brother had been fitted with a cast. Another accident courtesy of the Steele House ghosts, she thought with a shudder. She was still so grateful that it hadn't been a casualty.

Her hands felt frozen as she dug around in her purse for her car keys and awkwardly shoved them into her door's lock. From the corner of her eye she saw a twitch of movement, a figure all in white.

She jerked her head up. Her keys slipped from her grip, hitting pavement, but she didn't bother dropping to her knees to grope around for them. She felt as though she were falling, even though the ground was steady beneath her. She wanted to grasp hold of something, to regain her balance.

Eddie?

Her heartbeat pounded in her ears. It took a moment for the world to right itself. She scanned the trees. A cloud had passed overhead, sending a beam of sunshine blazing into the woods, like a sign from heaven.

Staring into the sun, Hendricks's heartbeat began to still. There was nothing there. She shielded her eyes and stared for a moment longer noticing as she did that there was something off about the trees themselves.

It was May, and most of the trees in Drearford had started awakening for spring. They had fresh leaves shivering from their branches, and there were birds poking around their roots, looking for worms.

But these trees were still bare. And more than that . . . their bark looked strangely ashen, almost diseased. The dirt surrounding their roots was dry and hard and black.

Hendricks shivered and looked away. She couldn't say exactly why, but it seemed wrong to look at those trees directly, like staring at someone who was badly ill.

Those trees . . . It was almost like they were dead.

CHAPTER
2

TEN MINUTES LATER, HENDRICKS SAT IN HER MOM'S CAR, fiddling with the buttons on the console.

Something was wrong with the Subaru. She hadn't been able to get the headlights to work on her way home, and for some reason the clock on the dash was stuck on 9:22. She'd tried to hook up her phone to the speakers, like she always did, but it wouldn't work this time. The radio would only play old stuff from the eighties that she didn't recognize.

"This thing is freaking ancient," she muttered.

Sighing, Hendricks locked her mom's car and hurried outside and up the steps to the front door of her new house. It had started to rain on her drive home. Not torrential rain, but the kind of rain that was more like mist, like the air around her was heavy and wet. Dampness crept up her sleeves and under the cuffs of her jeans.

She, her parents, and Brady had moved into the new place more than a month ago. When they were waiting for the bus to leave for camp, Portia's mom got talking to her dad and she told him about a recently available rental next door to their place. Hendricks's family had moved in by the time she was back.

It was a one-story ranch-style home with white siding and no porch. There were four square windows and a two-car garage and a front door that someone had painted robin's-egg blue. A single tree stood in the yard outside, surrounded by a small circle of packed dirt. It was possible that a few flowers might pop up once it got a little warmer.

If you asked a kid to draw a picture of a house, they'd draw *this* house. Hendricks half expected to look up and see that the sun was a yellow circle with a smiley face drawn on it.

When she'd first seen the place, Hendricks had been relieved. Her parents had always been the types of people who liked things to be *interesting* or *unique*. Like Steele House. It had been legit haunted, but her parents wouldn't shut up about the parquet floors and crown molding.

This house was too basic to be haunted.

"Anyone home?" Hendricks called, stepping through the front door. Inside, the house was just as generic as the outside was. Four white walls for the living room. Hall on one side, door to the kitchen on the other. She kicked off her wet boots and hung her jean jacket on a hook by the door.

"We're in the dining room," her dad shouted back.

Dining room was a rather optimistic way of referring to the tiny nook off the equally tiny kitchen. Hendricks crossed the living room and walked through the kitchen, finding her mom; dad; and baby brother, Brady, crammed around the circular Ikea table they'd bought to fit into the small space.

Her parents didn't look up as she walked in. They had coffee and blueprints spread out across the table, and they were bent over, studying them intently. Brady sat in his highchair across from her dad, carefully picking up individual Cheerios from the attached tray and dropping them onto the floor with delight.

"But if what if *this* wall wasn't here?" Hendricks's mom was saying, a deep V creasing the skin between her eyebrows. "Then we could merge the living room and dining room into more of an open greeting area?"

"Isn't that wall load-bearing?" asked Hendricks's dad.

Her mom scratched the top of her head with a pencil and said, "Huh."

Hendricks opened the fridge and closed it again without getting anything out. Her parents still didn't look up, but Brady started bouncing up and down in his high chair, squealing, "Ha-ha! Ha-ha!"

Hendricks beamed at him. *Ha-ha* was what he called her because he couldn't say *Hendricks* yet.

"Hey, bear," she said, and planted a kiss on top of his soft, sweaty baby head. "At least somebody here still loves me."

"Sorry, kiddo, we're just trying to figure this mess out." Hendricks's dad groaned and rubbed his eyes with two fingers, leaning back in his chair. The wood gave an ominous creak beneath his weight. "How was your party?"

"Depressing." Hendricks opened the fridge again, and this time, she took out an apricot La Croix. She messed with the metal tab on top instead of opening it. "Especially since Raven can't even blow out her own candles."

"God, that's heartbreaking," said her mom. "Her poor parents. Did you get a chance to talk to her mother at all?"

"No, she kind of stayed in the other room the whole time."

Her dad shook his head. "I can't imagine what this is like for their family. Didn't you say she had to take some time off work?"

Hendricks nodded. The only reason Raven wasn't required to stay at the hospital until she regained consciousness was because her mother was a nurse practitioner and knew how to take care of her at home. Portia told her that Raven's mom had taken a leave of absence from the hospital so she could care for her daughter around the clock.

Her mother stood and began moving coffee cups off the table so she could roll the blueprints up. "We should really do something for that family," she said. "Bring them a casserole maybe."

Hendricks nodded absently, but she was looking at the blueprints now. "What are those?"

"Do you want coffee, honey?" Her mom slid the blueprints onto the top of the fridge, her movements a touch more hurried than they'd been a moment ago. "We have that disgusting creamer you like. Hazelnut—"

"You're trying to change the subject and you're being super obvious about it." Another technique she'd picked up from CTE: being direct was better than being passive aggressive. Still, from the look on her mom's face, she thought she might've struck a nerve. Hendricks rolled her lip between her teeth, gnawing on it anxiously. "So, what's the deal? Are you, like, rebuilding it or something?"

It. Steele House.

Last Hendricks saw, Steele House was little more than a pile of blackened wood on a packed dirt clearing. She'd been hoping it would stay that way.

But those blueprints . . .

"Let's not get into this again," her dad said.

Hendricks crossed her arms over her chest. She could feel her muscles pulling tight, adrenaline pumping through her veins, her whole body gearing up for a fight.

It was a fight they'd already had a couple of times. First, they'd fought about whether to stay in Drearford at all. "Manhattan could be a really exciting way to spend your senior year!" her parents had argued. Like starting her life all over again could be some sort of adventure.

Hendricks didn't want to start over again. She'd made friends here. She had a life here, even after everything that'd happened. But she didn't want to go back to Steele House, either.

That was the part her parents were having a difficult time understanding, that she wanted to stay here, in Drearford, but that she didn't want them—or anyone else, for that matter—to live on the cursed bit of dirt where Steele House had once stood. Even though no part of their old house remained, that patch of land felt . . . tainted somehow. Like the earth itself was haunted.

In the end, they'd compromised. They'd decided to rent this house for the year while Hendricks finished school and they figured out what to do next.

"That place is messed up." Hendricks had to work to keep her voice from shaking. "People *died* there. You can't just let another unsuspecting family move in."

Her dad gave a deep, long-suffering sigh and pinched the bridge of his nose with two fingers. "It's our land, honey," he said, exasperated. "We paid for it. I know you have a bad association with that place, but we're looking at a huge loss if we don't get it back on the market."

"But—"

"This town is having a moment right now. It's on all sorts of best small-town lists," her mother added, cutting her off. "It's not just about recouping our losses. It's about saving for our future."

A million arguments sprung up in Hendricks's mind.

There were more important things than money, for instance, and *if you really cared about the future, you would make sure that house wasn't part of it.*

She opened and closed her mouth, feeling a bit like a fish on dry land. Desperate, dying. She'd tried those arguments before, along with many, many others. Nothing had worked.

Steele House was going to be rebuilt.

"I have some reading to do for history class," she said in a small voice, and drifted into the hall, toward her new, boring bedroom.

As she closed the door behind her, one last reason for leaving the grounds of Steele House alone played in her head. It was the *real* reason she was so staunchly against rebuilding on that land, and it had little to do with protecting the town or saving unsuspecting families from ghosts.

Steele House was where Eddie had taken his final breaths. It was where Hendricks had crouched in the dirt, holding his head in her lap as he died. The grounds of Steele House were sacred. If there was a chance that some small part of Eddie had remained in Drearford after his death, Hendricks knew that was where he would be.

And her parents wanted to cover it in concrete.

Thinking about that, Hendricks heard a roaring noise in her ears. Something deep within her began to shake. If that happened, she might never be able to reach the other side. And Eddie would be lost forever.

CHAPTER
3

HENDRICKS LEANED HER HEAD BACK AGAINST HER BEDROOM door and took a moment to breathe.

Steele House is going to be rebuilt, she thought.

She opened her mouth in a silent scream. She dug her hands into her hair and slowly slid down the door to the floor. It was hard to explain how she felt just then. Everything was falling apart, and the only way she could stop *herself* from falling apart was to curl into a very small ball and hold her body very close.

A minute passed, and then another. Hendricks didn't fall apart. She breathed in through her nose, and slowly, slowly, her heartbeat returned to normal. Her muscles unfurled.

Steele House is going to be rebuilt, she thought again.

This time, the need to scream wasn't quite so intense. Progress.

She decided to put it out of her head for now. Quietly, she dragged her desk chair across the room and wedged it beneath her doorknob, double-checking to make sure it was firmly in place. She doubted it would stop her parents from coming into her room if they really wanted to, but it might give her a second of warning before they did.

She dropped to her knees and dug under her bed for a cardboard box. She'd written the words *old clothes* across the top in Sharpie so her parents wouldn't snoop around inside.

It wasn't old clothes, though. Opening the box, Hendricks found every book she'd bought on the occult, her blessed salts and crystals, a Ouija board, and some black candlesticks and half-burned sage.

This stuff was all from Ileana's shop: Magik & Tarot. Since Eddie died, Hendricks had become something of a regular. She'd gotten into the habit of swinging by the shop most days after school, picking through the crowded shelves and tables, desperate to try something—anything—to make contact with the spirit world.

So far, every prayer, every spell, *everything* she'd tried had failed.

Hendricks dug to the very bottom of the box, finding Eddie's Zippo lighter. She flipped it, watching the little blue flame leap to life between her fingers. Then, with a sigh, she closed it again, and the flame went out.

She'd found the lighter two months ago, on the sidewalk in front of Steele House. It had seemed to appear from thin air, and at the time Hendricks had been positive that Eddie himself had left it, that he'd been trying to make contact with her from . . . well, wherever he was.

Now, though . . .

Hendricks released a heavy sigh, shoulders slumping. Now she felt foolish. If it was possible for Eddie to waltz out of the spirit world or wherever for long enough to leave his lighter behind, shouldn't it also be possible for him to talk to her? Or leave a note? *Something?* In the three months since his death, there hadn't been so much as a whisper of him. Hendricks was starting to get desperate.

She studied the various objects for a long moment before choosing a pack of tarot cards and Eddie's lighter, and setting herself up at her desk.

Hendricks wasn't very good at tarot. In fact, her current deck was still stiff and unused.

Ileana told her she needed to "make herself familiar" with her deck by shuffling and choosing cards daily. But Hendricks felt dumb doing that, so she'd only ever pulled the deck out on days like today, when she wanted to talk to Eddie so badly she thought she might explode.

She shook the cards into one hand and placed them to the side. Then she took up Eddie's lighter and held it in her hand for a long moment, letting the metal grow warm from her skin. Her eyes closed. As Ileana had instructed, she tried to conjure an image of Eddie in her mind.

He was wearing his familiar worn black T-shirt and faded jeans, his skin warm and soft, his dark eyes locked on hers. She saw him cock one of his thick eyebrows at her, the way he did when she said something he thought was ridiculous or funny. She could practically reach out and touch the faint spray of freckles on his nose.

She held the memory of him in her head until she could trace every line of his face.

And then, the memory changed.

Eddie's skin went horribly, deathly pale. Blood coated his face and clumped between his eyelashes. Though his dark eyes gazed up at her, they couldn't seem to focus on her face. They didn't seem to actually *see* her at all. She was holding him, sobbing, begging him not to leave her as fire and smoke surrounded them.

His lips parted, like he was going to say something, and Hendricks's heart went still inside of her chest as she waited for his next words, his last words. But the muscles in his face failed before he could utter them. He was just . . . gone.

A choked sob escaped Hendricks's lips. Her hand flew to her mouth, fingers trembling. This was how Eddie had looked the last time she'd seen him, dying in her arms.

She closed her eyes and, shuddering, pushed the image from her head.

She opened his lighter and placed it on the desk in front of her, the flame flickering. Ileana once told her that a candle was the only thing you really needed to communicate with the dead. You could ask yes or no questions and watch the flame. If it grew longer, the answer was *yes*. If it flickered, the answer was *no*.

Hendricks swallowed and said, her voice raspy, "Eddie? Can you hear me?"

For a very long moment, the flame stayed still.

Hendricks pressed her lips together. They felt dry, tight. Rain pelleted her window and somewhere farther into the house she could make out the rise and fall of her parents' voices. She kept her eyes on the flame, not daring to breathe. She curled her fingers into her desk, her fingernails pressing down on the wood—

Come on.

Slowly, the flame stretched up, up toward the ceiling.

Yes.

Air whooshed out past Hendricks's lips, a sudden exhale. *Yes*, she thought again, and bit back a smile. Blood rushed into her face, making her feel suddenly warm. He could hear her.

"I want to talk to you, okay?" she said, her eyes trained on the flame. While she watched, she shuffled the tarot cards in her hands, moving slowly, trying to imbue the deck with *intention*, like Ileana had taught her. "I need to know you're okay." Then, hesitating, she added, "I—I miss you."

Her voice cracked on the word *miss*, and she closed her eyes, her hands going still. The cards felt so stiff between her fingers. She took a deep breath and tried again.

"Just tell me where you are, okay? Tell me if you're all right?"

The flame stayed still.

Hendricks flicked the lighter closed and placed three cards before her. It was the simplest tarot layout there was, and the only one she really knew how to do. The position of the cards was like a question you were asking, and the cards themselves were the answer. The positions of the three-card layout could represent anything you wanted them to. *Past, Present, Future* was a popular interpretation. Another was *Current Situation, Obstacle, Advice*.

Hendricks liked to think that they represented *Body*, *Mind*, and *Soul*.

The flame flickered as she leaned closer, her eyes moving over the pictures on the three cards.

The first was the *Death* card, in the body position.

Hendricks felt a jolt move through her as she glanced at it, recognizing it immediately. It showed a sketchy black drawing of a skeletal bird, a few raggedy feathers still attached to its bony wings. Hendricks hated this card, but she supposed it made sense. She'd asked where Eddie's body was, and Eddie's body was dead. There was no other way to say that.

Again, she saw Eddie's dead face staring back at her. Those lifeless eyes, the pale cast to his skin . . . A strange feeling slithered up her spine. This time, it was harder to push the memories of his face from her mind.

It might be true that Eddie was dead, but that didn't mean she had to like it.

She moved to the next card, the one in the *mind* position.

This card showed two crossed swords at the center, a burning yellow sun between them. Hendricks frowned. She'd never gotten the Two of Swords before. She quickly located the card's meaning in her booklet:

Indecision, it read. *Stalemate. You are facing a challenging decision but are unclear of which option to take.*

Something prickled up Hendricks's neck. This was important,

she realized, tracing the edge of the card with one finger. Eddie might be dead, but he still had a decision to make. So, what was it?

Her heartbeat picked up, becoming a steady thrum in her chest. Could he be trying to decide whether to move on, to whatever came after death? Or come back here, to her? It seemed possible. What other decisions were the dead asked to make?

She looked to the final card, the card in the most important position of the layout. *Soul.* As her eyes moved over it, her heartbeat went still.

She'd gotten this card before.

The image was drawn in the same sketchy style as the others. It depicted a strange, monstrous creature, a claw with maggots crawling around it, two eyeballs rolling to either side. The claw creature was being struck with swords, nine in total.

Hendricks's skin crept as she considered it. She didn't have to look up the meaning of this card. The Nine of Swords stood for deep turmoil and anguish. It meant that things had gotten as bad as they possibly could.

Hendricks pulled the card almost every time she did a reading. It was the reason she hated coming back to this deck.

Things can't get any worse, the card kept telling her.

But it was wrong. Every day they got a little worse.

Hendricks slapped a hand over the card. Her shoulders drew tight around her ears, and her entire body slumped.

A choked sob erupted from her lips—and then, abruptly, it became a groan of frustration. She was *so sick* of being sad. She'd been sad for three months.

Annoyed felt better.

For a moment, she allowed herself to imagine that this was all part of some elaborate trick Eddie was playing, to mess with her. Anger flared through her.

"Damn it, Eddie," she gasped, clenching her eyes shut. Tears were gathering behind her closed lids, making her eyelashes sticky.

She sniffed, blinking them away. "We both know that ghosts are real, and you're the most stubborn person I've ever met. I don't believe for a *second* that you can't talk—"

Hendricks heard a buzz of electricity and smelled something like burned-out matches. And then, darkness.

The light bulb in her desk lamp had blown. The room was now pitch-black.

She felt a lift of hope. She snatched Eddie's lighter off her desk and held it before her. "Is someone there?"

Her voice shook, which bothered her. This is what she'd been waiting for, after all—contact with the other side. There was no reason to be afraid.

It's just Eddie, she told herself. *He's just trying to talk to you.*

But she was suddenly very aware of the rasping sound her breath made as it moved up her throat, and the way her chest seemed to constrict with every beat of her heart.

She held the lighter up higher, illuminating the four walls of her bedroom, her door, her furniture. Her palms had started to sweat, leaving the warm metal of Eddie's lighter slick beneath her fingers.

She watched the flame coming from the lighter. "Tell me where you are," she said, steeling herself. "Tell me that you're okay."

The flame flickered, steadily, mocking her.

And then, a sound.

It was like . . . *scratching.*

Hendricks turned around on her chair, scanning the shadows

in her bedroom for the source of the noise. This room was so much smaller than her room back at Steele House had been, barely large enough for her twin bed, narrow dresser, and tiny desk. Hendricks hadn't bothered putting anything up on the walls or displaying any photos of her friends. Half of her stuff was still in boxes.

It didn't take her long to look over everything in the room, to make sure it was all where it was supposed to be. Dresser drawers all closed, pajamas piled at the foot of the bed, objects from Ileana's shop scattered over the rug. The lighter's flame threw strange shadows over everything. When Hendricks moved her head, she thought she saw something flickering in the corner of her eye, but when she jerked back around again, the room was still.

Fear prickled up her neck. She didn't dare move, or breathe—

Scratch . . .

Scratch . . .

She stood so quickly she set her chair rocking back on two feet. Fear flickered like a match inside of her.

"Eddie?" she said, out loud. "Was that you?"

Silence. And then the scratching started up again, so faint that Hendricks wondered if she was imagining it. It seemed to be coming from the box of tarot cards on her desk.

Hendricks picked the box up, frowning. It was empty. Her tarot cards were scattered across her desk, and there wasn't anything else inside that could've been making the noise.

And yet—

She heard another low scrape, like a fingernail picking at cardboard. Heart hammering inside of her chest, she lifted the box to her ear.

She'd been right. There, muffled deep inside the box, was the sound of something scratching. Hendricks held her breath, the box pressed close to her head.

Something thin and hard brushed against her ear.

Hendricks jerked the box away. A sharp twist of fear blotted out everything else. Her hands felt thick and clumsy as she lifted Eddie's lighter, illuminating three long white fingers. They stayed curled around the edge of the box for a split second, and then they slithered back into the shadows and disappeared.

Hendricks gasped and threw the box to the floor. She felt like she couldn't breathe. She'd caught only the briefest glimpse of those fingers, but she'd seen that the skin along the knuckles was scaly, and long strips of it had peeled away from the bone. The nails had been curved and yellow and *sharp*.

A blood-curdling scream ripped from her lungs. Her scream was still echoing through the room when, in her ear, she heard a rasp of a voice, deep and gravelly:

"He'll be back for you."

CHAPTER
4

THE SUN DIDN'T BOTHER COMING OUT AT ALL THE NEXT morning. Cold air whipped into Hendricks's T-shirt, causing it to billow and flap against her goose bump–covered skin. She wrapped her arms around her chest, trying not to shiver. Fresh green weeds sprouted up between the sidewalk cracks, winking at her, as she made her way around the corner.

Dead Guy Joe, Drearford High's favorite coffee shop, crouched at the end of the street. Against the thin gray sky, it looked more like an abandoned garage than a place to buy food. Dirt clouded the windows, and a rusted hubcap rested against the concrete staircase leading up to the front door. Hendricks thought it was supposed to be art.

She pushed the door open to a small room crowded with thrift store tables and cracked vinyl chairs. The owner, Mike, leaned over the coffee counter, studying a crossword puzzle from beneath the brim of his battered straw fedora. He looked up when Hendricks walked in, a rare smile flashing across his deeply creased face.

"Morning, Mike," Hendricks called, and Mike tucked the pencil behind his ear and grabbed a cardboard cup off the leaning stack, pouring a cup of black coffee without waiting for her to order. Mike didn't understand anyone who didn't drink their coffee thick as tar. He only owned an espresso machine because the afternoon baristas had more patience for whipping up macchiatos and lattes.

Hendricks usually tried to force Mike to talk to her while he got her coffee, but today her mind was reeling. She thought of the hand reaching out of her box of tarot cards, those scabby, dead fingers brushing against her ear . . .

Her parents had come running after she'd screamed, but she'd told them that she'd just overreacted to seeing a spider. They'd believed her, but they still stuck around for a while to make sure everything was okay, and after a *long* talk about stress and PTSD, Hendricks had almost been able to convince herself that she'd just imagined the creepy fingers and strange voice.

Almost.

He'll be back for you, she thought, and shuddered so violently that Mike looked up from her coffee, frowning. She flashed him a tight smile, thinking, *Who?*

Eddie?

And then, her stomach twisting, *Grayson?*

Grayson was another ex-boyfriend. He'd been manipulative and emotionally abusive, and he was the reason Hendricks had moved to Drearford in the first place. She'd thought all that was behind her, but now she wondered. Could the voice have been warning her that he was coming back for her finally?

The thought sickened her.

Mike clapped a plastic lid on top of Hendricks's coffee cup, snapping her back to the present. "Thanks," Hendricks said, digging around in her pocket for a few crumpled bills. "And a maple éclair."

Mike got her pastry, and Hendricks balanced the coffee and doughnut bag in one arm, sticking a dollar in his tip jar on her way out the door.

Coffee dribbled out from under the plastic lid and seared the skin on her thumb as she reached for the door, then froze. Connor was outside.

Hendricks stuck her thumb into her mouth, frowning. Was he waiting for her?

She considered weaving to the other side of the shop, so she could go out the back door and spend the rest of her morning obsessing over the fingers and the voice, but at that moment Connor looked up and saw her through the glass.

He waved. She waved back.

You're friends now, she reminded herself, as she pushed the door open and joined him outside. *Stop being weird.*

She knew from experience that this was easier said than done.

"It's May, why the hell is it so cold?" Connor said, rubbing his hands up and down his arms.

"No idea," Hendricks said. Were they really talking about the weather? She glanced around the empty gray sidewalk, hoping Portia would materialize between the parked cars. They'd made tentative plans to meet at Dead Guy before class. "I don't mean to run, but I told Portia—"

"Portia and Vi are making out in the school parking lot," Connor said, a little sheepishly.

Hendricks felt her lips pull tight. *Oh.* "Well, then I'm free as a bird."

For a moment, they walked together in silence. Connor stared at the sidewalk, his hands bunched beneath his armpits. Hendricks studied the lid on her coffee cup. For a fraction of a second, she considered telling Connor about what she'd seen the night before but then immediately decided against it. They'd never spoken about what had happened that night at Steele House. She wasn't sure she wanted to open that Pandora's box just now.

Finally, Connor said, "Okay," on an exhale, air whooshing out from between his lips. And then. Again. "Okay, so here's the deal. Vi and Portia are planning to do the big, romantic prom night thing, but a bunch of other people were thinking of going in, like, a group. Sort of a casual thing, and I wanted to see if you were interested in coming with us. With me."

Hendricks lifted her coffee to her mouth and took a drink to buy some time before she was expected to answer.

The coffee was way too hot, and it burned her tongue.

"Shit," she said, jerking the cup away. Hot coffee spilled onto the sidewalk. "Shit."

Connor stopped walking. "You okay?"

"Yeah, I just burned myself." She pressed her lips together, grimacing. It wasn't a bad burn. She sort of wished it were worse, that blisters had popped up along her lips, or that the coffee had burned right through the layer of skin on the roof of her mouth. She would've had to rush back into the coffee shop then and get some sort of special salve from the first aid kit and maybe suck on an ice cube. Which would've meant that, at least for a little while, she would've be able to dodge Connor's question.

But she didn't have any blisters. Hendricks's mouth was starting to feel better and Connor was standing in front of her, eyebrows raised, and there was no reason at all why she shouldn't give him an answer.

This whole thing would be a lot easier if Connor weren't so cute. Not just cute in the good-looking sense—although he *was* good-looking. Cleft-chin, kind eyes, the usual.

But at CTE, she'd gotten to know another side of Connor. He liked nature and working with his hands, but he was also a tiny bit afraid of the dark. He hated s'mores, which was completely unacceptable and made her want to make him a dozen different types of s'mores, using all different types of chocolate and graham crackers until she found a combo he liked.

He'd played pranks on her and Portia almost every day. Dumb ones. Once, he'd left a fake rubber dinosaur in her sleeping bag. Another time, he followed them on a hike and kept trying to jump out from behind a tree to scare them, only he'd been really loud the whole time, and they could always tell exactly where he was.

He was . . . ridiculous and funny and completely wrong about s'mores.

In other words, he was the sort of guy she should *want* to be with.

But he wasn't Eddie.

Hendricks pulled her eyes away from Connor's and stared, hard, at the crack in the sidewalk. She should tell him no. It was the kind thing to do. She would just be thinking about Eddie at the dance, anyway. Connor deserved someone who wanted to be there with him.

She knew this. And yet, she couldn't quite make the word *no* form on her lips.

"Can I think about it?" she asked.

Not a no. But not a yes, either.

Connor's eyebrows flicked. "It's not a big deal, either way," he said too quickly, his gaze shifting down to his shoes. "Like I said, it's a casual thing. As friends. No big deal either way." He'd already said that.

"Right," Hendricks said.

Connor waved goodbye and took off in the opposite direction. As he walked away, Hendricks noticed that the backs of his ears were tinged red.

I'm such a jerk, she thought, hating herself.

With nothing else to do, Hendricks found herself pushing through the doors to Drearford High thirty minutes before the first bell. For a moment she just stood there, considering the dark hallways, the empty classrooms.

No one was here yet, not even the teachers. Or if the teachers were here, they were hidden away in the teachers' lounge or in their offices, where early-bird students couldn't bother them. There was a light switch to the left of the main doors. Hendricks flipped the switch, watching the cold fluorescents flick on, illuminating faded linoleum and battered locker doors.

For some reason, the light just made the halls feel emptier.

When Hendricks had first started coming to Drearford, Portia and Connor and their friends all congregated at a table in the cafeteria before school. Now that it was warmer, Hendricks noticed that students mostly hung in each other's cars, or nursed coffees at Dead Guy, or milled around outside in the parking lot. No one seemed to go inside early, but Hendricks had no interest in finding out what Portia and Vi were up to in the parking lot, and spending any more time with Connor felt strange now that she'd maybe'd his prom offer.

She tugged her bag farther up her shoulder and began walking toward her locker. Her footsteps echoed off the walls, the vibrations moving through the floors, making the locker doors jangle. A whiff of disinfectant hung in the air, along with the faint smell of food. Meat of some kind? Hendricks wrinkled her nose. The cafeteria workers must be here already, hunched over the stoves in the basement, cooking up lunch.

The light directly above her sparked. And went out.

Hendricks kept walking, unbothered.

Until a second bulb blew.

And then a third.

"The hell?" Hendricks stopped walking and looked up at the ceiling. Every single light bulb she'd walked beneath was now black.

The hair on the back of her neck slowly lifted. She chewed her lip, wondering if she should go back outside, find Portia or Connor or anyone really. Perhaps it had been stupid of her to come here alone, especially after what'd happened last night.

This was *school*. Nothing supernatural had ever happened to her here.

She thought of what she'd seen last night, those dead white fingers reaching out from her box of tarot cards. She'd assumed nothing bad could happen to her in that boring rental house, too. She'd thought the hauntings were only at Steele House.

Stupid, stupid.

She whipped herself around, muscles twitching beneath her light jacket, but she didn't see anything. She took a single, clumsy step backward, hearing her boot scrape across the linoleum. She was afraid to keep walking toward her locker in case more lights burned out, plunging her into total darkness. But she didn't know what would happen if she walked back down the shadowy black hall toward the front doors, either. She pictured those same fingers reaching out from the lockers, stretching toward her, grabbing for her—

She stood, frozen for a long time, dread building. Her eyes darted from one end of the hall to the other. What to do? Where to go?

A cold finger touched the back of her neck and traced down her spine.

Hendricks yelped and spun around, one hand grasping for her neck. "Who's there?" she shouted.

Her own voice echoed down the hall, bouncing off the lockers around her: *Who's there? Who's there?*

And then, in her ear, the same raspy voice she'd heard in her room last night:

"He'll be back for you."

The acid taste of terror flooded Hendricks's mouth. She lurched backward, toward her locker, and another light bulb fizzled and burned out.

"Who?" she shouted into the darkness. "Who will be back for me?"

No response, just eerie silence. Hendricks could feel her pulse thudding in her temples. She had the strange feeling that someone was waiting in the darkness, watching her, peering through the slats of her locker.

She said hesitantly, "Eddie?"

A sudden *bang!* echoed through the halls, and Hendricks whirled around in time to watch the school's front doors fly open. The lights switched back on as a small group of freshmen Hendricks didn't recognize filled the hall, talking and laughing. They cast strange looks at her as they drifted past. Probably wondering what she'd been doing standing here in the dark.

It took a long time for Hendricks's breathing to steady. She didn't know what else to do, so she shuffled toward her locker, the sound of her heart beating in her ears like gunfire. Her knees knocked together as she walked. The ground felt brittle beneath her boots, like thin ice that might crack open at any moment, swallowing her up.

Her fingers moved on autopilot, twisting her combination, fumbling with the latch, pulling the locker door open—

And then, she froze.

There, sitting on the bottom of her locker, was a single rose, its leaves curled like dead fingers, its petals shriveled and black.

CHAPTER
5

HENDRICKS'S FEAR SOURED THROUGHOUT THE DAY, EVENTUALLY curdling into anger. She'd gone three whole months without any contact from the other side. And now she was getting this? Not Eddie but flickering lights and dead flowers and cryptic warnings.

It was seriously messed up.

The anger cropped up in algebra, when Hendricks's teacher asked her if she understood the new formula and Hendricks snapped that she didn't know why they were bothering to memorize this stuff when they could just look it all up on their phones. It followed her to the principal's office, where she sulked and stared off into space while he lectured her about her "attitude" and threatened to call her parents.

And it was still lingering after school, when Portia materialized beside her locker.

"I heard they sent you to Principal Walker's after third," she said.

Hendricks slammed her locker shut. "I don't want to talk about it," she muttered, hitching her backpack up her shoulder. She'd thrown the dead rose away, but the smell of it still lingered in her locker, perfuming all her books. "Except to say that Principal Walker is a sad little man with way too much power."

"Well, duh." Portia's eyes lingered a second longer, concern flickering through them. "Are you sure you're okay?" she asked, in a softer voice. "You look a little . . . freaked."

For a beat, Hendricks considered telling her about the hand and the rose. As she had with Connor, she quickly dismissed the thought. Portia had been so traumatized by the last haunting that she hadn't spoken to Hendricks—or anyone else, for that matter—for weeks. CTE had fixed all that, but Hendricks didn't want to risk losing her again.

"I'm fine," she said. Portia fell in step beside her as they made their way down the hall. She changed the subject to something she knew Portia couldn't resist: *Vi.* "Why didn't you meet me at Dead Guy this morning?"

Portia pressed one hot-pink nail to her hot-pink lips, grinning. "I was . . . busy."

"Busy making out with Vi, you mean?"

Portia's grin vanished. "Who told?"

"Connor. He said you two were going at it in her car."

"We were hardly *going at it*," Portia said. "One kiss, *one*, and it was closed mouth and everything. We just wanted to . . . celebrate."

A blush had risen in Portia's cheeks. Hendricks knew she was supposed to ask what they were celebrating, but she kept her lips tight, making Portia wait for it.

After a moment, Portia glanced at her, looking disappointed. "Aren't you going to ask—"

"What are you celebrating?"

"As of this morning, we're *officially* official."

Hendricks lifted an eyebrow.

"She's my girlfriend," Portia explained. "I'm her girlfriend. We're girlfriends." Portia was bouncing, *actually* bouncing. "Oh my God, Hendricks, things are so good between us right now. You have no idea. It's like she finally wants to be together for real instead of just hooking up at parties when she's drunk."

41

"Lucky you," Hendricks muttered. She didn't mean to sound so annoyed, but she couldn't help it. Portia being all happy and giddy with Vi just made it that much more obvious that she was alone, miserable, and scared.

And then there was all the bouncing. Hendricks wanted to grab her by the shoulders and force her to walk normally.

"Are you psyched about prom planning committee?" Portia asked.

At this, Hendricks managed a real smile. "I am, actually. A little nervous, too." She didn't tell Portia this, but the two feelings were sort of mushed together in her gut, making her feel nauseated.

"Don't be nervous," Portia said. "It's going to be awesome, you'll see. This is exactly what you need."

Hendricks wanted to believe her. Her decision to join the prom planning committee was another thing to come out of CTE. Every night, after they'd finished hiking and fishing and chopping wood, Hendricks, Portia, and Connor and the other kids at camp would all gather around the fire. There, they'd pass a twig covered in ribbons and glitter—called the Feelings Stick—around the circle and talk about their emotions.

It was pretty cheesy. There was no other way to put it. But after a few days you sort of got used to it, and when it was Hendricks's turn with the Feelings Stick, she'd reluctantly admitted that, sometimes, she didn't really feel like she had a personality.

"My ex-boyfriend Grayson was really controlling. He didn't like it when I did things on my own," she'd admitted. For some reason, the mountain air and flickering fire made it easier to say this sort of thing out loud, and Hendricks found that, once she'd started talking, she couldn't stop. "He mostly wanted me to be there for him, like cheering him on at his soccer games, and hanging off his arm at parties and stuff. I was basically a prop. Now that I'm not with him anymore, I don't even know what I'm supposed to like doing."

The counselor had asked her what sort of things she'd been into before Grayson, and Hendricks had told her about how she'd helped out behind the scenes with her old school's theater department. Grayson always thought it was nerdy, and after they'd gotten together, he talked her into quitting. Hendricks still missed it, though. It had been fun.

"Our school musical isn't until fall, but the prom committee needs help with decorations," Portia had pointed out. "I'm prom president, I could probably get you signed up."

Which brought Hendricks here now, feeling nauseated but excited as she made her way into the gym with Portia. She inhaled, deep, pushing the nauseated feeling away. *This is good*, she told herself. It was the *one* thing in her life she was doing just for her, not for ex-boyfriends or ghosts. Or ex-boyfriends who happened to be ghosts.

"I come from a long line of prom presidents," Portia was saying. "It's practically a family tradition."

Hendricks frowned. "Don't you mean prom *queen?*"

"Queen?" Portia huffed. "The queen is nothing but an empty figurehead who stands on stage and wears a pretty crown. The prom *president* has the real power. I get to be in charge of every single facet of the event itself. My mom did it for her class back in '95, and my grandma before her, and my aunt planned the Drearford prom in '86 before she had a mental break and had to be committed." Portia said this with raised eyebrows, like it was something to aspire to.

"Impressive?" Hendricks managed to choke out.

"Since Raven can't help, you can be my vice. Don't worry, it's totally easy. I'll handle everything, you just have to sort of . . . pick up the slack when I can't. Cool?"

Portia pushed the doors to the school gymnasium open. "Hey,

guys!" she called, clapping. There were about twenty other kids gathered in the gymnasium. Most were milling about beneath the basketball hoops, but there were a couple of girls in bright, over-size sweatshirts and leggings crouched on the bleachers. Hendricks frowned at them. Drearford High was pretty small, only about three hundred kids total, and she'd gotten to know almost everyone in the school, but seniors ate lunch off campus, so there were still a few groups of kids whose names she wasn't sure of. The girls were unfa-miliar to her. They looked like Urban Outfitters mannequins come to life.

"I officially call this meeting of the prom planning committee to order," Portia said. "Can everyone gather around?"

The kids that had been standing beneath the basketball hoop huddled closer, but the girls on the bleachers stayed where they were. A new wave of annoyance fluttered through her. Hendricks glanced at Portia, wondering if she was going to call them out, but Portia didn't seem to notice them. Hendricks felt a flicker of curiosity. Maybe they were really popular. Or, like, bad girls. They would have to be if *Portia* was too intimidated to call them out.

"As you all know, Raven is currently recovering from a terrible in-jury, so I've asked Hendricks to step up and assume her duties." Portia motioned to Hendricks and there was scattered applause. Hendricks lifted her hand awkwardly. Bored eyes blinked back at her.

"Okay, first things first. Decorations committee, where are we at?"

A slender boy with Coke-bottle glasses said, "We just placed our Amazon order for basically everything we need for the SS *Drearford* theme, but we could really use some help assembling the balloon arch and decorating king and queen chairs."

"That's great, Oliver," Portia said. "We'll divide up to help you as soon as we're done here. Since the decorations are under control, could you to switch your attention to ordering tickets, invitations, and favors? If you don't have a good stationery place, see me after and I can give the contact info for mine."

Portia flipped to the next page in the binder. "Lydia? You were looking into a DJ, caterer, and photographer?"

A tall brunette with pale skin looked up. "DJ and caterer are booked, but, uh, photographers cost, like, twenty-five hundred dollars? I'm not sure we can actually afford one?"

Hendricks glanced at Portia. Prom with no photographer seemed like a disaster, but Portia just smiled wider and said breezily, "Everyone has cameras on their phones now, anyway. Let's set up a couple of selfie stations and figure out a prom hashtag where everyone can share their pics. Good? Okay, that's all I have for my checklist today. I want all of you to see Oliver to get your decorating assignments. Hendricks and I will take over the chairs. That's all."

Portia clapped again and the rest of the committee scattered. She kept her smile firmly in place until everyone else was focusing on their tasks, and then, to Hendricks's surprise, she pressed a hand to her mouth, her eyes closing tight. It took Hendricks a moment to realize Portia was trying not to cry.

"Are you okay?" Hendricks asked.

"Sorry . . ." Portia sniffed, pulling herself together. "It's just that thing about the photographer made me overwhelmed. Sometimes I feel like I'm the only one who even cares about *any* of this stuff. At least when Raven was here . . ."

Her voice cracked and Hendricks felt a sharp pang of pity. As much as she missed Raven, she knew Portia missed her more. She kept telling herself that Raven was going to be okay, but it had been three months. It was getting harder to stay positive.

"Raven's going to get better," Hendricks told her.

"Yeah, I know." And then, looking around at the other kids in the gym, Portia added, "Do you think they all think I'm a bitch?"

"Of course not!" Hendricks said. Portia gave her a look, and she admitted, "People just don't like strong women."

"I'm not trying to be bossy or whatever. I just want us to have a good prom."

"I know." Hendricks squeezed Portia's shoulder and said, in the most cheerful voice she could manage, "I don't care if you boss me around. What do you need me to do?"

Portia gave her a grateful smile. "The king and queen need thrones for when they're crowned. We have to cover them with glitter and stuff. Make them look regal."

Two tall, wooden chairs stood on the far side of the gymnasium, directly in front of the stage, which was loaded with boxes of ribbons and scattered balloons and tubs of glitter. Portia grabbed a roll of silver and began deftly weaving it around the chair back. When she'd finished, she twisted the remains of the ribbon into an effortlessly jaunty bow.

"See?" she said. "Easy, right?"

Hendricks re-created the bow on the second chair and moved on to the box of glitter, wondering if there was a way to use the silver to make it look like the chairs were all shimmering, like icebergs. That was on theme, wasn't it? Since there were icebergs in the ocean? Or was it tacky because of the *Titanic*?

It was easy work and after several minutes she found her attention shifting to the conversations scattered around her, everyone chattering about decorations and dresses and prom dates, their faces all lit up and worry-free. People were preparing for this party like it was the biggest event of their lives.

Hendricks felt her good mood fading. Her fingers felt suddenly clumsy. She couldn't make the glitter do what she wanted it to do.

She tried to regain her excitement for the iceberg chairs, but instead she found herself thinking about dead fingers touching her neck, her ear. The whispered warning echoing in her head. *He'll be back for you.*

She fumbled the jar of glitter and sent it scattering across the floor. Portia raised an eyebrow.

"Sorry," she muttered. As she tried to scoop the glitter back into the jar she found herself wishing she could be like every other girl in the gym, whose biggest problem was trying to decide between two equally beautiful dresses, or scouring Pinterest for hair inspiration, or saving for her share of the limo.

Portia's voice cut into her thoughts. "So, are you going to tell me what happened with Connor this morning or what?"

"Connor?" Hendricks asked, slapping a cap back onto the glitter. It took her a second to figure out what Portia was talking about. "He told you he was going to ask me to prom?"

Connor and Portia had been friends since they were in diapers. They told each other everything.

"He didn't, like, *tell* me, tell me," Portia said. "He just asked whether I thought it was a good idea, and I told him that you'd be at Dead Guy before school, and he told me that *you* said you were going to think about it."

"Do you even need me for this conversation?" Hendricks meant for this to be a joke, but her voice came out more snappish than she'd intended. She caught Portia's disappointed expression from the corner of her eye and felt a pang of guilt.

"Sorry," she added quickly. It wasn't Portia's fault she was in a mood.

It was hard to explain exactly *why* she was so upset. She was having a hard time sorting it out herself.

It was the memory of that hand reaching for her the night before, and the fact that the Steele House grounds were being repaved.

It was Raven, lying motionless in bed, her skin pale, and Eddie's coffin being lowered into the ground, his mother sobbing nearby.

It was the fact that bad things kept happening and Hendricks couldn't stop them, and she couldn't understand them and she definitely couldn't control them.

And Portia was all happy with her new girlfriend, and Connor wanted to go to prom, and they were covering chairs with ribbons so they looked like thrones.

Everyone else had gone back to normal.

It was like the other stuff wasn't even *there*. Like it didn't even *matter*. It made Hendricks feel like there was something wrong with her, because she couldn't be happy like they could. She didn't know how to move on.

"He said you were going to think about it?" Portia prodded.

Hendricks dropped her hands, giving up on her glitter for the moment. "Yup."

"What is there to think about?"

She shot Portia a look over the top of the chair.

Portia's shoulders slumped. "Eddie?"

Hendricks exhaled, her eyes closing. She felt a double rush of emotion. On the one hand, it was cool that Portia just *got* it, that she didn't need to explain.

On the other hand, she felt guilty that she kept pulling everyone into her grief when they were all trying their best to move on.

"Yeah." Hendricks stared down at the ribbon she was holding. "Eddie."

"He'll always be in your heart, you know," Portia said, her head tilted to the side. "My aunt Sam died earlier this year, and I still get so sad whenever I think about her."

Hendricks snorted. Losing Eddie was nothing like Portia losing her aunt Sam.

Out loud, all she said was "You sound like a Hallmark card."

Portia rolled her eyes at her. "Connor gets that you're still hung up on Eddie," she said. "He wants to be there for you, as a friend. What's so wrong with that?"

The way Portia said *as a friend*, made Hendricks realize that all this "friend" stuff had probably been her idea. "I don't know . . . I guess it feels like I'm betraying him, sort of."

"Betraying who?" Portia frowned. "Eddie?"

"I'm explaining it wrong," Hendricks said. "It's just . . . sometimes I feel like Eddie's still out there. Like, if I try hard enough, I could find him and . . . I don't know. Talk to him." *Maybe he could tell me what the hell is going on*, she added silently.

"Well," Portia asked. "Has it been working?"

Hendricks shoulders slumped. "No." She glanced at Portia, chewing on her lip. "I actually wanted to go back to Ileana's shop today. I think she might be able to help me figure out what I'm doing wrong."

She expected Portia to laugh at her. To tell her she was living in a dream world. That Eddie was dead, and she needed to let him go.

Or worse, go silent on her again, not wanting to get dragged back into her creepy supernatural world.

But Portia just dropped the ribbon she was holding back into the box and said, "Why not? Can you drive? My car's getting detailed."

CHAPTER
6

ILEANA'S SHOP WAS IN DEVON, A TOURISTY TOWN TWENTY minutes from Drearford. Portia fumbled with the radio the whole drive, singing along to every song she knew, switching to a new station before the last song was even over, scowling whenever she hit static.

"Can I plug in my phone?" Portia asked, after a full thirty seconds of static. "I have the new Ariana Grande."

"We're almost there." Hendricks drove past quaint coffee shops and farm-to-table diners and a retro movie theater. Then she took a left.

Here, the businesses were fewer and farther between, the houses derelict. Windows were dark and boarded up, and the yards were unkempt.

Hendricks slowed to a stop and cut her engine.

Beside her, Portia frowned. "What are you doing?"

Hendricks jerked her chin toward a Victorian house with boarded up windows. "We're here. Ileana's shop is in the basement."

Portia glanced at the house, her expression unchanged. "No, it isn't."

It was annoying how confident she sounded. There wasn't any part of her that believed that Hendricks had taken them to the right place.

"Hello? I'm the only one of the two of us who has actually been here before." Hendricks opened her door and stepped outside.

"But—" The car door slammed shut, cutting off Portia's voice.

A moment later she'd scrambled out of the car and was following Hendricks across the street, talking quickly. "But *that* is not a store. That is a creepy abandoned house. Haven't you had enough creepy abandoned houses for one lifetime?"

Fair point, Hendricks thought. Out loud, she said, "Portia, chill."

"Chill? That looks like the sort of place where psychopaths keep their child brides locked up in the basement. What do you mean *chill?*"

Really, it wasn't as bad as all that. The house was old, sure. The front windows were arched, reminding Hendricks of a church. Part of the porch seemed to be caving in on itself, and the house itself was painted such a dark green that it looked almost black. But the turrets were kind of cool, and there was intricate woodwork around the doors and windows. It was . . . pretty. Sort of. Creepy pretty.

Hendricks jogged around the side of the house and down the steps to the basement. There, she found a red-painted door with a small black sign with the words MAGIK & TAROT hanging off the worn wood. Occasionally, Ileana left signs on the door, declaring that the store was closing early for a moon day, or Imbolc, or other strange holidays that Hendricks had never heard of. But today the door was empty, and when Hendricks tried the latch, it swung inward.

The light inside the store was dim, a strange contrast to the bright spring day. It took a moment for Hendricks's eyes to adjust to the sudden change. The windows had all been painted black. Ileana had told her once that this was so that some of her more delicate products wouldn't be spoiled by the light—sort of like a wine cellar. The only outside light that drifted into the room was streaky and faint. Cluttered shelves lined the walls, filled with crystals and dried flower petals and demonic-looking statuettes. The smell of incense and something earthy and smoky that Hendricks now recognized as sage rolled over them.

Portia started coughing and waving a hand before her nose. "Oh my God, is that *pot?*"

"Shh," Hendricks warned her, eyes darting around the shop. She didn't want to offend Ileana.

"Why are you *shushing* me?" Portia was whispering now, but this didn't actually make her any quieter. "There's no one here."

But that wasn't true. At that moment, Hendricks saw Ileana standing at the far end of the room. She was very pale and had a lot of wild, dark hair, and she didn't blink nearly as often as you'd expect. This had freaked Hendricks out at first, but she was used to Ileana by now. She'd almost go so far as to say she was a friend.

Hendricks touched Portia's arm and nodded at her. Portia, frowning, followed her gaze. It took Portia a second to separate the woman from the shadows, and when she did, she flinched.

"Holy cow," she whispered, eyes wide. "Has she been here this whole time?"

If Ileana noticed Portia's reaction to her, she chose to ignore it. She pressed her hands together at her chest and bowed her head toward Hendricks and Portia.

It was the kind of gesture you expected of someone who was about to say, "Namaste," but Ileana just said, "Hey. What brings you into the shop today?"

Hendricks made her way across the room, Portia crowded close behind her.

"Oh my God, what's that?" Portia whispered.

She was looking at the cobwebby glass display case that Ileana used as a checkout counter. A stuffed fawn with two heads crouched inside the case, marble eyes staring at them.

"Be cool," Hendricks muttered, and Portia nodded, but the look of shock didn't quite leave her face.

Hendricks took a breath, the events of the last twenty-four hours flicking through her head like playing cards.

She remembered how she'd felt watching those withered fingers disappear into the empty tarot box, the ominous message whispered into her ear, and the cold that had spread through her when she felt something touch the back of her neck in the school hall. She could still smell that lone dead rose.

What would Ileana say if she told her about all of this? Would she get mad? Tell Hendricks that she'd done something wrong? Hendricks thought of a thousand different television shows and movies where the wizened old wizard chided the young ingénue for playing with powers she didn't understand.

She couldn't risk Ileana refusing to help her, telling her she'd gotten in too deep. If she could just contact Eddie, she was sure he'd be able to help.

So all she said was "I've been trying to get in touch with Eddie. I tried the tarot cards, like you said. But, uh, I don't think they worked."

"Mmm." Ileana's expression didn't change. "Well, that can happen."

Hendricks waited, hoping Ileana would say more, but she was silent.

Hendricks cleared her throat and rubbed the back of her neck. "I, uhm, I was hoping you might have another suggestion for how I might communicate with him."

Ileana sat down on a stool behind the counter and pulled out an old-school Walkman. She switched out the tape and then shoved it into her pocket, resting the headphones around her neck. She seemed totally unbothered by the fact that Hendricks and Portia were staring at her, waiting for an answer.

"Not all departed remain," said Ileana simply.

"What does that mean?" Portia asked. "Like, is Eddie not a ghost?"

Hendricks could feel herself clenching, growing tighter, anxious. She thought of the card she'd pulled last night, the Two of Swords.

Indecision. Stalemate.

"Eddie would've stayed if he could've," she rushed to say. It seemed important for Ileana to understand this. "I just have to figure out the right way to speak to him."

Ileana cocked her head to the side, considering her. Something about this movement seemed unnatural to Hendricks. The angle of Ileana's neck, perhaps, or the way her collarbone jutted out from beneath her skin. Hendricks suppressed the urge to shiver.

"There are ghosts around us all the time," Ileana explained, after a moment. "But most of them are just echoes or reflections of the people they once were. They aren't powerful enough to actually do anything, so they just sort of . . . exist. If you're right and some part of Eddie did remain, there's a way to call him forth, but it's involved."

Involved. The word blazed in Hendricks's mind, a match that had just been lit. "What is it?" she asked. "I'll do it."

"You can manually extract his spirit from the void." This Ileana said with a bit of a shrug, as though it were the only logical next step. "This unites him with whatever is left here, in our world. But it can be a lot of work. You need to be committed to the process."

"The void?" Portia asked, sniffing. "What *void?*"

"The other side. The beyond. The only way to summon a spirit that has already moved on is to perform a séance." Ileana hopped off her stool and started walking around the store, gathering candles, bundles of sage, a few crystals. "You'll need a circle. Three people, at least. Five is better." She picked up a black stone, lifted it to her nose and then, frowning, set it down again. "And a conduit. That's the most important part."

"What's a conduit?" Hendricks asked.

"A conduit is someone who exists on both planes." Ileana paused now, and for the first time, she seemed unable to meet Hendricks's eye. Instead, she just pulled her wild hair into a messy bun on the top of her head. Hendricks noticed that she had a *Legend of Zelda* tattoo on the nape of her neck. "Someone who exists in the physical world of the living as well as beyond, in the world of spirits."

Hendricks felt a chill work its way through her body. "I don't understand."

"You and I exist here, in the living world. But Eddie may no longer be on this plane or, at least, not all of him is. That's why you can't see him, can't speak to him. Because whatever he left behind isn't strong enough to form contact. In order for the séance to work the way you want it to you need someone who can bridge that gap. Someone who is still alive but can throw their conscious into the void, into the world beyond."

"How are we supposed to find someone like that?" Portia asked, blunt.

"There are a few mediums capable of throwing their consciousness into the void, but they're difficult to find," Ileana said. "Do you know anyone practiced in lucid dreaming or transcendental meditation?"

Hendricks and Portia both shook their heads.

"Well then." Ileana opened her mouth and closed it again, appearing to turn something over in her head. After a moment she continued, "I heard about a girl who was just released from the hospital. Someone in a coma?"

Hendricks felt a touch of nerves. Beside her, Portia stiffened.

"What do you mean you *heard* about her?" Hendricks asked.

Ileana didn't immediately answer the question.

"She's your friend, right?" she asked, aiming her flat, black eyes at Hendricks. "The girl in the coma?"

"She's my best friend," Portia said. For the first time since they'd entered the shop, Portia didn't sound freaked or weirded out. Her voice was edged in steel.

"People in comas naturally exist on both planes," Ileana explained. She started rummaging around the shop. "Their bodies act as an anchor, pulling them back to the world of the living, while their spirits are able to cross over. It is a very unusual state, very valuable. If you're really desperate to make contact—"

"No," Hendricks said, shaking her head. At the same time, Portia said, "Are you kidding me? Raven needs *oxygen* to breathe. Her parents can't even take her to the *bathroom* right now. We're not using her as some kind of . . . of *antennae*."

Ileana paused for a moment and looked at Portia. "Look, you feel so strongly about that, I won't push you. You can try the séance without a conduit. It won't be as powerful, though, so I suggest gathering a circle of seven. Seven is the most powerful number in all of magic."

She handed Hendricks the things she'd been gathering, already placed in a neat black bag. Hendricks reached for it, but Ileana didn't let go right away. She fixed her black eyes on Hendricks's.

"Summoning a spirit has its risks," she said, in a lower voice. "People change once they reach the other side. It's magic that even I don't fully understand. You may not actually contact the Eddie that you knew."

The look Ileana gave Hendricks left her feeling cold all over. "What do you mean?"

"Just be sure that you're willing to deal with . . . whatever comes back."

Whatever, not whoever. Hendricks took the bag, feeling something twist deep in her gut.

"How much?" she asked.

Ileana shook her head. "No charge." And then, with a small smile, she added, "I liked Eddie."

Hendricks and Portia didn't speak as they made their way back to Hendricks's car. Hendricks got the feeling that Portia was avoiding her. She hung back a few steps, and she hadn't looked up from her phone since they'd left the shop.

Hendricks hunched farther down in her coat, annoyed. Obviously, she had no intention of using Raven as a conduit, but something about the way Portia had said, "She's my *best* friend," left Hendricks feeling strange.

It wasn't quite that she felt left out. It was more like she was the consolation prize, like Portia was only hanging out with her in the first place because Raven wasn't an option.

For the most part, Hendricks thought jealousy was stupid, so she tried to brush it aside now. But she couldn't help wondering if Portia would've agreed to use her as a conduit if Hendricks were the one who was unconscious. A rush of shame coursed through her. It was such a dumb thing to obsess over. They had bigger things to worry about just now.

Like the séance. Hendricks wanted to do it. She felt like she *had* to. She was done with flipping tarot cards and looking for secret meanings in the flame of Eddie's lighter. Done with vague messages whispered into her ear and freaking *fingers* reaching out to touch her.

She wanted answers. Real ones.

But without a conduit Hendricks didn't see how she was going to make it work. She didn't have seven friends here. She had Portia and she had Connor, which barely met the three-person minimum Ileana had said they needed.

And that was assuming Connor even agreed to be part of a séance to help Hendricks get in touch with her ex.

Hendricks chewed on her lower lip. She had a feeling that wasn't what he'd meant when he said they could still be friends.

"Hey, where are we doing this thing?" Portia still hadn't looked up from her phone.

Hendricks opened the passenger door of her car and tossed the bag of supplies into the back seat. "What thing?"

"The séance or whatever. Your place?" Portia looked up. "I guess we could use mine. I have the rec room. Or is that not spooky enough?"

Hendricks motioned between the two of them. "We only have two people. Ileana said we needed seven."

"No, she said we needed at least three, five is better." Portia's eyes were on her phone again. "I have four confirmed, but they need to know where to meet."

Hendricks felt a lift of hope. *Four?*

"With you and me that's six," Portia continued. Then, frowning, she added, "Do you think it has to be odd numbers? Ileana said three, then five, then seven. Maybe *six* is bad for some reason?" She glanced back at Magik & Tarot. "Well, we should probably ask Ileana to help us, anyway. We don't know what we're doing. And that would bring us to seven."

"How did you find four other people?"

"I just promised we'd bring a case of Rolling Rock." Portia shrugged, like this was obvious. "Where there's beer, there's boys. So? Where should I send them?"

She had one thumb poised above her phone's keypad, waiting.

Hendricks's mouth felt suddenly dry. This wasn't playing with tarot cards and crystals in her room, watching the flame of Eddie's lighter for some sign that he might be listening.

This was a *real* séance. A real chance to speak to Eddie again, to get some answers. She needed to make it count.

"Hendricks? I need to know where," Portia said again, impatient. Hendricks felt something cold move up her arms and pulled the sleeves of her jean jacket down over her hands. She realized, a moment later, that the chill had nothing to do with the cool air. There was only one place she could think of to do this thing.

Portia, frowning at her, seemed to suddenly understand. She lowered her phone and said, "Oh. *Shit*. Really?"

Hendricks was already nodding. "Tell them to meet us there in an hour."

CHAPTER
7

STEELE HOUSE DIDN'T LOOK LIKE STEELE HOUSE ANYMORE.

The last time Hendricks walked down this street was a few months ago. There had still been rubble left on the lot, blackened bricks and splintered wood and broken glass. But a lot had changed since then. As of tonight, the rubble had all been removed, the remains of the house leveled, the yard torn up, leaving flat, packed earth in its place. In the middle of this was a slab of freshly poured concrete foundation.

Her skin crawled as she stepped onto the property.

It was the foundation that caught Hendricks's attention and made her breath stick in her throat. It looked like Steele House—or, at least, it looked like the outline of Steele House, which was more than Hendricks had expected to see when she got here. If she walked around the edges of the fresh concrete, she could point out where the living room would go, and the kitchen, and the staircase that would lead to the second floor.

Hendricks swallowed and looked up. She could see the Ruiz house through the spindly trees at the edge of the lot. The last time she'd run through those trees, it was to bang on Eddie's back door and beg him to help her.

Hendricks felt her chest tighten and tears welled in her eyes.

Portia bumped her shoulder into Hendricks's. "Hey, you cool?"

"Yeah, I think so," Hendricks said. She blinked rapidly, trying to clear her vision, but Portia didn't seem to notice.

"Help me with these," Portia said, unloading a few cases of beer from the back of Hendricks's car.

They'd picked the beer up at an auto service and gas station off the highway leading into Drearford. Hendricks had never been there before, and there hadn't been a sign hanging out front, but she'd felt a strange prick of familiarity the second she'd walked through the front door.

"Is this Connor's dad's shop?" she'd asked.

"Be cool," Portia said, through a clenched smile.

Hendricks's suspicions were confirmed when she saw a shorter, more muscled version of Connor standing behind the cash register. *This must be his brother*, Hendricks thought. He'd rolled his eyes when Portia walked in and said, "Make it quick. If my dad gets back before you're done, you're stuck drinking ginger ale."

Portia had just winked at him and chirped, "Love you, too, Donnie."

They'd gotten away with three cases of Rolling Rock before Donnie whistled at them, nodding at a tall, heavyset man approaching from the parking lot. Portia pulled a couple of twenties out of her wallet and slid them across the counter to him, whispering her thanks before tugging Hendricks out a side door.

Now Hendricks grabbed a case of beer and helped Portia haul it over to the site. The others were already there. There was Connor's other older brother, Finn, who—like Donnie—was like a strangely proportioned version of Connor himself. But Finn was taller and ganglier than them both. He also had a mop of dark blond hair that flopped lazily over his eyes and a cruel twist to his smile that neither of the other brothers seemed to possess. He was playing hacky sack with a guy from the track team named Blake. Vi and Connor sat cross-legged a few feet away, talking about cars.

"Parts for European sports cars can be really hard to find," Connor was saying. He paused to scratch the back of his head. "I don't know . . . I think you'd be better off getting something secondhand, the maintenance on that one is going to be rough."

"Yeah, but it's a *Jag*," Vi said. Hendricks hadn't spent a ton of time with Vi in the past, and if she was being totally honest, she didn't really understand Portia's infatuation. Portia and Vi seemed like total opposites. Portia was always incredibly put together, almost glamorous. Vi, on the other hand, was small and . . . well, a little mousy. She had shoulder-length black hair and brownish-gold skin. She never wore makeup or jewelry, and she seemed to have made it her personal mission to dress in the exact same outfit every day. Black T-shirt, skinny jeans, chunky black loafers.

Granted, her T-shirts always fit perfectly. It was the type of fabric that seemed to hang in a very specific way, like it was expensive and hard to find. Hendricks made a mental note to ask Vi where she bought them.

"Hey, guys," she said, and Vi and Connor stood up, dusting their pants off.

"Hey," Vi said, not smiling. Hendricks wondered whether she really wanted to be here or if Portia had pulled the girlfriend card.

"Let me help with that," Connor said, taking a case of beer from Hendricks.

"Do you honestly think she can't handle that single case of beer on her own?" Vi asked.

Connor groaned. "Don't tell me you're too much of a feminist to accept help with a case of beer." To Portia, he added, "Where do we want this?"

"Over there," Portia said, and pointed across the foundation slab to a bit of earth that would've been part of Steele House's backyard before everything had been leveled.

Hendricks realized, with a start, that it was the exact place where Eddie had died. A rush of emotions rose up inside her at once and she stood frozen, trying to sort them out.

I'm going to talk to him again, she thought. Eddie wasn't gone, not yet. She was going to find him.

She followed Connor, Vi, and Portia across the foundation and over to the place where Eddie had died.

Portia set the case of beer she'd been carrying on the dirt. Finn and Blake dropped the hacky sack they were playing with and drifted over to join the circle.

Finn nodded at her but didn't smile. Hendricks got the feeling that he didn't like her very much, though she couldn't figure out why.

"Beer!" Blake grabbed a can and popped it open, taking a long, deep swig. When he finished, he nodded at Hendricks and said, almost like an afterthought, "Hey, O'Malley."

"My last name is Becker-O'Malley," Hendricks said, smiling thinly. "It's hyphenated."

Blake shrugged and took another drink of beer. Watching him, Hendricks realized she didn't know Blake all that well, either. They'd been at a few parties together, but they'd never really talked to each other. She knew he was on the track team with Connor and . . . yeah, that was all she knew about Blake. He was very tall, with good, thick black hair and dark skin. His teeth were perfect.

He was *tall*. It seemed important to mention that detail twice.

Portia clapped her hands together, exactly like she'd done to call the prom committee to order. "Are we all here?" she asked, scanning the gathered people. Her lips moved as she counted. "One short."

"Ileana said she was going to head over as soon as she closed the store," Hendricks reminded her.

"Right," said Portia, nodding. "Well, I can get the rest of you caught up. Like I said in my text, we're going to do a séance to try and get in touch with Eddie Ruiz."

Hendricks pressed her lips together, bracing herself for the comments, the teasing. Before he'd died, Eddie had been an outcast in Drearford. Hendricks was well aware that none of the people currently gathered around her had actually liked him. Or, for that matter, known him at all.

Finn stuck his hands into his jacket pocket, and though the corner of his mouth curled, out loud all he said was "Cool."

Blake burped.

Hendricks cut her eyes at Portia, wondering what she'd told them. Did they all know that she and Eddie were . . . whatever they were?

Portia seemed to intentionally avoid her gaze. "In order to make contact with the other side, we're supposed to gather a circle of seven people, which we did. Yay us!" Portia clapped at them, grinning. "Okay, so, next step—"

A low rumble interrupted them. Hendricks turned and looked over her shoulder as a car pulled up to the curb. Hendricks didn't know anything about cars, but this one was red and vintage-looking and . . . well, *cool.*

"Nice," Vi murmured, and Connor nodded approvingly.

The engine cut, and Ileana climbed out. Next to the car, her bushy black hair and band T-shirt looked less crazy, and more like an intentional fashion statement. Witch chic.

"Oh good, she made it," Portia announced. Hendricks suspected she heard a dip in her friend's voice. Disappointment?

Portia glanced at Vi, who was still staring at Ileana's car, a look of awe on her face.

Ileana didn't bother introducing herself as she joined their circle. "We should get started before the energy shifts," she said instead. She added, "I'm not crazy about the air right now. Does it feel heavy to you?"

This she directed at Hendricks, who shrugged, unsure of how to answer. Ileana seemed younger than she did at the shop, less like an otherworldly priestess and more like a very cool college chick, or possibly someone in a band.

"I'm not usually one for group projects, but seven is good," Ileana continued. "Now participants are supposed to divide by gender. Can we have the guys move to that side, and the girls over here?"

Connor, Blake, and Finn shuffled to one side of the circle. Vi stayed where she was.

"Are you gender nonconforming?" Ileana asked.

Vi seemed taken aback by the bluntness of this question. "No," she blurted. Then, "I mean, I don't know. I just think gender is sort of stupid."

Ileana said, "Yeah, well, luckily magic isn't as close-minded as the rest of the world, and it holds the genderless in high esteem. Move to the head of the circle and I'll stand opposite you, for balance."

Vi looked a little unsure as she shuffled to one end of the circle, between Connor and Portia. Hendricks stood to Portia's right, with Ileana on her other side and the boys across from her.

Ileana closed her eyes and took a deep breath.

"This feels good," she said, cracking her neck. "Balanced." Turning to Hendricks, she asked, "Did you bring the stuff I gave you?"

Hendricks had the black bag she'd gotten from Ileana's store that afternoon at her feet. She picked it up.

"Cool," said Ileana. "So, everyone needs to take a candle. We need either three candles, or a number divisible by three, and the more the better. Since I'm the only one here who's held a séance in the past, I'll act as medium. Does that work for everyone?"

One by one, everyone gathered nodded.

"I also brought this." Ileana knelt and pulled a loaf of bread out of the leather bag at her feet.

"We get snacks?" asked Finn, sounding hopeful. Connor snorted.

Ileana gave them both a look and placed the loaf in the middle of the circle. "Spirits don't eat, but they really like the smell of food," she explained. "It reminds them of what it was like to be alive. Hendricks, make sure everyone in the circle gets a candle, except for me, and then place three additional candles in the center for a total of nine." Under her breath, Ileana added, like she was doing a complicated equation, "Nine is good."

Hendricks did as she was told. The candles were thin and tall and black. Once she'd handed them all out, she patted down her pockets—then paused, a sinking feeling filling her chest. She'd left Eddie's lighter at home.

"I got you, O'Malley," Blake said, reading her mind. He dug a lighter out of his pocket and started passing it around. Soon, nine flickering lights illuminated their small circle.

"Thanks," Hendricks said, and Blake winked at her.

"Now join hands," Ileana said.

Hendricks took Ileana's hand and Portia's hand. Around the circle, everyone fell quiet, doing the same.

"I'm going to need you all to repeat this chant after me," said Ileana.

Her voice was suddenly low and very strong. It made Hendricks think of roots stretching deep into the earth, of new life sprouting from tiny seeds. She felt like she was part of something larger than herself. She shivered. *Weird.*

"Our beloved, Eduardo Ruiz," Ileana said, her voice strong. "We bring you gifts from life into death. Commune with us, Eduardo, and move among us."

There was a brief moment of silence after she'd finished. Everyone looked around, wondering who would start.

Hendricks knew it should be her, but her throat felt suddenly thick, her mouth dry. It was that word, *beloved*, it felt so weird to say it in front of all these people.

She wet her lips—

And then Portia spoke, taking the lead. "Our beloved, Eduardo Ruiz," she said, and squeezed Hendricks's hand.

Hendricks, relieved, began to chant along with her, "We bring you gifts from life into death."

One by one, everyone else joined in. "Commune with us, Eduardo, and move among us."

"Again," said Ileana, once they were done.

And then, again and again.

"Our beloved, Eduardo Ruiz. We bring you gifts from life into death. Commune with us, Eduardo, and move among us."

The words layered over one another, reminding Hendricks of a song sung in rounds at nursery school, the voices weaving together like threads in a tapestry.

Once they'd completed the chant seven times, Ileana fell silent. Hendricks closed her eyes, her heartbeat thudding in her ears.

Please work, she thought to herself.

The night around her was still. Wind sighed through the trees, and new leaves twitched on their branches. Somewhere far off there was a low rumble that might have been the distant call of thunder, or might have been a car driving past on the next street. Hendricks's palms had begun to sweat.

Please, please work.

"Oh shit," whispered Vi after a moment. "I—I think I just felt something."

Hendricks's chest felt like a balloon that was about to burst, but it took her a moment to realize it was because she'd stopped breathing. This was it. Eddie, finally. Something inside of her began to hum—

"Yeah, I farted," Blake murmured, under his breath, and he and Finn burst into stifled laughter. Hendricks felt a jerk from the other side of the circle as Connor rammed one of them with his shoulder.

"Knock it off," he said. But Hendricks noticed his lips were twitching, like he was trying not to laugh, too.

Hendricks felt her hope slowly drain away. It was like she was inside a small room in the dark. This was a mistake. Nothing was happening.

She opened her eyes and saw that Ileana was already staring into the center of the circle, frowning slightly.

"Something's off," she murmured.

"What does that mean?" asked Hendricks. She felt like there was something caught in her throat. "Should we switch places or . . . or light more candles?"

"No . . . I just don't think this is going to work tonight." Ileana dropped Hendricks's hand. "I'm sorry."

Hendricks was confused. "I don't understand. We just started. Can't we try something else? A different chant, maybe?"

"The chant isn't the problem." Ileana motioned vaguely to the air around them. "It's like I said before, the energy of this place is . . . wrong. It's like milk gone sour. Can't you feel it?" Ileana made a face, like she smelled something foul. "The heaviness of it? It's . . . sticky."

Hendricks had no idea how to respond to that. It was like Ileana was speaking in riddles. How could energy be sticky?

She wanted to argue, but now Ileana was gathering the bread and candles, and Hendricks could see that there was no point.

The disappointment she felt was bad, but even worse was the sudden rush of embarrassment that followed it.

She'd been so hopeful. She'd *really* thought this was going to work. That hope still lingered in the back of her brain, whispering, *Please, please.*

The rest of circle had started to break up, too. Finn and Blake were looking for their hacky sack. Vi was asking Connor something about carburetors.

"Wait," Hendricks said. The word came out half-croak.

"We can try again some other time, Hendricks." Portia touched her shoulder, apologetic. "I'm sorry."

"Maybe when there's a full moon?" Ileana added. "A full moon is like the spiritual version of a car wash, it could help clean out the energy around here."

One by one, the group drifted off, until it was just Hendricks, sitting alone on an edge of the concrete foundation. She was cross-legged, her elbows balanced on her knees, her chin propped in her hands.

She was on the verge of completely giving up. Not just on Eddie. On everything. She felt like a failure. No part of her body seemed capable of holding itself upright.

"Why won't you talk to me?" she asked the spot of land where Eddie had died. She didn't feel hurt or embarrassed or disappointed anymore. Now she felt numb. She'd never thought she'd find herself missing the intense, all-encompassing pain that had taken her over after Eddie's death, but she did. Anything was better than this.

She slid off the edge of the foundation and walked over to the spot of dirt where Eddie had died. Little tufts of grass had begun to sprout up around the yard, but the spot itself was still mostly dirt. It was almost as though nothing wanted to grow there. She stared down at it for a moment. And then, she kicked it.

Nothing happened, so she kicked again, harder. And then again. The tip of her sneaker caught on a rock and pain shot through her big toe. She grimaced and kicked again. Again. Again.

Dirt flew into the air and scattered around the clearing. A few clumps sprayed the top of the foundation.

She didn't care. She kicked again. There was a shallow hole forming now, and nothing had changed so finally Hendricks stopped.

She'd sort of hoped that kicking the ground would make her feel better, but it didn't. She felt nothing. And now she was breathing hard and sweating a little. She couldn't quite catch her breath.

"Fine," she said, gasping. "I give up. Stay . . . wherever you are. In the void, or whatever. I hope you're happy there."

A tear pricked the corner of her eye, but she brushed it away, angrily, with the back of her hand. That stupid Two of Swords card— *indecision*—had made her think there was still some chance Eddie was planning to come back. Now she understood the truth. Eddie had already moved on. It was over.

She turned back toward her car.

A crow cawed as she walked back, and Hendricks began to feel an almost imperceptible tremble in the ground beneath her. It was subtle at first, the feeling of a train going by. She stopped short, wondering if she was imagining it.

But no, the shaking of the earth was becoming more intense. Then the wind started to pick up. A cold gust moved through the trees, making Hendricks shiver.

She turned in a slow circle.

A sudden crash of thunder made her jump. The sky lit up.

Hendricks stood stone still. Instinct told her to run. The last time she was in this backyard, the long-decayed corpses of three boys had clawed their way up from beneath her and attacked her friends.

And now the tremor grew stronger. It felt like the beginning of an earthquake. Like something big coming closer.

She looked around, half expecting to see hands reach up from the dirt, but there was only writhing earth.

She took a single lurching step toward her car, but the ground was shaking too violently, and it sent her crashing to her knees. Her teeth snapped down, hard, on her tongue, and the taste of metal filled her mouth. She lifted a hand to her lips. When she pulled them away, her fingers were stained red.

Another crash of thunder rumbled through the night, but no lightning followed. Instead, Hendricks heard a sound like smashing rocks. She whipped her head around.

A crack had appeared in the middle of the concrete foundation of Steele House. As Hendricks watched, it grew steadily larger. Beneath the sound of churning concrete, she heard other sounds . . .

Hisses . . . Whispers . . .

"Help," Hendricks whimpered. She fumbled for her phone in her pocket, but when she pulled it out, the screen was black. Dead. Minutes ago it had been fully charged.

Hendricks shoved it back in her pocket and took a ragged breath.

Maybe it's him. Maybe it's Eddie, she thought.

She slowly pushed herself to her feet, creeping closer to the foundation. The edges of the crack were jagged, and there didn't seem to be earth below, just a deep, hollow space. Staring at it, Hendricks remembered the Steele House storm cellar where little Maribeth Ruiz had died tragically three years ago. Had the construction workers built over the cellar without bothering to fill it in?

The crack grew. The sound of crumbling concrete echoed through the night. Hendricks cringed and clamped her hands over her ears. The crack was the size of her forearm and then, seconds later, it stretched longer than her leg. She watched in horror, her breath coming in harsh little gasps.

What the hell?

When the crack was the length of a body stretched out across the foundation, it stopped. The gnashing sound of breaking concrete ended, abruptly enough that Hendricks could still hear it ringing in her ears. The night was suddenly still.

Hendricks took a single step toward the foundation. And then another. Her armpits had begun to sweat. It was that cold sweat that smelled like fear. She could feel her T-shirt clinging to her skin.

She was still a few feet from the crack when the darkness below stirred. She froze.

Slowly, slowly, whatever was below began to crawl up.

Hendricks stifled a scream and took a quick step backward, one hand flying to her mouth.

The *thing* was dark and amorphous, shapeless and twitchy. It moved like an animal, but Hendricks didn't think that it was one. It felt dangerous.

She stood deathly still, worried that this *thing* might see her. Her heartbeat sounded like cannon fire in her ears, and the urge to inhale was so strong that it felt like her lungs might explode inside her chest. But she didn't move, she didn't breathe.

The thing pulled itself out of the crack. It still didn't have form, but there was a moment when it seemed to flinch, like a cat cocking its head because it had heard something.

The thing peered through the darkness, back at Hendricks. Hendricks thought she could make out the shape of a head and shoulders. Arms, legs, torso, head. But no face.

Despite her fear, Hendricks moved closer. This was the moment she'd been waiting for. She reached out her hand.

Wind rattled through the branches and shook the trees. Before Hendricks could brush her fingers against the strange, dark shape, it broke apart, first becoming thick wisps of black smoke, and then—

Nerves itched the back of Hendricks's outstretched hand. The smoke, it was thickening, changing. It seemed to take on form and weight. And there was a sound coming from it. A sort of . . .

Buzzing.

Horror trailed down the back of Hendricks's throat.

The smoke had become *wasps.*

They were only dim silhouettes in the darkness, but Hendricks recognized them immediately. Tiny, bullet-shaped bodies, vibrating wings. She screamed. Blood pumped through her skull, blotting out all other sound. She dropped to a crouch on the ground as the wasps formed a thick, grotesque swarm.

She could feel them on her skin, crawling, in her hair, brushing against her cheeks. One of them burrowed into her ear. She thrashed wildly, trying to shake it free as harsh little gasps that she couldn't control escaped her lips. Tears streamed down her face.

Distantly, she thought of what Ileana had told her.

Be sure that you're willing to deal with . . . whatever comes back.

Is this what she'd meant? Hendricks thought, numb. *Is this Eddie?*

And then, the wasps took a sudden turn. The swarm around her began to dissipate. Hendricks lifted her head. They were above her now, barely more than a black cloud blotting out the moon, the droning sound of their wings growing distant. Still shaken, Hendricks anxiously patted down her arms and touched her face, wanting to make sure that every last one of them was gone.

She hadn't been stung, she realized. Not once.

CHAPTER
8

HENDRICKS WENT BACK HOME—OR WHATEVER THE RENTAL house was. Not "home," but as close as she was going to get right now. She doubted she'd be able to manage normal human conversation, so she walked past her parents and Brady without acknowledging them. Down the hallway and into the bathroom. She took a vicious pleasure in the feel of her door slamming behind her, the force vibrating through the walls and floor. It wasn't until she heard her parents' concerned voices drift down the hall from the kitchen that she realized how loud she was being.

"... you think she's okay?"

"Someone should probably go talk to her ..."

She closed her eyes, groaning internally. Great. Now she'd freaked out her parents, too. She knew she should go back out there and assure them that she was all right, but she couldn't bring herself to open the door.

She thought of the crack appearing in the middle of Steele House's new foundation. The shadow ... thing that had crawled up from the earth and turned into a swarm of wasps.

Hendricks was suddenly itchy all over, like she could still feel the wasps crawling on her skin. She shuddered. She wanted to soak her entire body in bleach. She would settle for a bath.

Her new rental home did not have a big antique tub like Steele

75

House did. This one was small and plastic, and Hendricks knew it wouldn't cover her entire body once it was full, but she switched the faucet on anyway and waited impatiently on the toilet seat until the warm water filled the tub. The air grew thick and warm around her. Steam fogged up her mirror. She hugged herself, trying to ignore the phantom feeling of bugs creeping over her skin. Every nerve in her body felt like it was on fire.

Finally, the tub was full. Hendricks switched the faucet off with a flick of her hand, discarded her clothes on the linoleum floor, and climbed inside.

She'd been right, it wasn't big enough for her to lay down. She had to keep her knees bent and her head crooked awkwardly against the side of the tub itself, but a bath was still a bath. She tried not to focus on how cramped she felt and shifted her thoughts instead to the warm press of water against her skin, the steamy quality of the air, the steady drip of the faucet. Those sensations had never failed to soothe her before.

She closed her eyes and searched for a peaceful memory, like they taught her at CTE. *Find your happy place.*

Her happy place was a summer day at the beach from when she was little, back before Brady was born. She could feel the heat of the sun on her shoulders and how excited she'd been to wear her yellow swimsuit. Her dad let her get a treat from the ice cream truck, and she could still taste the creamy strawberry shortcake bar she'd chosen. Waves crashed against the shore, one after another, the sound so peaceful . . .

The sound shifted in Hendricks's mind, grew sharper, harder. It wasn't crashing waves anymore, but crumbling concrete, howling wind, roaring thunder . . .

Hendricks released a choked cry, her eyes flying open. She sat up so quickly that she sent a wave of water cascading over the side of the tub. Her heart was beating hard and fast inside her chest.

This wasn't working.

She scooted her body down the length of the tub, bending her knees until she could lay her head and shoulders down on the bottom. Hot water rushed up over her cheeks. She released a sigh that sent a trail of tiny bubbles up toward the surface. Better.

She'd gotten good at holding her breath over the years. There was something so peaceful about being underwater. The water acted as a strange lens, distorting everything in the bathroom. Some things seemed strangely close, others far away. Hendricks blinked, staring up at the ceiling above her. The only thing she could hear was her own heart beating in her ears.

And then, out of nowhere, Ileana's advice about the séance drifted through her head.

A conduit is someone who exists on both planes.

Hendricks blinked. She was starting to feel a little light-headed. She'd have to come up for air soon.

But . . . what did Ileana mean by that? Anyone on both planes?

She'd said they could use Raven because she was in a coma. But she'd also said that someone practiced in lucid dreaming or transcendental meditation could be the conduit as well.

Hendricks could feel her eyesight growing dim. Her head felt hot and full of air, a balloon about to burst. She reached out from under the water and gripped the side of the tub. But she didn't pull herself out.

How close would she have to come to death to act as a conduit? she wondered. Would she have to pass out?

Or would it be enough if she just got a little dizzy?

Hendricks dug her fingers into the plastic. Her toes curled into the bottom of the tub. Her chest was tight, her lungs raw, but still she didn't come up for air.

Talk to me, Eddie.

The muscles in her arms clenched tight. It took all the strength she had to hold herself under water as the oxygen drained from her brain. Her body began to shake.

Come on. Talk to me.

She became vaguely aware that her vision was narrowing. The edges of her eyesight had dimmed to black, and all she could see was the slow rise and fall of the surface of water directly above her. The rest of the world had faded away. It was like it didn't exist.

Her grip on the side of the tub began to weaken. She was losing strength.

Was it possible to drown in a bathtub? Hendricks had a sudden vision of how it would happen, almost like she'd floated out of her body and was watching from the ceiling.

She imagined how her eyes would lose focus, like Eddie's eyes had. How they would glaze over, and then go still as the last of the life drained from her body. Her fingers—still grasping the sides of the tub so tightly—would relax, her arms slithering back into the tub to come to rest at her sides—

Distantly, Hendricks thought she heard a snatch of music, some old eighties song.

Maybe I'm just too . . . maybe I'm . . .

It was man's voice, deep and urgent, the fast beat making her heart speed up.

The light hanging from the bathroom ceiling above flicked twice.

Off.

On.

The water in the tub seemed to chill and Hendricks saw a thin film of ice crawl across the surface. She caught movement at the corner of her eye, a flicker of white, and had the sudden sensation that she was no longer alone in the bathroom. There was someone standing in the opposite corner, behind her. Watching her. She felt like they—or it—was coming closer. Closer. Hendricks jerked underwater. She felt paralyzed, like when caught between a dream and waking.

A far-off scream ripped through the night, and Hendricks felt her paralysis release. She sat up, gasping for breath. She saw something twitch on the other side of the room and whipped her head around, her heart leaping into her throat. But it was just the mirror on the back of the bathroom door, reflecting her own movements back to her.

A relieved breath escaped her lips. She was alone.

The water in the tub was cold now, and Hendricks was trembling. She pulled her knees to her chest and wrapped her arms around them, trying to catch her breath. Her lungs felt rubbed raw, and tears had sprung to her eyes. Every breath was fire. Her heartbeat was so loud in her ears that she could barely hear anything past it.

And then, Hendricks heard it again. That terrible scream.

She stood, dripping, just as the screaming stopped. Her nerves twitched. It sounded like it had come from next door.

Portia lived next door.

She grabbed her bathrobe, pulled it on, and yanked the bathroom door open. Water trailed down her legs as she raced down the hall. Her feet left wet footprints behind her.

"Hendricks, honey, what's wrong?" her mother called as Hendricks darted past her and out the front door.

It was cold outside, and windy. Hendricks had to grip her robe tightly around herself to keep it from flapping open. Goose bumps shot up her legs. She raced down the stone steps, fighting back a shiver when her foot hit cool, damp dirt. But she didn't slow down.

Portia started screaming, again.

"Portia!" Hendricks raced up the steps to Portia's house and banged on the front door. When no one answered, she tried the door—Portia often joked about how no one locked their doors around here—and it turned easily beneath her fingers. *Thank God.* She raced down the hall to Portia's bedroom.

Portia was sitting upright in bed, her eyes wide and rimmed with red. She was shaking.

"Portia?" Hendricks climbed onto Portia's bed and grabbed her by the shoulders. Portia turned to look at Hendricks full on, her eyes focusing on her face.

Hendricks froze. A bruise was already starting to blossom along one side of Portia's face. It was massive, an ugly purplish yellow spreading across her cheekbone and down toward her chin. And cutting straight through the bruise was what looked like a *knife* slash. A two-inch-long gash, the edges starting to pucker, bleeding so badly that there was already blood crusted in Portia's hair and along the bottom of her jaw.

Hendricks felt a sudden dip in her gut. "Portia . . . Oh my God, what happened?"

Portia blinked, only just seeming to notice that Hendricks was there. She lifted a hand to her face, cringing. "It was Eddie. I—I felt him. He . . . he *cut* me."

Throat dry, Hendricks asked, "Eddie?"

"He was *here*," Portia said, her lower lip trembling. "Hendricks . . . he tried to kill me."

CHAPTER
9

PORTIA REFUSED TO SLEEP IN HER OWN ROOM THAT NIGHT.
She snuck out her window and curled up on Hendricks's floor, answering her questions with numb, one-word answers until the two of them finally fell asleep.

He was here. He tried to kill me.

Those words echoed through Hendricks's head all night, and all through school the next day, distracting her from the equations she was supposed to be memorizing in algebra, the lecture on African countries in geography, and the inedible lasagna they were serving at lunch. Hendricks knew what those words meant obviously, but she couldn't get them to come together in a logical way. Why would Eddie visit *Portia?*

If he'd really come back, wouldn't he visit her?

Eventually, she found herself back in the gym with the rest of the prom committee, balanced on top of an old wooden ladder, covered in glitter. She and Portia were constructing a selfie wall out of netting, streamers, and cardboard fish, and Hendricks's fingers were already a mess of paper cuts. Usually she wouldn't mind. She'd always enjoyed working with her hands, and there was something satisfying about seeing the results of her labor pay off immediately. Paper cuts plus sore arm muscles equaled awesome selfie wall.

Or, at least, the work would have been satisfying if she'd been able to focus on what she was doing.

"I still don't understand," Hendricks said finally, giving up on a streamer she'd been trying to untangle. "How do you know *Eddie* was the one who cut you? It sounds like you didn't actually see him."

"Haven't we been over this, like, twenty-five times?" Portia grumbled. "I didn't see anything but I felt, like, a presence. And then the room got really cold." She lifted her hand, absently fumbling with the Hello Kitty bandages she'd plastered across her face. She'd managed to cover the knife wound, but the bruise was still visible around the edges, deep purple and angry. "I could feel something on the edge of my bed, and then I heard a noise, and I woke up and that's when I felt it. *Him.*" Portia gave a sudden, hard shudder. "It was awful."

Hendricks thought of the shadow she'd seen climb out of the foundation of Steele House. It didn't have any defining features. It was just a shape, a darkness. It could've been anyone. "I still don't get how you know it was Eddie?"

Portia turned to her, blinking. "What do you mean, you don't *get* how I know it was him? We just did a séance to raise him from the dead. Who else would it be?"

Hendricks didn't know how to answer this, so she shrugged. "I don't know. Maybe it was a dream?"

Portia shot Hendricks a deeply annoyed look. "How could a dream do *this?*" she asked, gesturing to the bandage on her face. "Besides, do you really think I would've screamed like that over a dream?" She sniffed, muttering, "Give me a little credit."

"I'm sorry, it's just that . . . this doesn't make any sense. Why would Eddie come to *you?*" Hendricks's voice cracked on the word *you.* She wouldn't have admitted it out loud, but this was the part she was having the most trouble understanding. Her cheeks blazed. She added, "I mean, you barely even spoke to him when he was alive, right?"

Portia nodded, but she was looking past Hendricks now, staring into space. A laugh erupted from the other side of the gym, where two dozen kids were painstakingly constructing a twelve-foot-tall cruise ship out of papier-mâché and glitter.

When Portia spoke again, her voice sounded small. "I, like, made fun of him and stuff," she said. Guilt flickered in her eyes. "You remember, right? That night at the pizza place?"

Hendricks nodded. She remembered. One of the first times she'd ever hung out with Raven and Portia and Connor was at this pizza place on Main Street, Tony's. Eddie had come in to pick up some food to go. Raven and Portia had been pretty vicious.

Hendricks swallowed. Whenever she thought of that night, she felt a fresh rush of shame. She hadn't stuck up for him. She'd been too embarrassed, desperate to get her new friends to like her. She wished there was a way she could go back and rewrite what had happened. She would've done things so differently.

"That wasn't the only time something like that happened," Portia admitted. "Eddie knew we didn't like him. Maybe . . . maybe he's trying to get revenge."

"Eddie wasn't like that," Hendricks said.

"How do you know?"

"What do you mean, how do I know? I *knew* him."

Portia didn't look so convinced. "Look, I get that you guys were . . . involved or whatever, but Hendricks, you only knew him for, what? A month? I've known him my whole life."

Hendricks opened her mouth and then closed it, again. She didn't know what to say. The idea that she might not know Eddie as well as she'd thought she did upset her more than she'd liked to admit. She thought of telling Portia about how Eddie had told her about Valentina, the little sister he'd never had, or how much he hated this town, or how his mother used to tell him he should make wishes on tears instead of eyelashes. They were such small things, but they all added up to a person who was so different than the Eddie that Portia had known.

"I knew him," Hendricks said again. "I might not have known him my whole life, like you did, but I can tell you for sure that Eddie wouldn't try to hurt you just because you made some stupid jokes. He wasn't that kind of person."

"Except that he's not a *person* anymore, is he?" Portia reminded her. She had the streamers balled up in both hands, and now she was twisting them anxiously. "Ileana said he could come back . . . different, remember? Maybe that's what happened. Maybe dying, like, made him turn evil?"

Hendricks chewed on her lip. She'd had this same thought, of course. Ileana's warning had been tumbling through her head all last night, all day today. And whenever Hendricks closed her eyes, she saw that strange shadow crawl up from the Steele House foundation, she felt the drone of wasps surround her, and she wondered: What, exactly, had they brought back?

Anger knotted up her chest, but she wasn't sure who, or what she was angry with.

"I need to pee," she said. If she didn't take a second to catch her breath, she worried she might lash out.

"Take your time," Portia muttered.

Hendricks blinked at her. "Are you mad at me?" She *sounded* pissed.

Portia sighed. "No. I don't know. You just keep asking me what happened, but when I tell you, you don't believe me." She touched her bandage, cringing. "I'd rather not relive this whole thing again and again because *you* think I was having a bad dream."

"I'm just trying to figure this thing out," she said.

"No, you don't want to believe Eddie was behind it," Portia shot back.

Hendricks stared. She knew Portia was pretty freaked and that was why she was lashing out, but she couldn't quite bring herself to make nice. Portia hadn't even *seen* the ghost. The only reason she was insisting it was Eddie was because she hadn't liked him. Hendricks didn't think it was too much to expect a little proof.

She sucked a breath in through her teeth and tried one last time to keep the peace. "I feel like you're not listening to me," she said, once again using the "I feel" language they'd been taught at CTE.

Portia didn't look up from the streamers she was detangling. "And *I* feel like you should just head home," she said stiffly. "We don't really need your help here anymore."

"I don't want to fight." Hendricks dropped the streamers she'd been knotting together. "But if you want me gone, I'm gone."

The clock in the school hall was broken, the hour hand pointing at the nine, the minute hand twitching between the four and the five.

Hendricks glanced at it as she rounded the corner to the bathroom, a frown touching her lips, but before her brain could process why she thought it was odd, her eyes settled on a group of girls huddled beside the bathroom door.

A rush of relief. It embarrassed her how grateful she was to see them there, but ever since the morning all the lights went out, she'd been nervous about being in the school halls alone. The muscles in her shoulders relaxed slightly as she walked past them.

She recognized them, she realized. They were the girls from prom committee, the rude ones who'd huddled on the bleachers, ignoring Portia. Hendricks's relief turned to annoyance. Why weren't they in the gym now?

"We could use some help with the selfie wall," Hendricks muttered, as she reached for the bathroom door.

The head of the group seemed to be a girl in an oversize, pale pink jean jacket. She was facing away from Hendricks, but something about her reminded Hendricks of Portia, how Portia seemed to command whatever group she was in. The girl twitched at the sound of Hendricks's voice, but she didn't turn around.

Whatever, Hendricks thought, rolling her eyes. She pulled the bathroom door open—

She barely had time to register the sudden rush of footsteps and the blur of a boy running past before something flew through the air and bit into her arms. The girls around her shrieked and scattered.

Hendricks flinched, reacting seconds too late. The boy must've thrown something at them. She heard the rattling sound of dozens of tiny objects, like pebbles, scattering across the floor.

"Oh my God," said one of the girls, horrified. "They're . . . they're *teeth*."

Teeth? Hendricks opened her mouth soundlessly as her eyes landed on a tiny object lying on the ground near her shoe. It was yellowish and crescent-shaped and viciously pointed. One edge was rimmed in blood, and something thick and pink that might have been flesh. It looked like it had only just been pulled from a mouth.

Hendricks covered her mouth with one hand. Her stomach flipped over.

It *was* a tooth, she realized, but not a human one.

It looked like it belonged to a rat.

Hendricks looked back at the girls, but they didn't move. Their faces were pale with fear and frozen. Were they just going to let that creep get away with this?

"Hey!" Hendricks ran, darting down the hall and around the corner, after the boy. "Hey, what the—"

She slammed right into Connor, who stumbled back a few steps. "Whoa, hey what the hell?"

"Sorry." Hendricks recovered quickly and rose to her toes, trying to see past him. "What happened to that guy who just ran down here?"

"What guy?" Connor said, frowning.

Hendricks blinked at him. Something cold moved through her. She took a few steps back and checked around the corner. The girls were gone, the floors where they'd been standing clean.

No rat teeth, no blood.

The floor tilted below her. Had the girls been there at all? Had any of that—the boy, the teeth, the screaming—actually happened?

Her eyes flicked up. Now the clock above the bathroom read 4:10. Just like it was supposed to.

Behind her, Connor cleared his throat. "Hendricks? You okay?"

"Yeah," Hendricks said absently. She felt like her brain was moving slower than it was supposed to, struggling to catch up with what was actually happening. She lifted a hand to her head. "Yeah, I'm fine."

"I was actually about to come find you," Connor said. "I heard from Mr. Jenson that they're starting to do sign-ups for the fall musical. Not just cast, but crew and construction and stuff, if you're still interested in that. We usually start building the set over the summer."

Hendricks hadn't been expecting this subject change, and it took her a second to figure out how to respond. Her mouth was still dry, and her eyes kept flicking back to the area down the hall where, just a few seconds ago, those girls had been standing. "Uh . . . what?"

"School musical?" Connor repeated. He laughed sheepishly and ran a hand back through his hair. "Remember? I told you I usually help out with backstage stuff. Set construction, woodworking, that sort of thing. You said you were interested in doing crew again?"

With one last glance down the hall, Hendricks turned her full attention back to Connor. "Right, I was interested, I mean, I *am* interested."

Connor shoved the rest of his books into his bag, and the two began walking down the hallway. "Well, you're in luck. They're doing *South Pacific* this year, so they need someone to build an entire island out of cardboard."

"That sounds cool." Hendricks couldn't help thinking about how she would construct something like that, scouring the internet for places that sold fake plants on the cheap, maybe repurposing some of the prom decorations, the netting and cardboard fish, at least. "I think I'll sign up, too."

They walked in silence for a moment. Then Connor cleared his throat. He seemed to be trying very hard not to look at her.

He's going to ask about prom, Hendricks realized. Everything inside of her clenched tight.

"So," Connor said. "About—"

"Listen," Hendricks blurted, at the same time. "I think you're great."

Connor closed his eyes, a sharp breath escaping through his teeth. "But?"

Hendricks blinked, feeling a surge of uncertainty. She wanted to stop now, to backtrack and make a joke to break the tension between them.

This was *Connor*. She didn't want to hurt Connor.

But that's why she had to keep going, wasn't it? Because it was the right thing to do, even if it sucked. She'd only hurt him more if she kept leading him on.

And so she said, her heart stuttering, "Some girl is going to be so lucky to go to the prom with you."

Connor's expression darkened. "Just not you. That's what you're saying, right?"

"I need a friend right now, more than I need a date."

Connor stopped walking. He suddenly seemed very interested in something happening on the sole of his shoe. He scuffed it into the floor once, twice. "Is this because of Eddie?"

"No. I don't know." Hendricks pressed her lips together. She didn't know what to say. "I'm just . . . not ready yet."

"When will you be ready? Two more months? A year?"

There was something terrible about his voice then, desperate and sad. Hendricks hated that she was the one who made him sound like that. "Connor—"

"Or never?" Something shuttered in Connor's face. It was like a curtain being drawn; a door slamming shut. "Because you don't like me like that? Not like you liked him?"

"That's not what this is about." Hendricks reached for Connor's arm, but he took a quick step back.

"Don't do that, don't try to make it okay. I just want you to tell me the truth. Do you have feelings for me at all?"

"It's not that simple—"

"Actually, it *is* that simple. It's very simple. You either feel something, or you don't. Which is it?"

"If you need me to answer you right now, then—"

"Yeah," Connor said, cutting her off. "I think an answer now would be good."

Hendricks closed her eyes. Her brain turned slowly, trying to figure out the right thing to say, coming up blank. "Then I . . . I don't. I—I can't. I'm sorry."

There was silence, for a moment, a terrible, weighted silence in which everything seemed to change.

And then Connor sucked in a breath and said, in a low, angry voice Hendricks had never heard him use before. "Because I'm not him." The look he gave her cut through the air like a knife. "I can't compete with a dead guy."

Something inside of Hendricks's chest twisted. She couldn't believe he'd just said that, just as she couldn't believe that he was looking at her the way he was looking at her now, his cheeks red, the muscles in his jaws tight with tension. It took her a moment to choke out a response. "That . . . that was really cold, Connor."

"But true." He bit down hard on the word *true*, and Hendricks felt her stomach drop. She was caught off guard by how much it hurt.

What hurt even more was that it *was* true, if Hendricks was being honest with herself. She didn't know where they could go from here. She didn't know when, or if, she'd ever be ready to move on.

And then he shook his head and stalked off, leaving Hendricks alone in an empty hallway filled with ghosts.

CHAPTER
10

HENDRICKS DIDN'T KNOW WHERE TO EAT LUNCH THE NEXT day. Usually, she ate at the corner table with Portia and Connor, but Connor was pissed at her, and she figured Portia was still annoyed from their argument the day before. Somehow, in the space of about ten minutes, she'd managed to piss off every friend she had here.

She hovered at the cafeteria door, lunch bag in hand, before veering off down a narrow hall that led to the library.

The library was small and empty. It had orange carpeting and two dozen sadly stocked shelves. There wasn't a librarian on duty, at least not one Hendricks could see, but there was a line of computers against the far wall, humming faintly.

Technically, you weren't supposed to eat in here, so Hendricks kept her lunch bag hidden as she wove through the stacks. When she was sure she wouldn't be seen, she sat cross-legged on the floor and started digging in. It was only a few minutes before her phone started pinging.

Portia. *Where are you?*

Hendricks chewed on her lower lip and then opted to ignore it. She needed a break. But her phone kept pinging, and when she finally looked down, she saw that every message was from Portia.

Hendricks groaned and flipped the phone over. She pulled a baggie of baby carrots out of her bag and tried to distract herself by wondering where baby carrots came from, whether they started out baby or were they just normal carrots that someone cut down into tiny shapes. But her mind kept veering back to her friends. She hated when people were mad at her.

A book slid out of the shelf above her and thudded to the floor next to her leg. Hendricks thought she caught the smell of something. Cigarette smoke and baby shampoo.

Eddie.

She stood quickly and her eyes moved past the metal shelves holding row after row of dusty books, to the shadowy aisle on the other side. From where she was standing, she could see patches of orange carpet and another row of books, nothing else.

"Hello?" Hendricks called. The light bulb above her flickered. Her heartbeat quickened.

No one answered, but Hendricks thought she saw the shadows behind the bookshelf shift. Her breath stopped in her throat. She crept closer, closer, squinting through the shelves again—

Then, from behind her, giggling, followed by a girl's breathy voice. "Brandon, *stop!*"

Hendricks flinched. There was a shuffling sound of footsteps on the other side of the bookshelf, and then two kids rounded the corner, a boy and a girl. They were seniors by the look of it, and they were dressed kind of strangely. The boy's jeans were a touch too tight, and his hair swept away from his face in soft waves, reminding Hendricks of a villain from an old movie. The girl looked dated, too. Her curly hair wasn't quite in style, although her jean jacket looked like something Hendricks had seen people wear today. In fact, she was pretty sure Portia had the same one in her closet. Brandon had his arms wrapped around her waist, thumbs hooked into her jeans, and the girl was sliding her fingers up into his hair. He leaned in to kiss her—

Hendricks blushed and cleared her throat to let them know she was there. The girl pulled away, dark curls swinging forward to hide her face. She didn't look her way, but Hendricks recognized the pale pink jean jacket she was wearing and realized it was the same girl she'd seen the day before, the one who'd reminded her of Portia.

She even looked a little like Portia. She had the same dark brown skin and wide-set eyes, the same full lips. Her hair was different though, big and curly.

"Not here," the girl murmured. "Someone could see us."

"Come on, don't be such a priss," the boy said condescendingly. He tugged her close and gestured around them. "There's no one else here."

A soft sigh escaped from Hendricks's lips. *There's no one else here,* he'd said.

But . . . *she* was standing just a few feet away.

"You're ghosts," she said, on an exhale, understanding crashing over her. It was the only explanation that made any sense. This boy and girl were dead. She was watching something that had already happened, probably years and years ago.

This sort of thing had happened to her before, at Steele House. She'd watched as scenes from the past played out around her. Horrible things, mostly. Things she'd tried very hard to forget.

Her skin began to crawl. The last ghosts she'd seen had tried to kill her and had actually killed Eddie.

She needed to get the hell out of here.

She began to back toward the door—

There was a noise on the other side of the library, a shoe dragging over carpet, a soft exhale. Hendricks's eyes darted back to the bookshelves.

This time, she saw another set of dark eyes peering out from behind the books.

Hendricks swore and stumbled backward, nearly losing her balance. Her eyes darted back to the end of the aisle, but the boy and girl had disappeared. For some reason, this frightened her more than when they'd been standing a few feet away. If they weren't there anymore, then where were they?

The answer came to her instantly: anywhere. They could be anywhere.

The lights flickered, again.

Off.

On.

And now the girl in the pale pink jean jacket was standing directly in front of Hendricks, her nose inches from Hendricks's nose, a smell like spoiled meat clinging to her breath. Hendricks wanted to run, to scream, but she felt frozen, paralyzed in place.

The girl was different now. Her face had been mutilated, those thick, dark curls hacked away so that raw, bleeding skin showed through the few remaining tendrils. Her left eye was bruised and so swollen that she didn't seem able to open it, and her right eye was pitch black, as though her inky pupils had expanded to fill the entire socket.

Someone had carved an inverted pentagram onto one of her cheeks, badly, the cuts barely more than angry hacks in the meat of her face. Her skin was angry and raw and pink where the blade had dug into her. Blood trailed down her face in dark rivulets, gathering in the corner of her lips, the crease of her chin.

Hendricks watched, horrified, as the girl lifted a finger to Hendricks's face and traced the line of her jaw. Her skin was like ice, and it left Hendricks feeling cold straight down to her bones.

"He'll be back for you," the girl said. Her voice was throaty and deep.

The lights flicked off.

Hendricks's paralysis broke. Knees knocking together, she turned and fled, flying through the library door. She stumbled out into the hall, her heart thudding in her chest, tears streaming down her face. She felt like something pressing against her, holding her back. She tried to breathe but each inhale was a hard scrape in her throat, like something inside of her was trying to claw its way out.

She didn't dare look back to see whether anything was chasing her, but she could've sworn she felt a cold nipping at her heels, and the sound of buzzing in her ears. There was a sharp sting in her forearm, and when she looked down, she saw something moving just below her skin, like an insect trapped inside of her, trying to get out.

Hendricks froze, a scream building in her throat. She watched as two antennae poked up through her flesh, splitting the skin on her arm until it was large enough for a single wasp to crawl out of her, wings heavy with blood, eyes glassy and black.

Hendricks slammed back against a locker, clutching her throbbing arm.

The bell rang, making Hendricks flinch. She gaped wordlessly as students spilled out of the cafeteria and quickly surround her.

When she looked down, she saw that the wasp was gone. There was no scab on her arm, no blood—nothing but smooth, unbroken skin.

Hendricks didn't know how she made it through the rest of the school day. She was sliding into her desk for her first class after lunch and then, the next thing she knew, the final bell was ringing. At her locker, she was determinedly trying to ignore the lingering scent of roses and what seemed like a second later, she was shuffling down the sidewalk toward home, apparently having decided to skip prom committee.

She released a sudden breath, causing the hair hanging down over her face to flutter. Skipping prom committee was probably for the best. She couldn't imagine untangling streamers or painting glitter onto chairs after what she'd seen.

She made her way up the steps to her house and pushed the front door open.

"Diane?" called her dad from the kitchen.

"No," Hendricks said, fighting tears. She thought of that girl's black eyes, her mutilated face.

"Hendricks?" Her dad had appeared at the living room door, scratching his chin. "What's going on? Are you okay?"

Hendricks opened her mouth to say that she was fine and released a strangled sob, instead. She couldn't do this anymore. She couldn't pretend to be normal when everything was falling apart. She pressed a hand to her mouth, her face crumbling as she choked back fresh tears.

"Oh, honey." Her father was suddenly by her side, one arm slung around her shoulder. "What's the matter? I thought you had something after school? Like a prom . . . thing? Did you and your friends get into a fight?"

Hendricks shook her head. "No . . . it's not that, it's just . . . stress."

Stress. That was the understatement of the year.

Still, it seemed like the right thing to say. Something in her dad's expression softened as he said, "I know how hard this is for you, going back to school after camp and Eddie, and Raven . . ." he trailed off, clearing his throat. "But it's not going to get better all at once. Some days are going to be harder than others. The best you can do is just take them one day at a time, you know?"

Hendricks nodded miserably. "Yeah, I guess," she said.

"Come on." Her dad suddenly clapped her on the shoulder and stood. "Let's go for a drive. What do you say to burying our feelings with something sugary?"

Despite herself, Hendricks smiled. An ice cream cone or a

doughnut wasn't going to help, not really, but it touched her that her dad was trying so hard.

"Yeah, okay," she said, offering up a watery smile. "Let's go."

Hendricks and her dad hadn't spent much time alone together in the last few years. It wasn't that they didn't get along, it was just that Hendricks's family had always been a fairly tight, three-person unit. When Hendricks was little, she was always going on outings to the movies and trendy restaurants with her parents. And then Brady had come along, and her parents' house-flipping business had gotten busier, and Hendricks had started high school.

So she was touched to see that her dad was taking this outing pretty seriously. Meaning, he insisted they stop at Dead Guy to grab lattes, even though Hendricks knew he hated coffee, and he let her choose the music they listened to in the car. She appreciated the effort. And it seemed to be working—she *did* feel a little better.

Until dad turned down their old road.

"I just want to take a peek at the construction site," he explained, slowing the car as they approached the Steele House lot. Hendricks's heart began to beat louder and louder in her ears. Sweat broke out on her palms and under her armpits. She shifted uncomfortably in her seat, trying to look normal. As though that were even possible.

Her dad cut the car's engine. The music switched off, leaving them in strained silence. Hendricks, thinking about the wasps, refusing to look directly at the foundation. Tension crawled up the back of her neck. It didn't feel safe to be here.

Her dad leaned forward over the steering wheel, the skin between his eyebrows creasing. "What the hell?"

Hendricks swallowed and followed his gaze. Even though she knew what they were going to find, even though she'd seen it with her own eyes, she still wasn't completely prepared for the long, jagged crack that ran through the foundation. Evidence of the séance gone wrong.

Her dad swore under his breath and then threw the door open and climbed out of the car.

Cautiously, Hendricks followed him.

Some construction workers had gathered around the edges of the site. Her dad made a beeline toward them, but Hendricks veered off in the opposite direction, walking right up to the edge of the crack.

It jutted across the foundation, the edges rough. Now that Hendricks was looking straight down into it, she could see the ground below. So it wasn't a gateway to hell, then. The thought wasn't as comforting as she'd hoped it would be. The toes of her sneakers sent bits of rock and cement crumpling down over the sides of the crack and cascading into the darkness.

She sipped her coffee. Despite the sweet, syrupy flavor, it tasted bitter on her tongue, and she knew it was going to keep her up all night, but she drank it anyway. She needed something to keep her hands busy.

Until this moment, she hadn't really understood what Portia meant when she'd said she *felt a presence*. Had the temperature changed? Had she felt a breeze, or seen a shadow?

Now, though, Hendricks thought she understood. The air around the crack in the foundation felt charged. It felt . . . heavy. It was cold, like the deep part of the ocean was cold. Cold like a basement without any windows. Hendricks felt it under her skin and down in her bones. Everything smelled like burning wire, like ozone. It seared the insides of her nostrils.

It was such a deeply wrong feeling that Hendricks could only stay there for a short time before she began to feel light-headed. She dropped her coffee and stumbled backward, her bones shaking. Syrupy, caramel-colored liquid splattered across the cement and dripped down into the crack—

Hendricks blinked and when she opened her eyes again, it wasn't coffee dripping through the crack.

It was blood.

The blood was everywhere—red handprints swiped over the concrete and splattered across the tops of Hendricks's shoes, thick streaks stretching across the foundation like a child's finger painting. Like someone had been *playing* with it.

Hendricks felt her gut churn with horror. There was too much of it, far too much blood to have come from just one person. Some of it looked so fresh that she suspected it would still be warm to the touch, and some was so old it had dried to flakes of brown, like rust. The metallic scent of it filled her nostrils, making her want to wretch.

From the corner of her eye, Hendricks caught sight of something glimmering from deep within the crack, and she knew without coming any closer that it, too, was blood. A black pool of it. She glanced over at it, just for a moment, but that moment was long enough to catch sight of something below the surface of the bloody pool. Something *moving*. It left a ripple in the blood, and then it was gone.

Hendricks lifted a shaking hand to her mouth. She knew that whatever was down below that pool of blood was going to climb out and reach for her, and yet she couldn't bring herself to run away, couldn't bring herself to move at all. Hot tears pressed at her eyes. She clenched them shut, blinking the tears away—

When she opened her eyes, again, the blood was gone. The concrete was clean except for the spray of coffee, a scatter of dirty footprints. There was nothing beyond the crack in the foundation except for freshly churned dirt.

Still trembling, Hendricks leaned over and fumbled for her now empty coffee cup. There was something rotten at Steele House. They needed to leave. Now.

She felt a prick on the back of her hand, like a needle jabbing her skin.

When she looked down, she saw a single wasp hovering on her wrist.

CHAPTER
11

HENDRICKS HAD SPRINTED STRAIGHT FOR THE CAR. SEEING how upset she was, her dad followed, but on the way home he continued his pep talk about stress relief, adding in some new thoughts about meditation and the power of certain breathing techniques to help cope with PTSD. Hendricks had nodded along, staring out the window. As though breathing techniques could help her with *this*.

Later that night, Hendricks was sitting at her desk, her French book flopped open in front of her. She was trying to focus on verb conjugations and tense when she heard a little *tap, tap, tap* on her window.

Her spine went rod-straight. She looked up, her skin creeping.

And then she heard a voice. "Hendricks? Come on, open up."

"Portia?" Hendricks stood and threw her window open. Portia was crouched outside, in a pair of purple crushed-velvet pajamas and fluffy leopard-print slippers. She had a silk scarf tied around her hair. "What are you doing out here?"

Portia looked nervous. Her jaw was clenched, and there was a blush creeping up her neck. After a moment, she wrinkled her nose at Hendricks's oversize T-shirt and boxers and said, as though stubbornly trying to push the nerves away, "Is that what you sleep in?"

"I wasn't expecting company."

"Right." Portia tapped one fluffy leopard slipper in the dirt. "About that, are you going to let me in?"

Hendricks stood to the side, and Portia crawled in through her window with a soft grunt. One of her leopard-print slippers slipped off her foot, falling to the ground outside.

"Oh no," Portia said, peeking out the window. "Do you think it's okay? These are my favorite slippers."

"Portia, what are you doing here?"

Portia curled her toes into the floor. She looked down at them. "You weren't answering my texts."

Hendricks rubbed her eyelids. "I sort of needed a break."

A frown touched Portia's lips, gone a second later. Hendricks felt a shot of guilt. She'd hurt Portia's feelings.

"Friends don't take breaks," Portia said, her voice harsher than it usually was. "Friends talk to each other when they're pissed."

"You're"—she sighed—"you're right. I'm sorry, Portia."

"Is it because I told you I thought Eddie was trying to kill me?"

"No," Hendricks said. And then, when Portia gave her the look, she added, "Okay, yeah. I don't like that you just assumed it was him. You don't even have any proof."

"My proof is that we tried to raise Eddie from the dead and then something creepy and paranormal attacked me." Portia said this very slowly, like she was talking to a small child. Hendricks felt her annoyance flare up. She was about to start arguing again, when Portia raised her hand. "But," she added, cutting her off, "I get that that's not enough for you. So let's just table the whole Eddie thing until we have more to go on, okay? Can we both just agree that we don't know what attacked me last night and we need to figure it out?"

Hendricks chewed her lower lip, thinking this over. After a moment, she nodded. "Yeah, okay."

"Great." Portia exhaled, and Hendricks realized that she must've been really worried that Hendricks was mad at her. It made her feel guilty for ignoring all those texts.

"That's actually why I came over," Portia added, sheepish. "I was . . . uh . . . sort of hoping I could sleep at your place."

Hendricks frowned. "You said Eddie came to *your* room last night."

"Yeah, duh, that's why I want to sleep here."

"But if we're going to get proof, we should sleep *there*."

Portia pretended to think. "Maybe you can sleep there and, like, pretend to be me?"

"Like bait?"

"Exactly!" Portia looked excited for a second and then, realizing her faux pas, she quickly added, "I mean, not like bait, because he doesn't want to kill you. So, it'll just sort of . . . trick him."

"A, I'm not sure ghosts can be tricked. And B, he doesn't want to kill you." Hendricks ticked the points off on her fingers. "Maybe he just wants to tell you something?"

Portia rolled her eyes. "Yeah, I know that whenever I want to give my friends a message, I like to hide out in their bedrooms and carve lines into their cheeks."

Hendricks ignored her. "Let's go back to your place, and I'll prove it to you. If it was Eddie, you probably just misunderstood what he was trying to say. Ghosts can be scary even when they aren't trying to be."

"Right, because now you're the expert," she muttered, turning back to the window.

Hendricks frowned at her. "What are you doing?"

"Going home?" Portia had one foot propped on the window ledge.

"You know we can just go through the front door, right?" Hendricks pointed out. "It's, like, ten. My parents aren't going to be weird about letting me stay at your place."

"Oh, right," Portia lowered her foot, and smoothed out her pj's. "I guess I just got so used to doing that with Vi . . ."

Hendricks lifted an eyebrow, and Portia's cheeks went rosy. "Yeah, I'm definitely going to make you talk about that later," Hendricks said.

A half hour later, Hendricks was sitting at the edge of Portia's bed, watching in awe as Portia applied serum after serum to her perfect skin.

"It's a ten-step Korean skin-care routine," she explained as she patted something goopy onto her cheeks. "In Korean culture, they believe that you should spend just as much time taking your makeup off as you do putting it on."

"I have never seen someone spend so much time grooming herself," Hendricks said, cocking her head to the side. Portia grabbed another bottle from the top of her dresser and began pumping lotion into her palms. This one had a snail on it. Did that mean it was made out of snail?

"What's your skin-care routine?" Portia asked, frowning.

"Uh, soap and water?" Hendricks said.

"Yeah, but like, how do you take your makeup off?"

"Makeup?"

"You don't wear *any* makeup?" Portia swiveled around on her seat, her eyes wide. "Seriously?"

"I wear mascara if I'm, like, going on a date or something," Hendricks said, shrugging.

Portia groaned. "I seriously hate you. Your skin is so perfect that I just assumed you used some fancy white-girl foundation they didn't make in my shade." Portia gave her cheeks one final pat and put the cap back on her bottle of goop. "You should let me do your makeup for prom, though. I've been working on my eyeliner game."

Prom. The word sent tension twisting through Hendricks's shoulders.

"Did you hear Owen is taking *Samia Hart?*" Portia sniffed. "He certainly forgot about Raven quickly."

Hendricks felt heat climb her cheeks. It was only a matter of time before Portia asked about Connor. She picked up a stuffed bunny from Portia's bed and began fussing with its ears. "What's this guy's name?"

"Mr. Floppy Head." Portia narrowed her eyes. "Why are you changing the subject?"

Hendricks sighed and looked up. "I assumed you talked to Connor today?"

"No, he was weird at lunch. Why?"

Weird didn't sound good, Hendricks thought. Connor and Portia had been friends their whole lives. Hendricks took it for granted that they told each other everything.

"I sort of told Connor I couldn't go with him to prom," Hendricks said.

Portia's face fell. "What? Why?"

"It just felt . . . I don't know. Wrong. I didn't want to dance with him and hang out with him all night if I was just going to be thinking about Eddie. Connor's a nice guy and that's just not fair." Hendricks cleared her throat, looking down at her lap. "Anyway, that's why I didn't come sit with you guys at lunch. I figured he needed some space, and, well, I sort of thought you'd be mad at me."

Portia was quiet for a long time. When Hendricks finally looked up, Portia was frowning. "What?" Hendricks asked.

"We're friends, right?"

"Yeah . . ."

"Well, as your friend, I'm offended."

"Portia . . ."

"You just *assumed* I would choose Connor over you?"

"You've known him forever!"

"So? What about sisterhood? What about . . . what about femi-nism?" Portia stood up, huffing. "You should've given me more credit."

Hendricks laughed. "You're right, I'm sorry."

"I know that you're trying to get over Eddie. I've told Connor that he needs to move on and leave you alone but the boy is smitten. I'm actually sort of proud of you for turning him down. I was worried you were going to string him along and break his poor little doofy heart."

Portia sat next to Hendricks on the bed and lowered her head to Hendricks's shoulder. Hendricks leaned her head against hers. "Thanks for saying that."

"You're welcome," Portia muttered.

For a moment, neither of them said anything. Hendricks adjusted the pillows on Portia's bed and leaned back, resting her hands over her stomach. It felt good to be here, talking like this. It felt *normal*.

"So." Hendricks cleared her throat. "About you climbing into Vi's bedroom window . . ."

Portia sat up, and Hendricks saw two bright red circles appear on her cheeks. "I'm not sure I want to talk about that yet . . ."

She walked across the room and started fiddling with the bottles on her dresser.

"Are you going to prom together?"

"I asked her if she wanted to be my date, and she said that prom is a sadistic rite of passage designed to make outsiders feel like the other and celebrate gender-normative relationships," Portia said. "But then she texted later and told me she found a killer outfit. So . . . I think that means yes?"

"Well?" Hendricks grinned. "Come on, that's exciting."

"It is." Portia paused for a second, biting her lower lip. "I think . . ." She sat down on the bed next to Hendricks, again, looking suddenly giddy. "Okay, so don't tell anyone I said this, but I think I might want to . . . you know . . . be with her. For the first time."

"Whoa," said Hendricks.

"Like, on prom night," Portia added.

"That's a big decision."

Portia was nodding. "Yeah, I know. I just like her so much. She's so *smart*. She was telling me all about the Stonewall riots yesterday, and, Hendricks, I don't even like history, but the way she talks about it, it was like I was actually *there*. After we were done talking, I actually went online and ordered all these books about the riots because . . . I don't know, something about the way she was talking about them made them so interesting and important." Portia blushed. "That makes me sound stupid, doesn't it? Like I only care about important things because my girlfriend does."

"No, I get it." Without meaning to, Hendricks thought about how Connor had told her about getting into woodworking with his dad, and how excited he'd been when she'd mentioned she was interested in signing up to work backstage at the school play. Her chest twisted.

Instead, she grabbed Portia's hand and squeezed. "It sounds like you guys are really happy."

Their conversation dissolved into longer and longer stretches of silence while the two girls laid in Portia's massive king-size bed, until Portia's steady breathing filled the room. Hendricks was amazed by how Portia slept on her back, perfectly still, her hands folded across her chest, like a princess. Or a vampire. Hendricks had already kicked half the blankets off her legs and balled a pillow under one arm. And she still couldn't get comfortable.

Eventually, she felt her eyes start to close, sleep taking over. It had been a long day, and she was tired. She began to drift . . .

Portia's breath misted the back of her neck.

"Portia," Hendricks groaned, still half asleep. "Stop."

The breath was cold and dry. Lazily, Hendricks lifted a hand and tried to tap Portia to roll away. "Mmm . . . move over."

When the breathing still didn't go away, Hendricks rolled onto her back, intending to push her—

But Portia was still on the other side of the bed, lying perfectly still.

Hendricks sat up suddenly. She was wide awake now.

She knew she'd felt that breathing.

Slowly, she grabbed a pillow to put in her lap like it was a shield. It was too dark in the room to see anything but the outlines of shapes: Portia's figure on her side of the bed, the furniture pushed up against the walls, the thin sliver of moonlight coming in through the window.

Hendricks's heart began to climb up her throat.

"Eddie?" she whispered.

She strained to hear anything in the silence.

There was nothing.

And then . . .

There. A low, rumble of a laugh. It was more vibration than noise. Hendricks couldn't say for sure whether she heard it or felt it. She only knew it made her skin crawl. She and Portia needed to get out of this room.

She threw her legs off the side of the bed. The floor was cold against the bottoms of her toes, making her shiver. She hugged her arms around her chest.

"Who's there?" she asked.

The room was still, black. Hendricks swung her eyes from one wall to the other, clutching the pillow tight to her chest, her breathing coming fast and hard. Deep shadows had gathered in the corners and around Portia's dresser and bed frame, and Hendricks's eyes strained to see any movement in them, any shape, anything at all. He was nowhere.

Which meant he could be anywhere.

Hendricks perched at the end of the bed, poised for any sign of movement. Outside, an owl hooted. A tree branch rustled against the window. After a few moments, she loosened her grip on the pillow.

And then her phone screen lit up. Hendricks flinched and shuffled back onto the bed, trembling now. Her phone was sitting on Portia's side table, plugged into the wall. She glanced at the screen, expecting a text.

There were no texts. But someone had reached out of the darkness to touch the phone, the lit-up screen illuminating only their long gray finger. Hendricks gaped at it, her throat suddenly dry. The skin on the finger looked old, decaying. Bright red sores crawled up its knuckles, and flesh curled away from its bones like ribbons of old paint. Hendricks watched, horrified, as it slid back into the shadows.

Her phone screen switched off, and Hendricks was propelled into total darkness. It seemed heavier than before, claustrophobic and suffocating. She fumbled for her phone and stood up. Her fingers were trembling, but she managed to pull up the flashlight app and send a shaky white beam into the black.

She turned in a tight circle, illuminating every wall, every piece of furniture. Shadows danced away from her light. Something about the way the darkness moved bothered her. It was a fast, sort of twitchy movement.

Like wasps.

Hendricks shuddered, pushing the thought from her head. She

was just freaked out, that was all. She clutched her phone with two hands now, trying to hold the flashlight beam steady.

"Eddie?" she whispered.

Laughter drifted from behind her. It was a flat, humorless sound. It didn't sound like Eddie at all. Hendricks whirled around, her heart thudding in her chest. Light bounced off the wall of Portia's bedroom, the side table, Portia's sleeping body. There was no one there.

Something slithered up the back of Hendricks's head, snaking through her hair. Hendricks only had a moment to picture that decayed, rotting finger before it tightened around her skull, sharp fingernails digging deep into her scalp.

Pain exploded through her head. Her mouth hung open in a soundless scream. She could feel fingernails tunneling through her, breaking skin, drawing blood . . .

Those fingers . . . they were so cold. Like raw meat, like death. She wanted to swat it away, but fear and pain were holding her still. Tears filled her eyes. The phone slipping from her fingers and hit the ground with a soft thud. And suddenly, and there was only darkness again.

Breath against her neck. The pain in her scalp intensified as another hand snaked around her throat, tightening.

"*Please*—" Hendricks choked out. The air left her body in a single whoosh.

And then she was skidding, slamming into the far wall. He had *thrown* her. There was a throbbing in her back, and the strength in her arms gave out, sending her crashing to the floor. She cringed, trying to push herself back up to all fours. Her arms were shaking like crazy and there was something wet and sticky on her scalp—blood.

A scream tore through the darkness.

"Portia," Hendricks gasped, crawling toward the bed. She thought she could see make out a figure, some dark shape looming over Portia.

It seemed to be hauling her out of the bed as she desperately grabbed at sheets and blankets, kicking.

"Don't touch me," Portia shouted, her voice hoarse and terrified. "Let me go! Hendricks . . . *help!*"

Hendricks saw a flash in the darkness.

A *knife*.

She ran her hands over the floor, trying to find her phone so that she could see what was going on. Her fingers groped along the floorboards, finding nothing, and more nothing . . .

Footsteps thudded down the hall outside of Portia's room, and Hendricks heard Portia's parents calling, "Portia? What's going on?"

They tried the bedroom door, but it was locked. "Portia! Open up!" her mother said, more forcefully this time.

Hendricks crawled around the floor, the pain from those fingernails still throbbing through her skull, leaving her light-headed. Her hands brushed against her phone and she grasped it, fumbling for the flashlight app, her palms sweaty and slick against the screen—

"Help!" Portia screamed, again. "Let me go—"

The phone's light flashed on, illuminating black hair and a leather jacket. He had Portia on the ground. He knelt over her, a knife clutched in one hand, the other wrapped around Portia's chin, holding her cheek against the floor. Portia's breath was coming in harsh rasps, but otherwise she'd stopped struggling. Her eyes were black with fear.

He lowered his knife to Portia's skin, the blade hovering over her bruised cheek and the still-healing cut. Hendricks watched as her friend's face crumpled in pain, a howl shaping her lips. She heard a wet sound, like a blade slicing through raw steak, and then a sort of low spurt that made her stomach turn over.

Blood began to pour down the sides of Portia's face.

The ghost started to laugh, the sound mingling with Portia's weak, whimpered cries. It was too horrible to watch. Without thinking about what she was doing, Hendricks charged.

She hit the boy square in the chest, and the two went tumbling across the floor. Hendricks tried to scramble back to her feet, but the ghost grabbed her from behind, pinning both her arms to her sides. Her phone slipped from her fingers, and the light flicked off again.

"Let *go*," Hendricks groaned. The ghost chuckled in her ear and only held tighter. A moment later, she felt the cold touch of a blade against her own cheek.

"You want to play, girl?" he whispered. His voice didn't sound like a voice, but like a harsh, whispered rasp. He pressed the knife deeper against her flesh, leaving her acutely aware of how sharp the edge of the blade was, how he could slice her open with just a twist of his wrist, just like he'd done to Portia—

Hendricks flashed back to Grayson. It was almost as though *he* was the one behind her, holding her against the wall, whispering into her ear:

Don't you dare embarrass me here.

Cold fear coursed through her. Hendricks could practically smell the stink of Grayson's cologne, the lingering, sour scent of beer on his breath. The hands around her wrist, rough and strong, could've been *his* hands—

"Open this door!" Portia's dad roared from the hall. "Portia, do you hear me?"

Hendricks had made a promised to herself that she'd never be a victim again. She wasn't going to break it, not for anyone.

The ghost had her arms pressed down her sides, so Hendricks used the only weapon she still had at her disposal—she whipped her head back, crying out when it connected with something solid.

He dropped her, swearing, and she heard a few shuffled thumps as he stumbled back.

Adrenaline pumping through her, Hendricks spun around and kicked wildly into the darkness. Her foot met something solid. She heard a grunt.

The darkness stirred and then went still. Hendricks blinked into the darkness and saw nothing. The room was suddenly quiet, except for the sounds of Portia's parents still banging at the door.

"Portia? Open up—"

Hendricks felt the hair on the back of her neck stand up. Her heartbeat thudded in her ears. The silence felt loaded. It was as though something were standing very close to her, holding his breath. This wasn't over yet.

Hendricks found herself muttering into the darkness, "Come on, I know you're still there." Her fingers curled around her damp palms, tightening into fists. *I know you're still here, I know it.*

The blood pounding in her ears began to quiet, and now she could hear only her own ragged breath. She looked around the room, frantic, twitching when she saw something glint in the dark. A scream climbed in her throat—

But it was only Portia, kneeling in her bed with a sheet clutched to her chest. Blood still trailed down her cheek, reflecting off the dim light from the moon.

"Is he gone?" Portia whispered.

Hendricks swallowed. She didn't know. She couldn't see anything. Maybe he *had* disappeared. She took a single step toward the bed—

And felt cold fingers close around her throat.

CHAPTER
12

THE HAND TIGHTENED AROUND HENDRICKS'S THROAT. SHE could feel the rough edges of calluses, the pads of fingers pressing into her skin. She lifted her hands, grasping, but the hands held like a vise.

Her breath was coming in shallower and shallower bursts. Her heartbeat had gotten louder, a steady *thrum, thrum* beating directly into her skull. Her body was screaming.

She opened her mouth, gasping, but she couldn't get any air into her lungs. The hands gripped tighter. Her head felt thick, cloudy.

She thought she heard a sound like someone pounding on glass. Something in the darkness shifted, and then the hands let go.

Hendricks's legs gave out beneath her, and she dropped to the ground like a rock. For a moment, she just lay on the floor, desperately trying to catch her breath.

She heard voices, but she found that she couldn't lift her body. She was too weak. She maneuvered her hands beneath her shoulders and pushed herself up to a crawl, still gasping.

"Who's there?" she called. She lifted a hand to her throat, cringing. She tried to stand . . .

The lamp beside Portia's bed suddenly flicked on, casting a dim glow over the room. The sudden brightness made Hendricks cringe. She blinked a few times, waiting for her eyes to adjust to the light.

Portia was crouched on her bed, sobbing, her eyes wide with

terror. Another deep gash cut across her cheek, coming together with the first to form what looked like the pointed end of a triangle. Blood had been smeared all across her face and crusted in her hair.

Hendricks thought of the girl in the library, her mutilated face, the inverted pentagram etched onto her cheek . . . bile flooded her mouth.

Something moved in the corner. Hendricks started, but it wasn't the ghost. It was . . .

Connor?

He was currently standing outside Portia's window, pounding against the glass. Hendricks hurried over to the window and threw it open.

"Are you okay?" Connor asked, climbing into Portia's room. "I was coming over to see Portia, and it looked like you were being attacked but I couldn't see what it was . . ."

Hendricks blinked at him, trying to form a question, when the door behind her began to shudder again.

"Portia? Open up!" The door knob rattled, and then there was the sound of more pounding.

Portia crawled out of bed, both hands swiping at her face, trying to stop the flow of blood. "Closet!" she mouthed, nodding to a door on the other side of the room.

Connor bounded across the room and slipped into the closet without a word. Hendricks had a fraction of a second to think about how comfortable he seemed to be hiding in girls' closets before Portia was pushing her inside, too.

"Wait, why do *I* have to be in the closet?" Hendricks asked.

"Do you honestly think I'm allowed to have girls sleep over?" Portia hissed.

"Your parents don't know I'm here?"

Portia didn't answer. She pushed Hendricks into the closet with Connor and quickly closed the door.

Hendricks heard the sound of her footsteps padding across the room, then the creak of a bedroom door opening, followed by Portia's frantic voice. "I'm sorry! I had a nightmare and I got so freaked out. I didn't mean to wake you guys up."

A deep, male voice said, "Portia, your face!"

"I—" The rest of Portia's words sounded muffled, like she'd stepped into the hallway with her parents and pulled the door shut behind her.

Hendricks closed her eyes, exhaling heavily now that she no longer had to worry about staying quiet. She supposed she could go back into Portia's room now, but she couldn't bring herself to move. Her head was still pounding, pain beating at her temples and the back of her skull. She lifted a hand to her scalp and felt something wet and sticky. Blood, but not as much as she'd been expecting. The ghost had barely broken skin.

Sighing, she slid to the closet floor. Hendricks looked around trying to calm herself down. Mindfulness. That was another thing she learned at CTE. "When things get overwhelming, take stock of your surroundings," one her counselors had said. Hendricks's breath slowed she took in the details of Portia's closet. Unsurprisingly, it was monstrous. And color-coded. The wall to Hendricks's left was covered in a rainbow assortment of hanging dresses and silk shirts and neatly folded sweaters. The wall to her right held shelf after shelf of purses, bags, and . . . Hendricks was pretty sure those colorful round things were *hat boxes*. What teenage girl needed hat boxes? Directly ahead of her was a small stool, a wall of shoes.

Connor sat on the stool. The closet was big enough that they weren't exactly nose-to-nose. But still. It was the closest they'd been since the fight.

Her cheeks felt very warm, and she was suddenly aware that she was wearing an oversized T-shirt with no bra beneath. She hunched forward a little and crossed her arms over her chest.

"So," she whispered, on an exhale.

Connor nodded. "So."

His cheeks were flushed, and he was studying a lemon-printed sundress with the intensity of a religious scholar looking for meaning behind the pieces of yellow fruit.

"What are you doing here?" Hendricks asked, when she couldn't stand the silence any longer. Connor shifted on his stool uncomfortably.

"My house is just down the road. Portia and I used to climb into each other's rooms all the time, when we were kids." he said. "I was coming over her to . . . uh . . ." He scratched the back of his head, shifting his eyes down to the floor. "I guess I just needed to talk to her."

"About me?" Hendricks's cheeks flared as soon as the words were out of her mouth.

"Well, yeah." Connor glanced up at her, and then back down to the floor again. He sighed deeply. "Look, I feel like an ass about how I talked to you before."

"It's fine," Hendricks said quickly.

"It's not." Connor lifted his eyebrows. "I owe you an apology. You're going through a lot and . . . well, I just wanted to let you know that I can be whatever kind of friend you need right now. Okay?"

Hendricks didn't know what to say. She felt a little overwhelmed. She knew Connor still had feelings for her, and yet he was willing to put them aside to be there for her as a friend.

She wanted to tell him how much his friendship meant to her, but all she could manage to say was "Okay."

Connor seemed to hear what she hadn't said. He nodded, smiling slightly, and looked down at his hands. After a moment, he cleared his throat and whispered, "So. Uh, what the hell was in Portia's room?"

Hendricks swallowed, trying to think about how to explain. "The séance worked after all. We brought something back."

Hendricks stumbled on the word *something*. Connor raised his eyebrows. "What do you mean something?"

"I don't know." Hendricks could feel tears clog her throat. She hadn't realized how upset she was, but now that she thought about it, Portia had a point.

That shape in the darkness . . . it hadn't seemed like Eddie at all. But it had *looked* like Eddie. And Ileana had told them he might come back changed. Had she just been fooling herself, to think it wasn't him?

"The ghost or—or, whatever it was," Hendricks said, faltering. "I couldn't see his face, it was way too dark, but he had black hair and he wore all black . . . and . . . . ."

Hendricks closed her eyes. She couldn't keep going. It hurt too much.

"That ghost didn't seem like Eddie to me," Connor added. His voice was kind. Hendricks felt a wave of gratitude. "I didn't know Eddie too well, but from what I remember, he wasn't mean or hateful, even when he had a reason to be." Connor pushed a breath out through his teeth. "But the thing that was in here, well, it was different."

"That's what I thought, too," Hendricks said.

"But if it isn't Eddie, who—"

Before Connor could finish asking the question, the closet door flew open and Portia was standing over them.

"They went to find first aid stuff for my cheek," she said in a low voice, glancing over her shoulder. "But they'll be back soon." Then, her eyes zeroing in on Connor, she added, "What do you mean, you don't think it was Eddie?

Connor and Hendricks shared a look.

"Come on, Portia," Connor tried.

"Don't come-on-Portia me." Portia frowned. "We just did a séance to call Eddie's spirit or whatever back from the beyond, and now this shit is happening. What's your theory?"

"Eddie wasn't vengeful when he was alive," Connor pointed out.

"Yeah, Portia, he never mentioned anything to me about wanting to get back at you or anybody else."

"Like he's going to talk about me while you guys are sucking face," Portia snapped back. Both Hendricks and Connor flinched.

"Sorry," Portia added, softening. "That was a crappy thing to say. But come on, you have to admit that this all makes sense. I'm not proud of it, but I was one of his biggest bullies when he was alive, and now he's going after me. He barely touched you, Hendricks."

Hendricks swallowed, one hand moving to her neck. The skin was tender to the touch. It was going to be black and blue tomorrow. God, what was she going to tell her parents? That a ghost attacked her? They hadn't believed that the last time she'd tried that explanation.

And Portia was right, sort of. The ghost had seemed interested in her, not Hendricks. He'd brushed Hendricks aside, at first. It was only when Hendricks fought back that he'd seemed to remember she was there.

Hendricks flinched, her fingers brushing a raw spot of skin. That was the thing that was bothering her more than anything else.

When the ghost *had* remembered she was there, he'd gone in for the kill.

CHAPTER
13

HENDRICKS WASN'T FEELING VERY HUNGRY AS SHE MADE her way to Tony's, the pizza place on Main after school the next day. Dread sloshed around in her stomach. The only reason she was going was because Portia had sent out a group text that afternoon calling "a meeting of the seven." She'd actually written *the seven*, like that was a thing.

It was barely three in the afternoon, but the sky above was already dark gray and sludgy. It reminded Hendricks of the dirty snow you found stuck to the bottom of a car. Main Street had mostly emptied out, except for a handful of other students who'd made their way over from Drearford High after the final bell. A few waved at Hendricks and called, "Hey!" as she pushed through the pizza place's front doors.

Tony's was a traditional, old-school Italian restaurant, with plastic red-and-white-checked tablecloths, candles wedged into Chianti bottles, and massive framed posters of different shapes of pasta hanging on the brick walls. There was karaoke in the basement on Friday nights, and a few old arcade games slouched against the back wall.

Finn was playing the *Teenage Mutant Ninja Turtles* game while Connor and Blake huddled around him, cheering and groaning.

"Dude, I *own* you!" Finn shouted, pumping the air with a fist.

Hendricks made her way to the booth next to the games, where Portia and Vi had already gotten settled. To Hendricks's surprise, there was a large pepperoni pizza sitting on the table before them, untouched.

Seeing it, Hendricks felt hollow. The first time she came here, Portia and Raven had obsessed over the menu, trying to come up with the craziest combination of toppings for their pizza. Hendricks had always preferred classic pepperoni herself, but there was something a little sad about seeing it sitting in front of Portia just now. Portia and Raven had always said pepperoni was basic.

"Where were you after school?" Hendricks asked Portia. "I thought we were walking over together."

Portia and Vi shared a look, and Vi's cheeks darkened, confirming Hendricks's theory that Portia had been with her girlfriend. Hendricks arched her eyebrow, remembering her resolve to be more supportive of Portia's relationship.

"Never mind," she muttered, taking the seat across from them.

"Did you text Ileana?" Portia asked.

Hendricks frowned. "Was I supposed to?"

"Well, she *is* one of the seven. I was kind of hoping we could all be here for this." Portia chewed her lip. "Can you text her now? We can wait."

"I don't have her number," Hendricks said.

"Do we really think that chick owns a cell?" asked Finn. The boys had trickled over from their game, and now Connor slid into the booth next to Hendricks, while Blake and Finn pulled up chairs around the end of the table.

Finn nodded a hello to Hendricks, his lips twisted in a strange approximation of Connor's familiar, open smile—only Finn's was just a touch amused where Connor's always read as friendly. Hendricks smiled nervously back. She couldn't quite get a handle on Finn. He seemed so different from his brother.

121

"Yeah, I don't exactly see her rocking the new iPhone," said Blake, grabbing a slice of pizza and cramming half of it into his mouth. "Maybe we could call her using, like, smoke signals or something?"

A dribble of grease slipped over his lip. Vi made a face. "For a man of color, you're being super ignorant of other people's cultures," she said.

Blake frowned at her, swallowing. "I just meant that there's probably some mystical way of getting in touch with her. What's this about, anyway? You guys look all serious."

Finn snorted. "Let me guess. We raised a ghost the other night, and now he's trying to take us out, one by one."

He said this in a jokey, spooky voice, and did a creepy wiggle thing with his fingers. When no one laughed, the grin dropped off his face. "What?"

Hendricks wasn't remotely hungry, but she slid a slice of pizza out of the carton and onto a napkin and began picking at a piece of pepperoni.

Portia cleared her throat. "So, okay, we don't actually know *what* or *who* we raised," she said carefully. Eyes flicking over to Hendricks, she added, "But . . . *something* attacked me in my bed last night."

There was a beat of awkward silence. Hendricks flicked at the piece of pepperoni, sending a spray of grease over her napkin.

"Is that why you won't tell me where you got those scratches? Because they were from a ghost?" Vi was frowning, looking between Portia and Hendricks. "This is a joke, right?"

"Ghosts aren't real," added Finn.

"I felt it," Connor said, in a quiet voice.

Hendricks had now managed to detach the entire piece of pepperoni from the congealed cheese on her pizza, and she was holding it between two fingers, not sure what to do with it. She still didn't want to eat it, so she dropped it onto the napkin and grabbed another napkin to wipe the grease from her fingers. When she looked up, she saw that everyone else was staring at her.

"Oh, uh, yeah, I saw it," she muttered. "It was real. It tried to choke me."

"You keep saying *it*," said Blake. "How do you know it was a ghost?"

"Yeah," Finn added, "couldn't some pedophile dude or rapist have snuck in through the window?"

Portia was blinking very fast. "That's a comforting thought."

"It's more comforting than *ghosts!*"

"It disappeared into thin air when I tried to touch it," Hendricks said.

"It could've gone out the window," Finn pointed out.

"*I* was coming in through the window," Connor added. "I would've noticed if some guy came past me."

Finn said, "But you wouldn't have noticed—"

"Guys," Hendricks cut in, her voice rising above the rest of the argument. She took a deep breath, like they taught her at camp. "I feel like we aren't listening to each other. I know it was a ghost because . . ." She felt the words lodge themselves in her throat, and she had to work to spit them out. "Because I . . . I *saw* it. *Him.* The night we did the séance. After you guys left, I saw this thing crawl out of a crack in the foundation at Steele House. He looked like a boy at first, but all made out of, like, shadows. And then, just when I reached out to touch him, he broke off into a cloud of—of wasps." Her throat felt scraped raw, and she couldn't bring herself to look up from her pizza. "Rapists can't do that," she added quickly. "This was something else. It wasn't human."

There was a long stretch of silence. Hendricks finally looked around at them, uncertain whether they believed her.

Vi broke in at last. "You keep saying you *saw* it. But no one else saw anything, right?"

Connor and Portia looked at each other and shook their heads.

"It was dark," Portia said.

"I could see you and Hendricks moving around in the dark, but I didn't see anyone—any*thing* else. It just sort of felt cold." Connor shuddered. "It felt terrible."

"But *you* saw it," Vi said to Hendricks, frowning. "That's weird, right? That you saw it and no one else did."

Hendricks shrugged. "I don't know. I guess yeah, sort of."

"What did he look like, before he turned into bugs, or whatever?"

Hendricks started shredding her napkin. "I don't know. Just some guy."

"Hendricks, come on, tell us," Portia said urgently.

"Tall. Dark hair." Hendricks looked up and added, sighing, "I couldn't see him very well, but . . . he was wearing all black."

"Sounds like someone we knew," Portia murmured.

"Jesus, Portia, I'm telling you it wasn't Eddie."

"You said you could barely see him," Portia pointed out, eyes narrowing. "So how could you know for sure?"

"At least I saw *something*. You didn't see him at all!"

Portia looked like she was about to keep arguing when Vi touched her arm, "Hey, it's okay, we're all trying to figure this out."

"Yeah, I don't care whether this thing you saw was Eddie Ruiz or scary Gary the sewer clown, I'm still stuck on the part where we're talking about *ghosts*." Finn pushed his chair back, standing. "Ghosts aren't real."

"Dude, what do you think happened at that party three months ago?" Connor asked. "You think that fire was just some kind of freak accident?"

"Yeah, I do," said Finn. He lifted both hands to his head and dug his fingers into his hair. "Accidents happen all the time. The house was old, its wires were faulty, or someone left the oven on or knocked over a candle, or—"

"It wasn't a freaking *candle*," Hendricks said. "Steele House has been haunted for years. It's why Maribeth died—"

"*No.* Maribeth's older brother killed her," Finn said. His face was growing red. "And then he killed himself out of guilt. Everyone knows that."

"Why would Kyle kill his little sister? That doesn't make any sense." Hendricks could feel the anger rising in her chest. "The ghosts got Maribeth, and then they got Kyle, and two months ago, they took Eddie, too."

Finn was still shaking his head. "That's crazy—"

"You didn't think it was *remotely* strange that three kids from the same family all died in the same place?" asked Hendricks.

"No, I don't." Finn's face was red with anger. "Because those three kids were from the Ruiz family and everyone around here knows that family is messed up. The only reason you don't seem to get it is because you were screwing—"

Connor stood up very quickly. "Take a walk, man."

Finn lifted one shaking finger and pointed it at Hendricks. "Siding with your wannabe girlfriend isn't going to make her like you any—"

Before he'd finished, Connor had lurched across the table, giving his brother a hard shove that sent him skidding back into his chair. The glasses on the table rattled, and Portia said, "Are you freaking *kidding* me right now?"

With a jerk of his chin, Finn lunged for Connor, one arm swinging backward in the beginning of a punch. Blake sprung out of his chair first, shoving his body between the two of them.

"Whoa, man." Blake grabbed Finn roughly, his voice full of warning. "What the hell are you thinking?"

Finn shrugged Blake off, muttering something under his breath. Shaking his head, he turned stalked out of the restaurant. Blake followed him without a word.

Connor didn't go after them, but he stayed standing, his hands hanging open at his sides, his face bright red.

Hendricks didn't look up at him, but kept her eyes glued to the table, heat rising in her cheeks. She had the sudden desire to scream. At Finn for taking sides, and at Connor for starting a fight.

Instead, she dug her fingers into the tops of her thighs and stayed silent.

"So . . . what exactly are we saying, here?" asked Vi, after a long moment. "That Eddie's back?"

"No," Hendricks said, at the same time that Portia said, "Yes."

Hendricks cut her eyes at Portia, who pointedly wouldn't look at her.

"And we need to kill him before *he* kills me!" Portia added.

"How do you kill a ghost?" asked Vi, frowning. "You think Ileana knows?"

"No one's taking anyone down," said Connor.

"Excuse me?" said Portia. "As the only person sitting here who is actually being haunted, I would like to take him down."

"Will all of you just . . . stop?" Hendricks closed her eyes. A headache had begun pounding at her temples, the pain a steady thud, beating in time with her heart. "We don't know even know that it was Eddie and if it was, we don't know why he came back, or what he wants, or—"

"What he wants?" Vi interrupted her. "Portia just said that he attacked you last night. It seems like he made it pretty clear what he wants."

"That's not . . ." Hendricks wasn't sure what else to say.

Tears were pressing at the corners of her eyes, threating to spill over onto her cheeks. For some reason, it was the tears that made her more frustrated than anything else. She had survived so much. She'd always been strong, even when truly terrible things had happened to her. But something about this moment was getting to her. It was sitting here, trying to explain to her new friends that the boy she'd fallen in love with wasn't the monster they were all making him out to be.

Finn's words echoed in her head. *The only reason you don't seem to get it is because you were screwing—*

"You didn't know him," Hendricks said, sliding out of the booth. "None of you actually knew him."

She made her way toward the front of the restaurant, walking fast. The tears hadn't started to fall, yet, but she could still feel them there, gathering behind her eyelids. She tried to blink them back.

She was almost at the door when Connor caught up with her.

"Hey," he said. "Let me walk you home. It's not safe out there."

Hendricks hesitated. She was still annoyed about the fight with Finn, and there was a part of her that wanted to turn him down. But he was right, shit kept happening to her when she was alone. It wasn't safe.

She nodded. "Yeah, okay."

The sky was still its usual gray, but the cloud cover seemed to be holding in the warmth. Hendricks left her jacket unbuttoned. The air smelled like rain and dirt.

She stared at the sidewalk, at the little green plants growing up from between the cracks. They seemed strangely hopeful, those plants.

Even though it had been gross and gray and cold for so long, they still believed spring was coming. Hendricks exhaled through her teeth. "I wanted to say that . . . well, that I'm sorry, I guess. For being weird lately."

Connor cut his eyes toward her. "You haven't been weird."

"I feel like I've been . . ." Hendricks remembered what Portia had said and added, "Stringing you along."

Connor cleared his throat and stared off at some point in the distance. A car disappeared around the corner. "You know, I always knew how you felt about Eddie. Even before."

Hendricks raised her eyes. "Before?"

"Do you remember that night in my car? After we jumped into the quarry?"

Hendricks blushed. That was the night they'd first kissed. "I remember."

"We saw Eddie walking along the side of the road. And you didn't really say anything about him or anything, but there was a look on your face when you saw him, like a . . ." Connor paused searching for the right word. "A spark," he said eventually. "I know that sounds cheesy, but I don't know how else to describe it. I remember thinking, that guy's going to be a problem."

Hendricks closed her eyes. "I'm sorry."

"Yeah," Connor said. "Me too."

Hendricks didn't know what to say.

"He sacrificed himself to save me," she said eventually. "Back at the house. I was going to let the ghosts take me, but he wouldn't let them. He gave his life instead. I don't know how I'm supposed to move on after that."

Connor was silent for a long time. "I get it," he said finally. "You're a good person, Hendricks."

Hendricks looked up at him. "You really think that?"

"I really do."

They were outside of Hendricks's house now. She could see the lit-up windows, and she knew that her parents were probably in the kitchen, waiting for her to come in so they could all have dinner.

"Thanks for walking me home," she said to Connor.

"Thanks for letting me." He stuck out his hand. "See you later, friend."

Hendricks couldn't help laughing out loud. "Yeah, see you later," she said, and shook it.

There was a warmth in his hand that felt like it spread into her arm. Hendricks kept thinking about it, even after she climbed the steps.

CHAPTER
14

HENDRICKS HESITATED OUTSIDE HER FRONT DOOR, ONE hand grasping the doorknob. She could hear her parents inside, the steady rise and fall of their voices. She knew that, if she went in, they'd have dinner as a family, and Brady would be gurgling happily in his highchair, and her dad would want to talk about the construction on the Steele House lot, and her mom would want to know whether anyone had asked Hendricks to prom, and Brady would smile at her and throw his peas.

She sighed deeply. It was all so normal, so happy, but the idea of sitting through a whole night like that made her feel claustrophobic. And she still had so many unanswered questions swimming in her mind. She took her hand off the doorknob and backed down the stairs. She couldn't do it. She was still too raw.

Pulling her jacket tighter around her shoulders, she turned and jogged the rest of the way down the stairs. Once she reached the sidewalk, she just started walking.

She wasn't sure where she was going. Without meaning to, she thought of the walk she'd taken with Eddie around the neighborhood back when they were first becoming friends.

You don't get it, he'd told her. *There's something rotten here.*

Rotten, that was the word he'd used to describe the town. It made Hendricks think of something black and decaying just beneath Drearford's sidewalks, something crawling up toward the surface, like mold. She suddenly realized how selfish it had been of her to try and get Eddie to come back here, now that he'd finally gotten away. Eddie had hated it here. Did she really expect him to return, for her? Because she missed him? How selfish was that?

If he had turned into that dark, evil thing she'd seen last night, she knew she was to blame.

She shuddered and kept walking. Down block after block. Around corners and across streets. Hendricks stared at her feet, watching her shoes rise and fall over the cracked and dirty pavement. She wondered whether she could just keep walking, out of this town, this life.

But when she finally looked up again, she realized she'd circled back without meaning to, down Eddie's old block, right up to Eddie's old house.

She exhaled through her nose. The house looked just like she remembered. The paint had long ago faded, showing weathered gray siding and rusted gutters. Old plastic toys littered the yard, and a car without wheels sat on cinder blocks beside the back shed. A few of the upstairs windows had cardboard taped over the glass. Wherever Eddie had ended up, it had to be better than this.

"Where are you?" she whispered.

The wind blew past, the sound a low moan in the trees. Hendricks closed her eyes and saw flickering candlelight, Eddie's dark hair. She was back in the cellar at Steele House. She'd just told Eddie about everything that went down at her old school with Grayson, but instead of trying to make it better or convince her that it was all over, he'd just listened. He'd told her that the ghosts they made up themselves were more dangerous than real ones, and for the first time, Hendricks felt like there was someone in the world who understood what she'd gone through.

That had been the moment she'd realized she'd really liked Eddie. Maybe even more than liked. It hurt to think about it now.

She started walking again. Slowly, at first, her head hunched against the wind, watching her feet like before. And then she lifted her head, a thought occurring to her. She walked a little faster, and then she started running.

She suddenly realized where she wanted to go.

The Drearford Cemetery was about five blocks from Eddie's house, bordering the edge of town. Hendricks had run the whole way there. When she reached the wrought-iron fence that surrounded the grounds she doubled over, hands propped on her knees, breathing hard. It took her a minute to catch her breath.

Finally, she straightened, wiping the sweat from her forehead. It felt strangely peaceful over here. There weren't any people, and the only light came from the old-fashioned-looking lanterns that dotted the winding sidewalks. The air smelled like flowers and freshly turned dirt.

Hendricks began to walk. She hadn't been to the cemetery since Eddie's funeral, and she was surprised by how pretty it all was, more like a park than a graveyard. The grass was lush and well maintained. Large oak trees shaded the path, and there were little patches of flowers, tulips and daffodils and daisies, planted every few feet. Even the gravestones were beautiful, in a strange way. The marble caught the light of the setting sun and seemed to glow.

It all made Hendricks feel vaguely ill. It was a lie, she thought. This wasn't a park at all. There were bodies buried beneath the lush green lawn, the swaying flowers. Hundreds of corpses lay in boxes under her feet, rotting. Eddie's was one of them.

Just a few months ago, she'd kissed his lips and run her fingers through his hair and touched his shoulders, his back. And now he was just meat and bones.

The thought caused tears to spring to her eyes.

It kept hitting her over and over again, how much she missed him.

She wandered through the cemetery, winding around the sidewalks, closer and closer to Eddie's grave.

Cicadas hummed. The sun dipped behind a distant hill. Shadows stretched toward her, long and dark.

The mood shifted, a chill coming over her. She could see Eddie's gravestone in the distance now, a small concrete slab jutting up from the earth like a crooked tooth. The shadows were so heavy over here that it wasn't until Hendricks was standing just a few feet away that she realized there was someone *there*, some hunched figure kneeling before the gravestone.

Her heartbeat sputtered. Deep in her soul, a small part of her had hoped he would be here.

She stepped off the sidewalk and cut across the grounds, her sneakers kicking up bits of dirt and leaves. The figure in front of Eddie's gravestone had his back to her, but she could tell that it was a teenage boy wearing a black leather jacket, black jeans, and scuffed combat boots. Dark hair hung over his face. Seeing him, Hendricks felt like someone was squeezing her lungs between their hands. She knew that hair. She'd run her fingers through it.

She stopped walking, feeling suddenly frozen.

"Hi," she said, her voice a croak.

The boy straightened.

Hendricks didn't know what to say. Her mouth felt impossibly dry. Her heart was beating so loud inside of her ears that she couldn't hear anything over it, even her own thoughts. It was Eddie, finally, after all this time, after everything she'd done to try to reach him.

He stood, very slowly.

She took another step toward him, reached out, and touched his shoulder. He turned around.

Hendricks stared for a long moment, confused.

This boy wasn't Eddie.

He was young, like Eddie had been, but his face was rounder and boyish, a strange contrast with his tall, broad-shouldered body. He had a patchy mustache that didn't quite connect to the hair on his chin, and though he had black hair, up close it didn't look like Eddie's at all. Eddie's hair had been thick and wavy, but this boy's hair was thin and straight. His roots were growing in a deep ginger that made it look like his scalp was bleeding.

His eyes narrowed on Hendricks's face. He was wearing thick black eyeliner that made them look very small and beady.

"Who are you?" he snarled through chapped, cracked lips.

Hendricks couldn't quite find her voice. "I—"

She stopped speaking as a smell rose up from the ground below her. It was a dank, slightly sweet smell. Fruit gone mushy. Fresh manure. Decay.

Hendricks covered her mouth with her hand, gagging.

Rotten, she thought out of nowhere. That was exactly what this smelled like. It was as though there was something rotting in the ground beneath her, the smell only just reaching her nose.

When she looked up again, she saw that the boy's face had changed. His teeth looked longer than they'd been a moment ago and crooked, like they didn't all fit inside of his mouth. There was something between them, something blackish and . . . *oozing*. The cracks in his lips had grown deeper.

"Who . . . the fuck . . . are you?" Now the boy's voice seemed layered over other, unearthly voices. His words echoed around her.

Hendricks couldn't breathe. This was familiar, all of it, so, so familiar. Fear solidified inside of her, leaving her entire body cold. She took one stumbling step backward.

"I—I'm leaving," she said, and she lifted her hands, like the boy was a wild animal she was trying to keep calm. "I'll go. Okay?"

The boy's mouth split into a laugh. The cracks in his lips began to bleed. "Bullshit."

Then, with a sound like raw meat hitting a cutting board, a chunk of his skin peeled off the bones of his face. It curled away from his cheek, still attached by a thin strip of flesh. A wasp landed on the meat of the boy's face, its tiny wings twitching.

Hendricks balled a hand at her mouth. She felt sick.

She took a single, slow step backward, and as though waiting for this, the boy's hand shot out, his fingers curling around her upper arm. He held her roughly in place.

"Hold still," he said in that strange, layered hiss of a voice. The putrid scent of his breath washed over her, making it hard to breathe.

"Let *go*." Hendricks pushed the words through clenched teeth, trying hard to keep herself from inhaling the scent of him, the rot.

She felt a cold wave of fear wash over her. She tried to pull away, and the boy shot his other hand out, now grasping both of her arms. She screamed and arched her back, trying to break free, but he held her so tightly, his fingers pressing against her skin, making her cringe. Laughing, he lifted her off the ground.

She stretched her feet down, down, trying to brush the tips of her shoes against the grass—

He pulled her harder, up, up, up.

"Please. Let me go," Hendricks said. The boy grinned, showing decaying black teeth. Hendricks squeezed her eyes shut.

"Okay," he muttered. "I'll let you go." He gripped her tighter, then

135

jerked her body away from him, throwing her to the ground.

Hendricks screamed as she landed, *hard*. The air left her in a whoosh, and for a long moment, all she could think about was the pain. It lit up the entire left side of her body, pounding through her hips and shoulders, making her head scream.

She rolled onto one side, hands grasping at her ribs, wondering if she'd broken anything. It took her a couple of tries to force her eyes open again.

The boy looked her over, grinning. The smell of his breath was enough to make Hendricks start coughing again. Her head began to swim. She couldn't breathe.

"Please," she murmured, turning her face into the dirt, as far away from this boy as she could manage. "Please ... don't...."

He dragged her off the ground, rocks and sticks slicing at her arms, and pinned her against a large, crumbling headstone. Hendricks grunted, her head lolling forward. She was having a hard time regaining her strength. Darkness flickered at the edges of her eyes. Everything hurt.

And then, she heard something else: a low, throaty gurgle. It seemed to travel a great distance before reaching her ears, and it took her a long moment to realize it was coming from the boy. He was *laughing* at her pain. Anger flickered through her, and without thinking about what she was doing, she began to drag her hand over the ground, fingers searching for something, anything ...

There, a rock. Hendricks gripped it clumsily. *I'm not a victim anymore*, she reminded herself.

With a grunt, she lifted the rock and brought it down against the boy's skull—hard. He released a groan and crumpled, his grip on her arms loosening.

Hendricks jerked her knee up, catching him right in the gut. He doubled over, crying out in pain. "*Bitch.*"

Hendricks darted around him and started to run. He turned with a grunt and caught the sleeve of her jacket, pulling her backward, and the momentum sent both of them stumbling to the ground.

Hendricks pushed herself up to all fours, gasping. The ghost got her by the leg, but she was still holding the rock, so she swung out wildly, trying to smash it against his skull. He was too quick. He grabbed her wrist and wrestled the rock away, tossing it to the ground. Hendricks noticed that his fingernails were long and painted black, the polish chipping. She felt a prickle in her skull, remembering how he'd dug those fingers into her throat.

And now, he dragged her backward, pulling her off her knees so that her face slammed into the packed earth. Her teeth cut into her tongue. The taste of dirt and blood filled her mouth. Choking, she tried to push herself up. Her arms trembled. She'd only just managed to pull her knees below her body when he grabbed her by the shoulders, flipping her over so quickly and with so much strength that white stars burst around the edges of her vision. An ache like fire burned through her back. The ghost's black eyes bore into hers. She could smell his rotten breath.

He pulled a knife out of his pocket, opening it with a flick of his hand. There was still blood dried along the blade.

Hendricks drew in a sharp breath. She could die right here, she realized. Just like Maribeth had died. Just like Kyle and Eddie.

Her heartbeat slammed in her temples. The sound of it blocked out all other noise. Gathering the last of her strength, she kicked out, not aiming, just *thrashing*.

The ghost grunted and stumbled backward. Hendricks scrambled away—but not fast enough. His hand shot out, fingers catching around her wrist. She yanked her arm back and those long black nails left a jagged gash along her skin, stretching from elbow to her wrist. Blood bubbled up along the scratch.

She screamed and lunged for another rock, hurling it without looking to see where she was throwing. She missed.

"Stay the *hell* away from me!" she shouted. There were no other rocks to throw, nowhere for her to run. "Stay—"

Her voice died in her throat as the grass around her began to whither. It curled in on itself, turning first brown and then black. Ice crawled up each individual dying blade. The temperature around Hendricks grew several degrees colder. She felt her jaw grow tight.

The boy stared at her, his eyes a deep, solid black, his long teeth hanging over his chapped lips. But he didn't come any closer.

And then, strangely, he began to *sink.*

Down, down, down. First his ankles, then his hips, then his torso disappearing into the earth.

Hendricks stood there, frozen for a long moment, one hand pressed to her chest. She watched the ghost's head sink down below the ground and that's when she noticed that the dead grass had formed a perfect circle around her.

Almost like something had been protecting her.

She closed her eyes, her head dropping forward. She took a few deep breaths, trying to steady herself, and then she moved away from the tree. On instinct, she pulled her cell phone out of her pocket and checked the time.

9:22, it read.

She blinked, and the time changed. Now, it read 7:43, the correct time. But Hendricks knew what she'd seen.

All she could think about was how badly she wanted to get away from here. But first, she glanced over at the tombstone where the boy had been kneeling. He'd left an inverted pentagram drawn in blood next to the name.

It wasn't Eddie's tombstone.

Instead, it read *Samantha Davidson, 1970–2019.*

CHAPTER
15

HENDRICKS DIDN'T REALIZE HOW BADLY SHE WAS BLEEDING until she pushed the front door to her house open, and her mom screamed.

"Oh my God! Baby, what happened?"

Hendricks stood there, numb, while her mom raced across the room and began fussing over her arm.

The scratch she'd gotten from ghost's long, creepy-ass nails looked much more . . . *garish* in the light. The deep, jagged cut stretched all the way from her wrist to her elbow, and it was still gushing blood. Hendricks looked down and noticed that there was a dark brownish-red smear down one side of her body, over her jacket and her jeans, splattering her shoes.

Damn, she thought distantly. *I liked those shoes.*

A ruined pair of shoes probably shouldn't have mattered just then, but it was the one thing Hendricks could think about as her mother knelt beside her, gingerly touching the edges of the cut with her finger. All of the other thoughts were just too horrible. She just felt numb now.

"This might need stitches," she murmured, grimacing.

"Were you attacked?" This came from her dad, who was hovering nearby, a wriggling Brady in his arms. His face was stony and grim. He was speaking in a voice that Hendricks had only heard him use a few times before, deep and angry. "Was it that boy again? Did he come here?"

That boy. He meant Grayson.

Sometimes her life felt like an endless cycle of one drama after another.

Hendricks shook her head. "No, it wasn't a boy. I was trying to hop a fence over by Tony's and my jacket got caught on the metal wire. I fell."

The lie just popped into her head. It was a pretty terrible lie, now that she thought of it. There weren't any fences over by Tony's, for one thing.

Her father frowned at her. He must've been squeezing Brady too tightly, because Brady began to squirm in his arms, saying, "Daddy, *down.*"

"I swear, Dad," Hendricks rushed to say. "A boy didn't do this to me." At least not a *living* boy, she amended silently. "I fell, that's all."

Her father seemed to deflate some. "Well," he muttered, still looking unconvinced. "Either way, that cut looks terrible. We should go to the hospital."

The hospital. Hendricks had already been there once, when Brady got hurt a couple of months ago. She remembered the harsh fluorescent lighting and the thick smell of antiseptic in the air. She shuddered.

"Dad, *no.* No hospital." She looked at her mom with pleading eyes. All she wanted to do was take a shower and climb into bed and think about what she'd just seen.

The ghost in the graveyard. The gravestone he'd been kneeling beside. *Samantha Davidson.*

Hendricks didn't know who Samantha was, but if she was the reason this boy had returned from the dead, she had to figure it out.

The idea of wasting time that could be spent researching made her skin itch.

"Please, it's fine. I just need to clean it up and slap on a few Band-Aids."

A muscle near her dad's eye twitched. Hendricks figured he was thinking about how badly he wanted to avoid the nightmare that was the emergency room at this hour, too. He was already in the worn sweats he wore around the house when he knew he wasn't going to have to leave again, and there was an open beer on the table behind him, condensation still clinging to the glass.

After a moment, his shoulders sagged, and a silent, weary cheer went through Hendricks's head. She'd won this round.

"You just make sure to put some antiseptic on that cut," her mom called after her, as she drifted down the hallway. "And clean it well! Soap and water! I don't want your arm turning green and falling off."

"Promise," Hendricks called back over her shoulder, and ducked into the bathroom.

It took several wads of tissue for Hendricks to soak up all the blood from her arm, and by the time she was done, the bathroom looked like a crime scene. There was blood dotting the porcelain sink and a spray of it across the mirror. A pile of bloody tissues sat next to the toilet.

Hendricks ran her arm under warm water from the tap and dug a bottle of first aid ointment and Band-Aids out of the hall closet. It took five Band-Aids snaking up her arm and into the crook of her elbow to cover the whole cut, but she was fairly sure her arm would be okay.

After she'd cleaned the sink and tossed the last of the bloody tissues into the trash, Hendricks fished her cell out of her pocket and texted Portia.

She pressed send. She hadn't even managed to move her thumb from the return key when she got a response.

Come over, Portia texted back. I can't leave my room

Hendricks frowned. Huh? Why? You grounded?

Three little dots appeared, telling Hendricks that Portia was typing. Then they vanished. Hendricks waited for them to appear again, but they never did.

She set her phone down on the sink and walked over to her bedroom window. She could make out the shape of Portia's shadow moving behind the thin curtain of the house next door. She waited for Portia to throw the curtains back and lean outside, but she didn't. Weird.

Hendricks doubted her parents would be cool with her leaving again after she showed up with a freaking *gouge* up the side of her arm, so, as quietly as she could manage, she slid her bedroom window open and crawled outside. The grass was cool beneath her bare feet and a little crunchy with frost. She crept across the ground between hers and Portia's bedrooms and rapped on the glass.

The window slid open almost immediately. Portia hovered on the other side. "Good, you came."

"You were being cryptic enough," Hendricks said. "Why can't you leave your place?"

But Portia's eyes had already swiveled to the bandages snaking up Hendricks's arm. A deep crease formed between her brows. "Holy shit, are you okay? What happened? And why were you at the cemetery? Did you hit your head? Did he *choke* you? He totally tried to choke me."

"I'm *fine*, Portia."

"Do your parents know you're over here?" Portia asked, scandalized. "Are you going to get in trouble?"

"Not if you let me come inside."

"Oh, right." Portia stepped aside so that Hendricks could crawl through her window and into her bedroom. "Okay, now I need you to start from the beginning. Why were you at the cemetery, of all the creepy-ass places? Tell me absolutely everything that happened."

Hendricks dropped onto the frilly pink stool in front of Portia's makeup table, groaning. Her arm throbbed. "Why you aren't allowed to leave your room?" she asked, instead of answering Portia's questions. "Did you get in trouble?" A smile twitched at the corner of her mouth. "Did you parents catch you with Vi?"

"What? God, no," Portia said, blushing. She sat at the edge of her bed and leaned close to Hendricks, lowering her voice. "Actually, my parents can't know about this, okay? If I tell you, you're sworn to secrecy."

Hendricks mimed zipping her lips shut.

"Okay." Portia exhaled. "So, the truth is that I was feeling pretty freaked out after Tony's. I didn't really want to go home so I . . . sort of went to Ileana's."

Hendricks blinked, certain she'd heard her wrong. "You what?"

"Eddie—I mean, the ghost," Portia amended when Hendricks shot her a look. "He's attacked me in this room *twice* now. How am I supposed to feel safe here? God, Hendricks, how am I supposed to *sleep?* So, anyway, I thought maybe Ileana would have an idea, like a spell or a ritual we could do to keep the ghost or whoever out of my bedroom. I told her what was going on, and she agreed to . . . to do a spell for me. Just a little one."

"A spell," Hendricks repeated. She tried to picture Portia standing inside of Ileana's shop, surrounded by yellowed skulls and crystals and statues of naked goddesses, calmly explaining to the witchy girl that she was being haunted.

It felt strange, like trying to picture Portia throwing out all of her skincare products or wearing a pair of boot-cut jeans.

"Yeah, a spell." Portia started fumbling with something hanging from her neck. It was a small burlap satchel attached to a length of thick twine. Hendricks frowned. Not exactly Gucci. "To protect my bedroom."

Now that she was looking, Hendricks couldn't help noticing a couple of other things, like the thick line of salt sinking into the carpet directly in front of Portia's door, or the tiny mounds of crystals, balanced like pyramids, glinting mysteriously from the corners of her room. Black candles flickered from the tops of Portia's dressers. The entire room smelled like sage.

"Portia," Hendricks murmured, eyes flicking back to her friend's face. "You can't be serious."

Portia looked suddenly defensive. "Of course I'm serious. This whole *thing* is serious. A ghost keeps trying to carve up my face. I'm scared to, like, *move* right now. I could *die*." She hesitated before adding, "And you didn't seem remotely interesting in helping."

Hendricks flinched, stung. She cleared her throat. "You really think all this is going to work?"

"It has to. Only . . ." Portia trailed off.

"Only what?"

"Well . . . the spell only works in my bedroom. So, I can't, like, leave it."

Hendricks felt her lip twitch, certain this was a joke. "You're not going to leave your bedroom?"

"Not until the ghost is gone, no."

The smile dropped off Hendricks's face. Portia didn't sound like she was joking. "What about school?"

"I told my mom that the school nurse diagnosed me with mono. I've never missed a day of school, like, ever, so she bought it pretty easily. Vi and Connor are going to bring me my assignments here, although I was going to text you to see if I could share your World History notes? They're both taking Mrs. Murphy's class and we're in Mr. O'Donnell's, so the material won't be the same."

"Yeah, sure," Hendricks said. "Whatever you need."

"And do you mind checking in on Raven? I've been trying to go most days after school, but now I can't."

Hendricks felt a pang of guilt. Why hadn't it occurred to her to check on Raven? "Of course," she said.

"Okay, my turn now," Portia said, crossing her arms over her chest. "You said you saw him in the cemetery. Explain, please."

Hendricks told Portia everything. How she saw a boy crouching at Eddie's grave, how she thought it was Eddie when she saw his leather jacket and his dark hair, but then he turned around and she realized that it wasn't Eddie at all. She shivered, remembering the boy's red roots, his chapped lips.

Portia looked confused. "I don't understand," she said, cutting Hendricks off. "You saw the ghost's face?"

"Yeah, I did, and, Portia, he was someone else. Someone I didn't recognize."

"But why would he have been at Eddie's grave if he wasn't Eddie?"

"He wasn't at Eddie's grave. He—"

The tone of Portia's voice suddenly changed. "You know, it's a little convenient that you're the only one who can see him. We're all just expected to take your word for it that you're telling us the truth, even though there's all this other evidence saying something else."

Hendricks reeled backward. "You think—you actually think I would lie about something like this?"

Portia cocked her head, studying Hendricks's face. "I don't know what you would do. You've been weird ever since we did that séance. It's like you don't want to face the facts."

Hendricks needed a second to catch her breath. It felt ragged, like she'd just run a marathon. There was a part of her that wanted to keel over, head between her knees, close her eyes until the room stopped spinning.

She'd figured Portia was going to have a hard time believing that the ghost following her wasn't Eddie, but she'd never expected Portia to accuse her of lying to protect her dead boyfriend. It hurt that her closest friend here didn't trust her.

She sucked a breath in through her teeth and tried again. "You aren't listening to me—"

"No, *you* aren't listening. I can't leave my room. Don't you get that? I keep getting attacked. I'm terrified that I'm going to get seriously hurt, that I'm going to die. I'm tired of having this argument with you. It's not my fault you don't want to deal with the truth about who Eddie was."

"And who was that?" Hendricks asked, her voice stiff.

Portia met her eyes and said coldly, "A creepy outsider who no one liked."

CHAPTER
16

SAMANTHA DAVIDSON, HENDRICKS TYPED INTO HER search engine.

It was late, and she was lying in bed, trying to distract herself from the fight she'd just had with Portia.

Portia was wrong, she told herself, bristling. *The ghost had nothing to do with Eddie. It was someone else.*

She just had to figure out who.

She hit enter.

A second later: *17,900,000 results.*

Hendricks chewed on her lower lip. *Okay then*. She was going to need a way to narrow this down. Remembering the dates on the tombstone, she added, *1970–2019.*

This time, only three results popped up. One of them was an obituary.

Hendricks clicked, and a photograph of a woman in her mid-forties filled her computer screen. She leaned in closer, her heart beating so loudly she could hear it. *Samantha.*

If Samantha had ever been beautiful, those days were long past. In the photograph, she was skeletally thin, her face made up of harsh angles, sharp cheekbones and a well-defined jaw coming to a drastic, narrow point of a chin. Her dark brown skin looked ashen in the strange light of the photograph, and there were deep shadows under both of her eyes, turning them monstrous, hollow. Her dark brown hair had been scraped back in a ponytail, and a gnarled scar took up one side of her face.

Hendricks shuddered. Even though the scar was long healed, she could tell that it had been a pentagram. Just like the girl in the library. Just like the blood-smeared tombstone.

Below the photograph was a short obituary.

Samantha Cherie Davidson died Wednesday, January 14, 2019, at the Longwood Farm Community in Dover Plains, New York. She was born October 19, 1970, and is survived by her family.

Funeral services will be 3 p.m. Saturday, January 24, 2019, at Cedar Grove Baptist Church in Drearford, New York. Interment will follow in Cedar Grove Cemetery in Drearford under the direction of Marks Funeral Home of Magnolia.

In lieu of flowers, the family requests donations be made to Longwood Farm Community.

Hendricks read through the obituary twice. Two things stood out immediately.

The first was that the obituary didn't actually mention specific members of Samantha's family. Hendricks knew this was strange because she'd attended the funerals of two grandparents and one uncle, and all three times her name and her parents' names had been mentioned in the obituaries. She remembered reading that her beloved family members were "survived by" her and feeling a strange, weighty shiver, like she suddenly had a job to do, that it was up to her to up-hold their legacy. But here, Samantha was just "survived by her family." No names.

The second strange thing was where she'd died. Not at a hospital, or at home surrounded by her family, but at a place called Longwood Farm Community. Her family even requested that donations be sent to this Longwood Farm Community, so it had to have some special importance.

Hendricks typed the name into her search engine and clicked on the first result. A red webpage with a little farm graphic popped up.

Longwood Farm Community read the scripted font. Below was a photograph of a group of adults grinning at the camera, along with a short paragraph:

> Longwood Farm Community is a residential therapeutic community dedicated to helping adults with mental health and related challenges move toward recovery, health, and greater independence through community living, meaning-ful work, and clinical care.

"Adults with mental health and related challenges," Hendricks read out loud. Had Samantha been mentally ill?

She clicked through the photo gallery. Picture after picture showed an idyllic-looking farm, rolling green hills covered with horses, ador-able families of ducks, and smiling people planting flowers or milking cows. It didn't look like the sort of place where people with serious mental illnesses lived. It looked . . . nice.

Eventually, Hendricks found the contact page of the website. She was thinking she'd give the place a call or shoot them an email, when a little map popped up. Hendricks hesitated, eyes narrowing in on the map.

Longwood Farm was only a twenty-minute drive.

The next morning, Hendricks skipped first period to drive out to Longwood Farm.

The sun was just rising above the distant hills as she steered her mom's Subaru off the main highway and onto a twisted dirt road lined with massive boulders and spindly trees. The car shuddered over small rocks and gravel, causing Hendricks to shake violently in the driver's seat. It was barely a road at this point. If Hendricks didn't have a map pulled up on her phone, she would've doubted she was going the right way. She squinted through the tree branches, trying to make out the distant rolling hills, the gray lake, and barn.

The road narrowed the farther she drove, the tree cover growing denser, creating the feeling of being in a small, dark tunnel. Branches scratched at Hendricks's windows, the sound reminding her of bony fingers.

The gravel road was completely dark and it left her feeling uneasy, as though whoever was in charge of the grounds had let the trees grow unruly on purpose, to make it that much harder to see anything beyond. Bits of grass and far-off barns flashed between the gaps in the trees, gone too quickly for Hendricks to get a good look.

"Creepy . . ." she murmured to herself, slowing her car to a crawl as the road curved up to meet the barn. A wood sign swayed in the wind, lopsided letters reading LONGWOOD FARM COMMUNITY FRONT OFFICE. Below was another sign, this one in the shape of a little arrow pointing straight ahead, to a squat white farmhouse with peeling paint and dirt-smudged windows.

Hendricks pulled to a stop in a gravel lot out front, working through her cover story as she jogged up the front steps to the porch. She figured a place like this wouldn't give some random teenager private information just because she showed up asking for it. She needed another reason for coming here without any parents, asking questions about one of their patients.

The feeling of neglect hung over the farmhouse like a stench. Paint peeled from the walls and stacks of paperwork and files teetered from the tops of every surface. A soupy brown stain stretched across the ceiling. Though the front window was cracked, the breeze that moved through the room was oddly thick. It smelled of manure and wet dog.

Hendricks approached the front desk, where a woman with aggressively red, cat-eye-shaped glasses was typing away on a computer.

Behind the glasses, her eyes flicked up. "Can I help you?"

Hendricks cleared her throat. "I hope so," she said, mentally running through her prepared story one last time. "My name is Hendricks, I'm a junior at St. Joseph's."

St. Joseph's was the name of the college down in Drearford. Brady's nanny, Gillian, went there, and Hendricks thought she might be taken a bit more seriously if the receptionist thought she was speaking with a college student.

The receptionist nodded, one bob of her small, pointed chin, and Hendricks continued, "Right, so I'm helping my mom check out facilities for her, uh, brother? Charlie? She'd heard good things about Longwood Farm and asked me if I could stop by, and, like, look around the grounds for her."

The receptionist's lips pinched together, a small, pouty frown. "We're a mental health facility," she said, speaking slowly, like she thought Hendricks might not understand. "Do you happen to know your uncle's diagnosis?"

Hendricks felt a momentary touch of panic. She really should've researched different diagnoses to prepare for this. "He has . . . bipolar disorder," she said quickly, remember the words from the Farm's website. "But my mom doesn't actually talk about the details of his illness with me. She just wanted me to swing by to see whether this place seemed . . . nice."

Now the receptionist looked really suspicious. "Our tours are by appointment only. Did you call ahead?"

"Was I supposed to?" Hendricks could feel the heat climbing her cheeks. She was screwing this up. "I'm really sorry, I don't do this often. We were interested in this place because my mom, uh, went to high school with one of your former, er . . . residents. Maybe you knew her? Samantha Davidson?"

The receptionist tilted her head to the side, blinking rapidly behind the thick lenses. "Your mom went to school with Sam? Was she a cheerleader, too?"

Cheerleader, Hendricks thought, tucking that bit of information away. "Yup," she said easily. "That's totally how they met."

"Oh, well it's really nice to meet one of Sam's friends." The receptionist didn't say *finally*, but Hendricks thought she heard the word lingering in the air. She glanced over her shoulder and then, turning back to Hendricks, added, "Usually our tours are a *touch* more formal. We like to make sure the prospective resident is present and have them talk with the doctors we have on staff, and take a look around the dorms, things like that. But seeing as you were referred by Sam . . . I guess I could show you around quickly, just the highlights. That way you have something to tell your mom."

She stepped out from behind the desk, straightening her paisley-printed pencil skirt, which she'd, inexplicably, paired with mud-splattered Hunter boots that went up past her knees. "My name is Miriam, by the way. Would you like a pair of rubber boots?"

Hendricks quickly understood the need for the rubber boots. Mud sloshed up around her feet as they headed across a patchy, gray field filled with horses and sheep. The trees weren't quite as dense out here, and she felt her nerves ease a bit as the sky opened up above.

The feeling didn't last. The sky was low and dark. The animals didn't bother looking up as Hendricks and Miriam approached, and Hendricks noticed that they looked . . . well, mangy. Their coats were patchy and rough, and she could see the thin curves of ribs poking through their sides. Flies buzzed around their flicking tails.

Miriam navigated the field easily. She had a dancer's posture, even in the oversize boots, and Hendricks found herself marveling at how her feet didn't seem to slip and slide in the mud the way Hendricks's did. "Longwood Farm was established as a not-for-profit organization in the late seventies by New York native Donna Radley," Miriam explained. "It was built in honor of Donna's daughter, who sadly lost her battle to depression in 1986. Longwood is the only therapeutic farm community in New York and one of only a handful in the United States. We are licensed to serve up to forty adults and we employ approximately sixty full-time, part-time clinical, direct care, and administrative staff. Our aim is to help individuals understand the importance of their medications and develop the skills necessary to live more independently."

"Wow," Hendricks said, struggling to keep up with Miriam in her own clumsy, too-big boots. She hit a particularly slippery patch of grass and skidded a little too close to a goat, who danced away from her, grunting. "That's . . . that's sort of cool."

"It is, isn't it?" Miriam said, beaming. "We help adults who've been diagnosed with everything from major depression and bipolar disorder, to schizophrenia, like Sam."

Schizophrenia. Hendricks tried to keep the excitement off her face as she added this new piece of information to the growing list of facts she knew about Sam.

Cheerleader. Not a lot of friends. Schizophrenic.

She even knew a little about schizophrenia. She was pretty sure it was the disease where you heard voices.

"Did Sam have any friends here?" Hendricks asked.

Miriam frowned. "No, Sam pretty much kept to herself. Reality was . . . tricky for her. As I'm sure you know."

She darted a look at Hendricks, as though to confirm that Hendricks did, in fact, know that. Hendricks nodded. But her mind was reeling.

Miriam continued the tour, pointing out the greenhouse, a cracked, dirt-smudged glass building with walls covered in creeping vines, and explained that residents were encouraged to grow their own plants. She showed Hendricks the decrepit barn where they helped take care of the farm animals. Every now and then, Hendricks would spot another resident, and they would wave and smile back. They were strange smiles, though, the corners of their mouths pulled too wide, their eyes not quite focusing on Hendricks's face.

Eventually, Miriam led Hendricks back to the main farmhouse, the tour winding down. "Our highly qualified staff creates an environment of caring and acceptance while providing first-class, licensed mental health services at our CARF accredited mental health treatment center," she said in her soft, even monotone. "If you think your mom would be interested in any more information, I'd be happy to send you home with some brochures."

"Uh, yeah, sure, brochures would be great," Hendricks said, not wanting to blow her cover. Miriam told her she'd be right back and disappeared inside.

The second she'd gone, Hendricks felt uneasy. The gray sky seemed a bit lower than it had a moment ago, the far-off fields and goats and horses just slightly closer.

It was as though, now that Hendricks was alone, the farm itself was closing in. She thought of a hand reaching up from behind her, fingers slowly closing around her neck . . .

A shudder moved through her. She whipped around, eyes ticking off the horses and fields and fences. All right where they were supposed to be.

Of course.

Hendricks knocked her boot against the side of porch, trying to shake the feeling off.

Then a noise on the other side of the house, a soft cough. Fear shot through her.

"Get a grip," she muttered to herself and poked her head around the side of the house.

A girl in her early twenties was sitting on a bench, watching a crowd of chickens peck at the ground. She was a little pale and thin and super freckly. The freckles covered her whole face and both of her arms—almost but not quite hiding the cuts crisscrossing up and down the skin between her wrists and her elbows. She wore a loose-fitting tank top and sweatpants, no shoes. There was mud dried to the bottoms of her bare feet, between her toes and under her toenails.

Hendricks hesitated at the side of the house, wondering whether she should say something, when the girl said, without looking up, "This isn't a zoo."

Hendricks started. "Uh, what?"

"'This. Isn't. A. Zoo," the girl repeated, slower. "It's rude to stand there and gawk at the freaks."

"I didn't mean to . . . gawk," Hendricks said. She was about to go back to the porch when the girl scooted over on her bench, wood creaking noisily beneath her skinny thighs. Hendricks went and sat next to her.

"Sid," the girl said. Her voice was low and scratchy.

"I'm Hendricks."

"Inmate or a visitor, Hendricks?"

"Uh, visitor?" said Hendricks hesitantly. "What do you mean inmate? Isn't this place nice?"

Even as she asked the question, Hendricks thought of those strange, too-wide smiles, the skeletally thin animals.

"Maybe if you're willing to drink the Kool-Aid like the rest of the zombies." The girl leaned back against the bench, long, skinny arms stretched along the back rungs. "But if you don't get all hot from mucking up animal shit and planting pretty flowers, it's not exactly the place to be." She cut her eyes toward Hendricks. "Who are you visiting?"

"Oh, no one?" Hendricks said. "My mom wanted me to check this place out for, uh, for her brother, just to make sure it was nice, you know."

Sid raised her eyebrows, the corner of her lip twitching. "Is that right?"

Hendricks's cheeks flared. She felt caught.

"Look, I'm not going to bust you," Sid said, her voice a touch softer. "Honest. But why are you really here?"

Hendricks rolled her lip between her teeth. It's not like she had anything to lose. She'd been about to take off, anyway, and if this girl was one of the residents here, she might be willing to divulge a bit more information that Miriam had been.

"Did you know Samantha Davidson?" Hendricks asked.

Sid lifted her eyebrows. "No shit. You knew Sam?"

"I know someone who's looking for her. I came here to see if I could figure out why, but Miriam is being a little cagey."

"Yeah, well, Miriam's a bitch." Sid sniffed and turned back to the chickens. After a long moment, she said. "I miss Sam, though. She was the only person around here who was actually interesting."

"So you did know her?"

"We weren't bestest friends or anything, but we talked, yeah." Under her breath, Sid added, "She was the only person in this place who acted like I was even there." And she thumped the heel of her bare foot against the bench, so hard it made the wood tremble.

"What was she like?" asked Hendricks.

"Batshit crazy." Sid laughed, staring off at some distant point in the muddy field. After a moment she added, almost like a dare. "Sam used to say she could see the other side."

Hendricks's heart hit the back of her throat. "The other side? You mean . . . ghosts?"

"If you believe in that crap." Sid pulled her feet onto the bench and hugged her knees to her chest. "Sam was cool, though. She was this hot shit cheerleader back in high school, but then she had a total mental break and had to be sent here. She used to run around this place with, like, knives and shit, trying to defend herself from the evil spirits." A wicked grin. "It certainly made the farm more interesting."

"That sounds awful," Hendricks said.

Sid shrugged. "Depends on your definition of awful. I thought it was amazing. This place has totally sucked since she left. No one's any fun."

There was a noise, the sound of a door swinging open and shut, and then footsteps coming around the side of the house. Hendricks turned just as Miriam reappeared, a bunch of brochures fanned between her fingers.

"There you are! I see you found Sidney's bench," Miriam said, picking her way around the side of the house. "I've always thought it was such a nice spot to just sit and think."

Hendricks nodded. "Yeah, we were just talking."

Miriam frowned deeply. This wasn't her small, pouty frown, but one that seemed to involve every muscle in her face. Her eyes pinched, and the skin beneath her brows furrowed.

"Right," she said, like she was choosing her words very carefully. "Anyway, you've got the brochures. The office number's on the front, just there." She pointed to a number at the bottom of the brochure. "Give me a call if you want to schedule something more official, okay?"

Her eyes flicked to something behind Hendricks, and then settled back on Hendricks's face. A quick smile, there and gone, and then she was hurrying back around to the other side of the farmhouse, like she couldn't get away from Hendricks quickly enough.

"You're right," Hendricks said, turning back to Sid. "She really is a—"

The word *bitch* died in her throat as her eyes landed on Sid's face.

Sid had . . . changed. Hendricks stood up quickly, stumbling back from the bench. But she couldn't bring herself to look away. Deep wrinkles had appeared around Sid's eyes and mouth. Her skin looked dull and dry. She stretched her thin lips into a smile and her teeth had turned yellow.

The longer Hendricks looked at her, the more she noticed. Like the mud on Sid's feet . . . it wasn't brown, it was green, and it smelled putrid, like sewer and garbage disposals and rotting trash. And now she was way, *way* too thin. Not thin in a skinny way, but in a substantial way. Hendricks could actually see through her.

Hendricks tried not to gag. Sid didn't seem to notice. She slapped at something on her wrist. A small buzzing fly.

Hendricks suddenly noticed that there were lots of flies around her. They swarmed around Sid's hair in a gray cloud. They landed on her ears, wings twitching.

"See what I mean?" Sidney said. Her words had grown slow and slurred, stretched out like taffy. "Miriam acted like she didn't . . . even . . . see me."

The word *me* had barely left Sid's tongue when she was suddenly . . . gone. What was left of her thin, wispy body broke apart, becoming a thick mass of buzzing flies. Hendricks leapt back, horror climbing her throat. She pressed her knuckles to her mouth, forcing herself to breathe through her nose.

There was something small and glinting on the bench where Sid had been sitting. Nose wrinkled, Hendricks leaned closer to see what it was. A plaque.

IN HONOR OF SIDNEY RADLEY, the plaque read. BELOVED DAUGHTER, TRUE FRIEND. YOU WILL BE MISSED. 1968–1986.

Hendricks read the inscription twice. It took a long time for her heartbeat to steady.

CHAPTER

17

BY THE TIME HENDRICKS GOT BACK TO HER CAR, SHE HAD
five new texts, all from Portia.

> Are you going to prom committee today after school?

> I left the binder with Oliver, but I was hoping he could hand
> it over to you

> Are you still pissed because of what I said last night?

> Look, I'm sorry, but I'm being HAUNTED.

And finally, Maybe we shouldn't talk about it anymore? At least
until the ghost is gone? I don't want to wreck our friendship.

Hendricks sat in her car for a long moment, staring at her phone.
She wanted to tell Portia what she'd learned about Samantha Davidson
and the farm and the freaking *ghost* she'd just had an entire conversation
with. Even Portia had to admit that this had nothing to do with Eddie.
How would he have even met Samantha Davidson?

Her fingers hovered over the keypad, trying to figure out how she
could put everything she had to say into a text—

And then her eyes flicked back over Portia's messages. Maybe we shouldn't talk about it anymore? I don't want to wreck our friendship.

She felt her shoulders slump. Portia was right. Every time they talked about the ghost, they fought. Hendricks didn't have a ton of friends in this place. She couldn't afford to alienate any more of them.

I'll be at prom committee, she texted back. Stop freaking out.

And send. She dug her teeth into her lower lip, watching her message disappear into the ether. It felt weird to be keeping so much from Portia, but she knew that for now at least, it was the right thing to do. She might know a little more about Samantha, but she still didn't know who this ghost was or why he was after them.

Until she found out, she'd just have to keep her research to herself.

Hendricks stood in front of the prom committee after school, trying to balance Portia's massive binder in one hand while she scanned her friend's impeccably neat, color-coded notes.

"Okay, uh . . . it looks like we need an update from the decorations committee?" she said, glancing up.

The gathered students all looked at each other, and then back at her again. Without Portia there to lead them, they seemed a little lost.

"Portia was going to see whether we had any leftover decorations from last year's production of *Anything Goes*," Oliver offered. "It was, like, this musical set on a cruise ship, so she thought they might have some cruise stuff we could use. Did she tell you whether she had a chance to check the props closet?"

"No." Hendricks chewed her lower lip, thinking. "But I could go take a look now. Someone just needs to tell me where the props closet is."

"End of the hall, down the flight of stairs, and to the right," Oliver said.

Hendricks dumped Portia's prom binder into his arms, grateful to unload the responsibility of leading the committee onto someone else. "You guys keep going. Portia's pretty much written step-by-step instructions on what's supposed to happen next. I'll be back in a bit."

She made her way past rows of lockers, empty classrooms, steadily dripping water fountains. The sun was just low enough that it shone right through the glass doors at the far side of the school, illuminating each individual particle of dust in the air. Shadows cut down the hall like long, thin blades. Hendricks heard distant laughter, the sound of someone slamming a locker door shut, the snap of metal on metal making her flinch.

She rubbed the nerves from her arms. She hadn't really spent a lot of time in Drearford High after school hours. It felt a lot different than it did when it was filled with people. Older.

Hendricks hadn't given much thought to what Oliver meant by "down the flight of stairs" until she actually reached the staircase. Drearford High only had one story. So, "down the flight of stairs" meant the basement. Hendricks peered into the dark, windowless stairwell, and wished she'd sent someone else to find the damn decorations. Since coming to Drearford, she hadn't had a lot of luck with basements.

"Don't be a wuss," she muttered to herself and placed one foot onto the top step. The wooden stair groaned beneath her sneaker, a warning. She snatched her foot back, swearing under her breath.

It's just a creaky old wooden stair. It's totally normal.

She leaned into the stairwell and groped along inside of the wall until her fingers found the light switch—*there!*—but when she flicked it up, down, and up again, nothing happened.

She glanced over her shoulder, thinking. She could go back now, tell them she looked but she didn't find anything. What was the worst that could happen? It wasn't a life-or-death situation, after all, it was prom, and if they didn't have enough cardboard anchors, it really wasn't the end of the world.

As if on cue, music suddenly poured down the hallway, coming from the gym.

This is what it sounds like . . .

Hendricks felt her shoulders inch up toward her ears. Her heart beat steadily in her palms. She'd heard that song recently. The radio in the Subaru was still broken, playing old eighties music on a loop.

She walked down the first five steps. Nothing happened. Okay then. She took the last four steps quickly, holding her breath, and then she was in the basement, and the props closet was just around the corner.

She inhaled, deep. The air down here smelled off. It made her nose wrinkle. She found a door and reached inside, her fingers quickly locating another light switch on the wall. This time, when she flicked it on, a dull glow filled the space. Hendricks turned in place.

She was standing in a narrow room filled with floor to ceiling shelving. All around her were vintage hats and bags and shoes, racks of musty clothes, ancient-looking television sets and lamps and record players. There were cardboard boxes covered in scrawled handwriting. *Ancient Rome—Antigone* read one. Another, *Mental Hospital—One Flew Over the Cuckoo's Nest.* Hendricks felt a little overwhelmed. She wasn't sure where to start.

She turned in place, eyes moving over the scattered props, when something leapt out of the darkness above the door, something with thick fur and long, sharp teeth—

Hendricks screamed and slammed into a shelf. Metal jammed into her back, sending pain shooting down her spine.

The lion mask from the school mascot uniform hung above the

164

door. Hendricks shuddered and turned away, but she could feel those empty eye sockets following her as she moved around the room. Watching.

Goose bumps climbed her arms. She didn't want to spend any more time down here than she had to. She moved quickly around the small room, gathering anything that looked like it might belong on a cruise ship: sailor's hats; a life raft; an oversize, fake champagne bottle (they served champagne on cruises, right?). And then, satisfied that she'd made enough of an effort, she headed for the stairs.

The song drifting down from the gym started over again.

Hendricks's eyes drifted up, up, toward the ceiling. Why did they have it on repeat?

The prop closet must've been directly under the gym because she could hear the prom committee moving overhead. Footsteps thudded, and voices rose and fell above her. It didn't sound like a half a dozen students quietly discussing prom plans. It sounded like hundreds of students, dancing.

Hendricks's heart started beating a little bit faster. Something was . . . strange. She inched toward the stairwell, suddenly wanting to be upstairs again, in the sun, where there were other people and . . . and light switches that worked, and no freaking *lion masks* hanging from the wall above her, staring down with strangely vacant eyes and those long, curved teeth, teeth that seemed really inappropriate for a school mascot now that she actually stopped to think about it. She reached the door, stepped into the hall.

The prop closet lights switched off.

On.

Off again.

The ceiling creaked above her and then, Hendricks heard a voice. It seemed to speak directly into her head.

I . . . see . . . you . . .

Nerves crept up her skin. She swallowed. "Samantha?"

Silence answered her.

"I know he did something to you," Hendricks said out loud. "That's why I went out to the farm. I was hoping you could show me what it was."

A shadow twitched in the corner of her eye.

The shelves in the prop room began to shake, clothes rustling like laughter.

The voice came again.

You . . . see . . . her . . .

Hendricks frowned. "Are you talking about Sidney?" she asked. "I did see her, I—I mean I *saw* her. Is she important?"

The low sound of laughter filled the room.

There was silence for a long moment. The room went still. Hendricks felt her shoulders drop. She was missing something, she was sure of it.

And then, the voice came again. It only said one thing.

Watch.

The lights turned back on.

Hendricks froze. She felt a scream building in her throat, but she swallowed it down. Something about the small room was different. Her eyes flicked over dusty props, bowler hats from the forties and swishy, fifties-style dresses, and cat-eared headbands and wigs. Had they been there before?

She jerked around to look at the lion's head hanging above the door. She wasn't sure what she'd expected to see, maybe the lion's expression would be different now, smiling at her instead of scowling, or maybe there would be real eyes behind those vacant holes.

But no. The mascot head was exactly the same. Matted fur, sharp teeth.

Screw it, she thought, turning for the door.

Behind her, the sound of wood scraping against wood.

Hendricks froze. Her skin felt damp and itchy, and something sour had filled her mouth.

She felt something behind her, something lurking . . . *watching*. The skin on the back of her neck crept. She had to know what it was.

Slowly, she turned.

This time, she saw what was different about the small prop room right away. It was the wall between two racks of costumes, it had sort of *opened up*, revealing a small, dark crawl space on the other side.

For a moment, Hendricks just stared. Her heart was rising and falling inside of her chest, steady and hard.

The wall had opened up.

"Hendricks," she whispered to herself. "Do not even think of going into the strange, dark crawl space. Nothing good can come of exploring the strange, dark crawl space."

But she couldn't make herself look away. The darkness seemed to pulse, like a beating heart.

It felt like . . .

It felt like it was calling to her.

Hendricks took a single step closer. Then, swearing, she dropped to all fours and crawled inside.

There was damp wood beneath her knees and cool musty air all around her. The sounds of music and dancing were suddenly muffled. Once she was just inside the doorway, Hendricks pushed herself back onto her heels and dug her cell phone out of her pocket. Every muscle in her body felt pulled tight. Her pulse was light and fluttery in her chest.

She found the flashlight app on her phone and switched it on.

Jerky white light bounced off smeared black paint, melted candle wax. Hendricks wrapped her opposite hand around her wrist to hold the cell phone steady so she could see what she was looking at.

Pentagrams covered the walls, the paint heavy and black. Black candles had melted into the floor, and someone had written HAIL ARGBÁKTU across the walls. Scattered in the corners of the room were small white objects that looked disturbingly like animal skulls. Hendricks moved her light away quickly. She didn't want to look at those. She exhaled, noticing as she did that her breath hung in a white cloud before her mouth. It wasn't just the skulls and the cold. It was the *feel* of this place, the heaviness in the air, and the way nothing seemed steady. It almost felt . . .

Cursed.

Hendricks felt a sharp twist of fear. The skin on the back of her neck pricked.

All of a sudden a voice reached out from the darkness, singing, "Why do we scream at each other? This is what it sounds like, when doves cry."

Hendricks froze. That voice. It sounded so close. She pressed herself up against the side of the crawlspace, suddenly afraid to move. She felt light-headed. She curled her fingers into her palms to stop them from shaking.

There was a footstep on the other side of the door, a low scrape, like someone dragging their boot across the wood. Hendricks's throat seized up. Someone was *in* the prop closet.

A higher, clearer voice said, "Actually, Justin, I don't think we need the disco ball after all. I—I'm just going to go back upstairs, okay?"

"Come on, Sam, it's right in here." Justin hummed a few more bars of "When Doves Cry." "Prince is such a pussy. I don't know why chicks love him so much."

"Yeah," the girl said. She sounded nervous, and Hendricks felt a twitch of sympathy. "Whatever."

Gathering her courage, Hendricks crawled toward the entrance of the crawl space and peered into the prop room.

A girl stood in the middle of the room, her back to Hendricks. She wore a floor-length, floaty white dress, her hair twisted into a complicated knot at the back of her head. Hendricks couldn't see her face, but even so, she could tell the girl was beautiful. Like something from a fairy tale.

Justin stood behind her, looking just as he had when Hendricks had seen him in the graveyard. Black leather jacket. Dyed black hair that was just starting to show at the roots.

Samantha crossed her arms over her chest, shivering. "Did you find it?" she asked.

"Yeah," Justin said. But he wasn't holding a disco ball, he was holding a small, torn dishrag. Hendricks frowned as he crept up behind Samantha, the muscles in his shoulders going tense. "I found it."

Hendricks knew what was going to happen a second before it did. She wanted to scream, to warn Samantha, but her cries got stuck in her chest. She pressed her knuckles to her mouth and bit down, fear twisting through her. Every inhale scraped up the insides of her throat.

Justin grabbed Samantha from behind, holding her arms down with one arm while, with his opposite hand, he pressed the dishrag over her mouth and nose. Samantha released one sharp choke of a scream, but the sound of music drifting down from the ceiling covered it. Hendricks watched horrified as the girl's shoulders slumped, her head dropping to the side.

"Good girl," Justin said. He ran one finger down the side of Samantha's face, almost lovingly, and Hendricks felt a disgusted shiver move through her. "This will all be over soon."

Justin carried Samantha's unconscious body back up the stairs and through the school halls. Following them, Hendricks saw that the whole school looked different than it was supposed to. The lockers were painted an ugly, muddy green instead of black, and the floor was old linoleum, not wood. A banner on the wall read CONGRATS CLASS OF '86!

On instinct, she glanced at the clock hanging on the gym wall.

9:22, it read.

CHAPTER
18

HENDRICKS REMEMBERED DRIVING TO THE TOP OF PIKES Peak in Colorado with her parents when she was eight years old. By the time the three of them had reached the summit, her head was swimming and she'd felt sick to her stomach. She'd actually thrown up and had to lie down, sipping warm bottled water in the visitor's center with a cold compress on her forehead until the swimmy, light-headed feeling passed. Altitude sickness, her parents had told her. It happened because the air at the top of the mountain was too thin, and not enough oxygen was reaching her brain.

The exact same feeling hit her the second she stepped off the side-walk and onto the Steele House construction site. She had to pause for a moment, one hand propped against a tree, eyes clenched shut, just trying to breathe normally.

She didn't want to be back here. The air here felt *wrong*, too thin, like there wasn't enough of it to go around. She drew her arms around her chest, shivering. She'd kept her distance as she'd followed Justin from the school, to be sure he wouldn't see her. *Watch*, the voice in the prop closet had said, and that's all she intended to do. Watch. Learn.

Even so, she'd known from the moment they'd stepped outside that *this* was where Justin was going to take his victim. All roads led back to Steele House.

Justin didn't carry Samantha toward the house itself but around to the back of the lot, where a copse of spindly pine trees separated the Steele House lawn from the Ruiz family's house and yard just behind it. Once Hendricks caught her breath, she followed them, her skin buzzing.

Wind moved through the trees, rattling the branches. Somewhere in the darkness, an owl hooted. Hendricks drew her arms around herself, shivering. Everything looked warped and strange. Sounds seemed too close, like the wind and the owls were whispering directly into Hendricks's brain. Twice, she thought she heard an insect buzzing around her head, and she flinched and swatted but felt only air.

Justin dropped to his knees in the dirt and carefully placed Samantha on a bit of packed dirt ground. Hendricks hovered behind a tree a few feet away, as close as she dared come. From where she stood, she could see that the hem of Samantha's beautiful white gown had been smudged and torn where it had dragged along on the sidewalk, and her hair had started to come loose from its bun, bits and pieces sticking to the sweat on her face. Samantha must've woken up during the walk, because her eyes were wide and terrified, shifting anxiously around the clearing, as though she was looking around for someone to help her. Tears trailed down her cheeks, smudging her eye makeup. She made a grunting noise, and that's when Hendricks realized that Justin had shoved something into her mouth, gagging her.

Hendricks felt her lower lip begin to tremble. This was horrible. Everything she'd eaten that day churned around inside her stomach, threatening to come up.

She wanted to *do* something, to scream for help, or call the cops, something to change this.

But it had already happened, in the past. The only thing she could do now was watch.

A few feet away from where Samantha lay, Justin began to build a fire. Hendricks watched him work for a few long moments, uneasy. Something about his movements bothered her, but she couldn't figure out what it was.

Then, all at once, she realized. Justin hadn't had to go rooting around in the woods for dry logs and branches. He hadn't had to clear the brush away from his little circle of dirt. The stack of wood and kindling had already been there, the fire pit ready and waiting for him.

Whatever he was about to do with Samantha, he'd been planning it for a while.

It took Justin a few tries, but eventually, red-orange flames leapt to life among the pile of wood, illuminating his hollow-looking face, his greasy hair.

Samantha's sobs grew louder. The firelight reflected off her wide black eyes. Fear made them look animal-like and strange.

"Stop crying," Justin muttered, casting an annoyed look her way. "This isn't going to take very long."

Hendricks didn't find that promise very reassuring, but Samantha's crying subsided a little. She tried to say something, but the gag muffled her words.

Groaning, Justin leaned over and pulled it out of her mouth. "What?"

"Wh-why are you doing this?" Samantha choked out. Her voice was thick with tears and fear. "What—what did I ever do to you?"

Justin's eyes moved over Samantha's face, studying it. Next to Samantha, he looked strangely flat. He tilted his head to the side, and Hendricks felt a chill shoot straight down her back.

"I've been watching you for a while now," Justin said. "You're . . . different."

"I'm . . . I'm not, really, I'm not."

"You see things."

Samantha closed her eyes, a sob bubbling past her lips. "I don't, I swear."

"You don't have to lie to me. I know that no one else believes you. But I do. You see ghosts."

Hendricks felt a cold finger touch her spine.

You see ghosts.

Samantha sniffed. She looked a bit calmer than she'd been a moment ago, curiosity replacing some of the fear in her eyes. She asked hesitantly, "Do you . . . do you see them, too?"

Justin's eyes darkened. "My dad died last year. Did you know that?" He shook his head before she could answer. "No, I bet you didn't. None of your friends, those popular shitheads you hang out with, none of them know that the rest of us exist."

"I'm sorry. I—I never meant to ignore you, we didn't mean anything—"

"Shut up," Just snapped, bitter. "I don't care about that, it's not why I brought you here." He threw a couple more sticks into the fire, and for a moment there was only the sound of flames crackling, twigs shifting in place.

Fear flickered in Samantha's eyes. "Justin—"

"I found this spell," Justin continued. "It's supposed to transfer the power of the sight from one person to another. I figured you wouldn't mind. I mean, you don't even seem to appreciate it, and the whole ritual's pretty easy, too. All you need is a little smoke, a little sage . . ." Justin lifted his shirt and pulled a hunting knife out of the waistband of his jeans. A leather case covered the blade. He tilted his head and, grinning, added, "And a sacrifice."

Samantha jerked like a fish on dry land. "What do you mean by sacrifice?" She pulled at the bindings around her wrists, but even from her position behind the tree Hendricks could see that the rope wouldn't budge. "What's that for?"

"It shouldn't hurt too much." Justin removed the leather case and let it drop to the ground between them. The blade glinted in the fire-light, the edge wicked, sharp. "My dad used to take me hunting. He taught me how to make it quick."

Samantha thrashed against her bindings, shrieking. Justin grabbed her by her hair and lifted her head off the ground, twisting her neck back at an unnatural angle. He pressed the flat edge of the blade to her cheek—

"No! Justin, don't, Justin, please—"

"Hold still, you little bitch." Justin slammed the butt of his knife into her eye, and Samantha released a sharp bark of a scream that quickly dissolved into more sobs.

Behind her tree, Hendricks clamped her hand over her mouth. In her whole life, she'd never heard a sound as terrible as those sobs. They seemed to go on and on, causing the hair on her arms and legs to stand straight up.

Justin brought the knife to Samantha's cheek again, and this time he sliced down, cutting a thick gash into her skin. Hendricks flinched. Blood poured down Samantha's face in a dark, glimmering sheet. Her lips were trembling, but she looked too terrified to keep fighting. She held perfectly still as Justin fisted his fingers more tightly in her hair, holding her in place so he could cut her face four more times.

When he was done, an upside-down star marred her cheek.

"Shh . . ." Justin said. "Almost done." He twisted the knife's blade around the scar, to form a jagged circle.

"Please, please, please . . ." Samantha was crying again, a low, desperate whimper. Blood covered her face like a mask, leaving her skin completely red except for the space around her eyes and mouth. The inverted pentagram Justin had carved into her cheek seemed to pulse, gushing fresh, dark blood onto Samantha's skin.

Hendricks felt vomit rise in her throat and gagged. She closed her eyes and swallowed it, desperate to remain silent.

Finally, Justin lowered the knife. He grabbed Samantha beneath her armpits and dragged her over to the fire. For several long moments, there was only the sound of her struggling to breathe through her cries, the wind in the trees, and the crackling of the fire. With a final grunt, Justin dropped her and knelt beside the flames.

"Father Argbáktu . . ." As Justin spoke, he sawed roughly through Samantha's hair, his blade cutting close to her scalp, drawing yet more blood. "I beg you, accept my humble sacrifice."

He dropped a handful of Samantha's hair into the fire. The flames surged.

Samantha flinched as she watched her hair go up in flames, and something flicked through her eyes. It wasn't fear anymore but something stronger. She swallowed, and the muscles in her shoulders grew tense.

Justin held his own hand above the crackling flames. He was crouching, knees bent, balanced on the balls of his feet, and he was facing away from Samantha. Hendricks saw the way that Samantha's eyes moved over his body, calculating. She dug her fingers into the bark of the tree, thinking, *Get up. Fight.*

Justin pressed his knife into the palm of his hand, cringing as the blade drew blood . . .

Samantha sucked a breath in through her teeth and jerked, slamming her shoulders into Justin's leg, just behind his knee. He crashed forward, grunting, hands landing in the pile of flaming wood. He screamed and dropped the knife. It landed on the ground just beside him.

Samantha reached out with her bound hands, grasping for the hilt. Justin was still screaming and cursing, but he recovered quickly. He whipped around and got the blade between his fist—

"Nice try," he snarled, and he started to pull the knife out of her grip at the exact same moment that she thrust the weight of her body forward—

The knife slid into Justin's chest, all the way up to the hilt.

Samantha whimpered with fear and let go. But it was too late. The knife stayed where it was.

Justin looked down. His hands were still grasping the blade and now he tried, unsuccessfully, to pull it out. It was dark and his T-shirt was black, so Hendricks couldn't see the blood until he moved his hands away. His fingers were bright red, stained with it.

He lifted his head, eyes black with fear as they struggled to focus on Samantha's face.

"I'll be back for you," he said.

And then he slumped forward, hitting the dirt shoulder first. A shudder went through his body, jerking his limbs, and then he was still. The only sounds left in the clearing were the steadily cracking fire, and Samantha's desperate cries.

CHAPTER
19

HENDRICKS DIDN'T GO HOME. SHE GOT INTO HER MOM'S CAR and drove straight to Magik & Tarot. The shop wasn't open. There wasn't even a sign hanging on the door this time, it was just locked, and it wouldn't budge, no matter how desperately Hendricks yanked on it.

"Ileana?" Hendricks called, banging on the door. "Are you there? I really need to—"

The door swung open, and Ileana stomped outside, an apple wedged in her mouth.

"Oh hey," she said, removing her apple. "Can we do this while walking? I'm running late."

Ileana looked different than usual, Hendricks noticed. She'd seemed to attempt to wrangle her bushy hair into a bun at the nape of her neck, and there was a pair of gigantic black glasses perched on her nose, the lenses making her eyes bug. She had a Spider-Man backpack slung over one shoulder.

"It was the only one they had left," she explained, when she saw Hendricks studying the backpack. "And it has a lot of pockets, so I don't mind."

"Are you still in school?" Hendricks asked, eyes on the backpack.

"Night school," Ileana explained, yanking the backpack higher up her shoulder. "I take an accounting class at Devon Community College."

Hendricks wrinkled her nose. "Accounting?"

"Yeah. The school's only a few blocks away if you want to walk with me." Ileana led Hendricks to the end of the street, past decrepit Victorians with boarded-up windows, overgrown yards, and trees with knobby branches and no leaves. She was walking quickly, and her legs were longer than Hendricks's, so Hendricks had to practically jog to keep up with her. The sidewalk was uneven. Hendricks stumbled twice.

"So," Ileana said, rounding the corner, "what's up?"

Hendricks hesitated. Images moved through her head, making her brain feel mushy and slow. She remembered how Justin had covered Samantha's mouth with that dirty rag, how he carried her through the school halls.

And then she saw the clearing, the fire, Samantha lunging for the knife, burrowing it in Justin's chest . . .

Justin's final threat echoed in her head.

I'll be back for you.

Heart pounding, she told Ileana all of it, right from the beginning. She felt drained by the time she'd finished with her story. She waited for Ileana to provide her with some sage wisdom or mysterious spell, but Ileana only took another bite of her apple, her forehead creased in a slight frown.

A sudden rush of wind moved down the street, rattling a bit of cardboard that had been taped over the windows of a nearby house.

"So," Hendricks urged. "What I am supposed to do?"

Ileana chewed thoughtfully on her apple. "Ghosts don't come back every day," she said, swallowing.

"I sort of figured that part out. I just don't understand why *this one* came back. We didn't do the séance for him, we did it for Eddie."

"When you call a ghost using a séance, think of it more like using an intercom at a department store. You can hope that the correct person answers the call, but there are no guarantees. Steele House is supposed to be this location of great spiritual energy." Ileana finished her apple and chucked the core into the dandelion-covered lawn of an abandoned house. "I bet a lot of people have passed at that location."

"You think we called for Eddie and got the wrong ghost?"

"You wanted to call Eddie from the void, right?" Ileana said. "But all sorts of things can happen when you open the door to the other side. People who've passed on can be called back, sure, but ghosts who are already here can also be made stronger. It's tricky stuff, especially if you aren't using a conduit."

Hendricks bit her lip. Ileana's mention of a conduit reminded her that she still needed to swing by Raven's house.

They'd reached Devon's main street. Unlike Ileana's neighborhood, Main Street was cute and touristy. They hurried past a little market, the windows filled with fresh produce, and a coffee shop called the Sparrow.

Ileana turned to Hendricks. "This ghost you saw, you said his name was Justin?"

"That's what Samantha called him."

"That rings a bell, but . . ." Ileana seemed to think for a moment. "There's someone I think you should talk to," she said finally. "This guy at my school"

"A teacher?"

Ileana laughed. "Crow is definitely *not* a teacher."

Hendricks felt a twinge of doubt. *Crow?*

"Trust me," Ileana assured her. "Crow knows everything."

Devon Community College was a short walk from Main Street. It was a small campus, just three flat brick buildings crowded around a stone fountain that had long ago gone dry. The surrounding grass was all dead and brown, weeds swaying in the stale wind.

Hendricks followed Ileana past the fountain and toward the center building. A bell tower sat on the roof like a hat, and if Hendricks squinted, she thought she saw movement in the shadows. She shivered. This place looked more like a mental asylum than a school.

She followed Ileana up the short staircase and through green-tiled floors with dim lighting until finally they'd reached a small room without any windows. There was a smattering of desks inside the room, a few students already milling about: a young woman in a shapeless white shirt-dress hunched over a desk in the second row, an older man writing something on the chalkboard, a group of students huddled near the windows, talking in low voices.

Ileana ignored them, making a beeline for a man sitting in the back row. "Hendricks," she said, stopping before the man's desk. "I'd like you to meet John Crowski."

John Crowski was a bald, middle-aged Black man. He wore a navy-blue polo and jeans, a silk scarf draped over his shoulders like a shawl.

"Call me Crow," he said, eyes flicking over Hendricks and then back to Ileana. "Did you bring my black tourmaline?"

Ileana pulled a small black crystal out of her Spider-Man backpack and handed it to Crow, who moved it through the air around him as though cleansing the space.

The group of teens near the front of the classroom glanced over at him curiously, but none of them said anything

"Crow's in my witch group," Ileana explained, sliding into the desk next to him. She shrugged off her backpack and motioned for Hendricks to take the desk in front of them, explaining, "He's the one who told me about this class."

"Someone had to help you out," Crow said, rolling his eyes. He finished with his crystal and placed it on his desk, sighing deeply.

"Your books were a *mess*. It's amazing you can still afford the rent on that little shop of yours."

Ileana pulled a notebook out of her bag, frowning. "They're getting better."

Crow didn't have eyebrows, but a muscle in his forehead popped like he was trying to raise one. "Are you still keeping track of sales in that *sad* little spiral notebook?"

"Anyway," Ileana said, a blush creeping up her neck. She swiveled around in her seat and nudged the back of Hendricks's chair with her boot. "Hendricks here had some questions about Steele House, so I thought I'd bring her to the expert." To Hendricks, she added, "Not only has Crow been practicing witchcraft since before either of us were born, but he actually grew up in Drearford. He even went to Drearford High."

One of the guys suddenly leaned back, sending his chair balancing on its back two legs. He released a sharp laugh before slamming the chair back down on all fours. Around him, his friends dissolved into giggles and howls.

Hendricks glanced at them, frowning, wondering what was so funny. Crow was studying her now, a curious from on his face. But all he said was, "I graduated in '88."

Hendricks thought of the banner she'd seen in the flashback: CONGRATS CLASS OF '86! Samantha would've only been a couple years older than Crow.

She leaned over the back of the chair. "Did you know Samantha Davidson?"

Crow gave a short snort of a laugh. "Did *I* know the cheerleader who went crazy and killed that kid? Girl, *everyone* knew Samantha. You forget, we didn't have reality TV back in the eighties. We had to watch *each other*. And Sam . . . well, Sam was like our version of a Kardashian."

"The kid she killed . . . his name was Justin, right?"

"Mm-hmm, Justin Morrelly. He was certainly a piece of work, always following Sam and her friends around, watching them, doing messed up things to small animals." Crow pressed a hand to his chest, sighing deeply. "*Personally*, I think that little freak had it coming, but the cops and Justin's family didn't see it that way. After the murder, Sam was committed."

The boys were laughing again. One of them said loudly, "You have *got* to be kidding me." Hendricks felt her eyelid twitch. It was taking a lot of energy to tune them out.

"To that Longwood Place?" she asked Crow.

Crow raised his eyebrows. "Yes, Sam was sent to Longwood. Technically, I believe she was diagnosed a schizophrenic, but you and I both know that's not really what she was." The muscle in his forehead popped again. "Don't we?"

Hendricks stared blankly, and eventually Crow sighed and said, "Okay, so the whole history of Drearford is pretty messed up, but the absolute craziest shit that ever happened in that town has to do with the Steele family. You know about the Steele family of course."

"Wait, there was a Steele *family*?" Hendricks asked.

"Maxwell and Thelma and their five daughters," said Crow. "They came to town in . . . let's see . . . it was 1886, I believe? They were cultists, worshipped some insane god. Long story short, they sacrificed their daughters to this god, and now people think their sacrifice opened, like, a portal between the living and the dead, which, by the way, is why the whole town is overrun with ghosts." Crow glanced lazily at Hendricks and said, "It also, I think, explains why *you're* here."

Hendricks was about to ask him to elaborate, but at that moment one of the other guys suddenly climbed onto his desk. He was holding some old textbook, and without any warning, he dropkicked it, sending it flying across the room. It landed on the floor with a thud that made Hendricks flinch, just a few feet from the woman wearing the shapeless dress.

The woman took no notice of the book but only twirled a strand of hair around her finger muttering to herself. The man standing at the front of the classroom glanced over one shoulder, scowling.

The boy's friends doubled over, hooting and howling with laughter.

"Jesus," Hendricks said, turning back around. "What's wrong with them? Haven't they ever been in public before?"

Ileana looked at Crow and raised her eyes. "What did I tell you?"

"What?" Hendricks asked, looking back and forth between the two of them. "What did she tell you?"

"Ileana thinks you're the new medium," Crow explained. "That's what they call someone who can see and talk to ghosts. Ever since Drearford became ghost central, there's always been a medium." Crow held up one finger. "But just one. It was Samantha Davidson for the last thirty or so years, but she died back in January, which I'm guessing is about when you were called."

Hendricks swallowed. "How did you know?"

Crow suddenly leaned forward, eyes bulging. "Take a look around right now. How many people do you see in here in this room with us?"

Hendricks looked. There was the girl in the shapeless dress, and the guy at the chalkboard, the three rowdy students. "Uh . . . five? Not including the three of us."

Crow blinked at her. "Honey, Ileana and I meet here before class because it's a nice, quiet place to go over her notes." He made a show of looking around the room, his eyes drifting over the other five people without seeming to see them. "Right now, the three of us are the only ones here."

CHAPTER
20

HENDRICKS COULDN'T SPEND ANOTHER MOMENT IN THAT room. She said a quick goodbye and thank-you to Crow and then it was through the hallway and back outside, where she doubled over, breathing hard.

It was getting dark. Hendricks's parents would be sitting down to dinner soon, and they were going to be wondering where she was. Hendricks couldn't bring herself to care. The weight of everything she'd just heard had settled over her like a thick blanket. *Ghosts, medium, chosen.* She pulled at the collar of her jacket, feeling like she couldn't breathe.

The door creaked open and closed behind her, and Ileana said, "You okay?"

Hendricks tried to answer but only managed a strange, strangled laugh. Okay? She didn't know whether that was a word she could use to describe herself anymore. She was a medium. She could see ghosts.

The last medium was *committed.*

Tears blurred her eyes. "You knew?" she managed to choke out. "Crow said you knew."

Ileana hesitated. Hendricks straightened, forcing herself to meet the woman's eyes.

"I only suspected," Ileana admitted, after a long moment. "You said that you could see things back at Steele House, and you showed up here right around when Samantha died. But I didn't know for sure, Hendricks, I swear."

Hendricks felt suddenly ill. She brought a hand to her forehead and said, almost to herself, "If I can see ghosts, why can't I see Eddie?"

"I don't know." There was pity in Ileana's eyes as she added softly, "I'm sorry, but there's something else we have to deal with now. Justin is getting too strong. If we send him back to the void without cutting off the means of his return, he'll just come back again. We need to close the seal for good. As the medium, *you* need to close the seal for good."

If they closed the seal, Eddie would be gone forever.

"When?" she asked.

Ileana lifted her eyes to the sky, where a nearly full moon was just peeking out behind the scattered community college campus, turning the early evening sky purple.

A few students had begun to trickle up the stairs of the adjacent building, but Hendricks was too nervous to ask Ileana whether or not any of them were actually there.

"Tomorrow night is the full moon," Ileana said. One of the students waved, and Ileana lifted her own arm to wave, lazily, back. Hendricks breathed a sigh of relief. At least *that* one was real.

Ileana continued. "I recommend that we gather as much of the original circle as we can and meet at Steele House then, at midnight."

"What about the catalyst . . . or conduit thing?" Hendricks faltered. "Or . . . is that *me*?"

"No, we can't use you." Ileana sighed and sat down on the top of the steps, her elbows sliding onto her knees. "Very few mediums are capable of throwing their consciousness into the void. And you're new, you've never tried anything that complicated before. It's best that we use someone who exists on both planes naturally—"

"I told you, we can't use Raven." Hendricks sat beside Ileana, stretching her own legs down over the steps. "She could get hurt."

"Fine." Ileana plucked a weed up from beneath the stone steps and wove it between her fingers. "I'll figure something else out. You just make sure everyone is there."

"I can do that," Hendricks said.

She sat next to Ileana for a long time, watching students mingle around the dried-up fountain. And when she finally pushed herself back to her feet, it was with a sense of unreality. She felt changed.

She started down the stairs.

"Hendricks?" Ileana called after her. Hendricks turned back around. "I don't know if this helps but . . . if Eddie *is* trying to communicate with you from the other side of the void, it's possible that it doesn't look like what you'd expect."

"What do you mean?" Hendricks asked.

"There's a theory that flashing lights, even certain smells are all spirits from beyond the void trying to communicate with their loved ones." Ileana shrugged. "I've even heard stories about people receiving gifts or finding spots of dead grass on their lawn and knowing that it was the departed trying to reach them. Or even inexplicable rain."

The hair on the back of Hendricks's neck stood up. "But . . . why would the grass be dead?"

Ileana only smiled, a little sadly. "Who knows? Some things about the afterlife are a mystery, even to me."

It was gray as Hendricks drove back to Drearford, and so foggy that she couldn't see the tops of the trees or houses that lined the streets. A crow cawed outside her car window, but she only saw a slight stirring in the gray, and nothing else.

She shivered and drove a little faster.

It wasn't just the weather that had Hendricks feeling off. It was everything. It was Samantha and Justin. It was the fact that they were going to close the seal for good. It was having to leave Eddie behind, forever.

And that's if they were able to close the seal at all. The closer Hendricks got to Raven's neighborhood, the more she thought of the terrible meeting at Tony's the other night, everyone arguing and talking over each other. Vi and Finn taking Portia's side, refusing to believe that the ghost was anyone other than Eddie, Blake not quite managing to accept that there was a ghost at all.

Just thinking about that argument made Hendricks's shoulders creep up toward her ears, the muscles in her back and in her jaw coiling tight. Things were still weird between her and Portia. Was she still on the outs with everyone else, too? If she decided to do the séance after all, would anyone even come? Or was it going just going to be her and Ileana and a moldy hunk of bread?

Out of nowhere, she felt a deep pang of sadness. She was glad that she going to visit Raven. She missed her. When she first got to Drearford, Raven had acted as a kind of antidote to Portia. Where Portia was intense and overbearing, Raven was chill and laid back. To Hendricks's surprise, she felt tears prick the corners of her eyes as she thought about her friend, all alone in that house, machines beeping around her.

Hendricks parked at the end of the block and climbed out of her car.

Raven lived in a big craftsman-style home with a brick porch and a wide, open front lawn. Hendricks took the steps to her porch two at a time and knocked.

A short Asian woman dressed in a no-nonsense outfit of cropped khakis and a gray sweatshirt answered the door. "Hendricks," she said, looking a little surprised. "It's so good to see you, come in."

Raven's mom's name was Cheryl, Hendricks remembered. Everything about her read as efficient and intentional. Her hair was cropped in an easy bob, and she wore no jewelry or makeup. In other words, she was the exact opposite of Raven.

Despite this, Hendricks couldn't help but notice the dark circles under Cheryl's eyes, the lines that seemed to have appeared along her forehead and around her mouth overnight. She looked tired, stressed. Hendricks was suddenly ashamed with herself for showing up empty-handed. She should've brought a casserole or a pie or something. What type of food did you bring people in times like this? Lasagna? Ziti?

Cheryl ushered Hendricks into the front hall. "Can I get you something? Coffee? Tea? We have chamomile."

Hendricks's voice felt suddenly stuck inside of her throat. She remembered how Raven used to bring the little packets of chamomile tea to school with her and steal hot water from the teacher's lounge.

"No thank you," she said, when she could speak again. "I actually can't stay long. I just wanted to say hey."

"Of course." Cheryl smiled kindly and led Hendricks to Raven's bedroom. "Take however long you need," she said and pulled the door shut behind her.

Raven was lying in the center of her bed, looking even smaller than she had on her birthday.

Now that Hendricks was in the same room with her, she found that she didn't know what to say or how to act. The only times she'd come to visit Raven before this had been with Portia.

This is Raven, Hendricks reminded herself, sinking into the chair next to her bed. *She doesn't act like a person until she gets her morning coffee and she wears little boys' T-shirts that she finds at the Goodwill and she's obsessed with anything creative or artistic.* Hendricks swallowed.

She refused to let things be awkward between the two of them.

She grabbed the arms of her chair and scooched forward. "Raven?" She hesitated, and then—remembering her vow not to let things get awkward—she took her friend's hand. "Hey."

Raven didn't look like herself at all. Gone were her fun accessories and bright makeup. Her skin looked dull, her hair limp.

Hendricks felt a lump form in her throat. She suddenly wished she had a cute bracelet or some earrings that she could give her friend, to help her feel more like herself.

She cleared her throat. "So, school's been super weird without you," she said haltingly. It felt strange to be talking to someone who looked like she was sleeping, but she forced herself on. "Portia needs a lot of attention. I guess I didn't realize because you took care of that when you were, uhm, awake. But yeah. She can be a lot."

Hendricks paused, like she was waiting for Raven to answer. But the only sound was the softly beeping hospital machines. *Beep . . . beep . . .*

"I'm making it sound like she's not worth it," Hendricks hurried to add, feeling guilty. "She's been great throughout all of this. She tries really hard to be a good friend."

Beep . . . beep . . .

"And then there's the whole Connor drama." Hendricks laughed softly. "I'll spare you the details of that. It's complicated. I wish we could just go back to being friends."

Beep . . . beep . . .

"Owen misses you." Hendricks suddenly remembered the sweet, poetic boy that Raven had developed a crush on before she fell unconscious. "He hasn't said anything, but I can tell. He canceled his prom date with Samia and is going out of town that weekend instead. Everyone knows it's because of you." Hendricks's throat felt tight.

190

"Maybe . . . maybe if you wake up before prom, we can make a plan for you to ask him? Feminism and all that, you know? Girls shouldn't wait for a boy to ask them anymore."

It was exactly the sort of thing Raven would do: walk up to a boy she had a crush on, tell him how she felt, and ask him to prom with her. Hendricks could practically picture it happening.

Suddenly, she couldn't continue. She doubled over just as a sob bubbled up to her lips. She pressed her knuckles to her mouth, trying to calm herself down. For all she knew, Raven's mother could hear everything. It seemed selfish to break down when she was already going through so much.

"Wake up, Raven," Hendricks whispered, once she'd managed to swallow her tears. She took Raven's hand and squeezed. "I need you, okay? I need you to—to wake up and tell me that Eddie's gone and that closing the portal is more important than wanting to see him again. And I need you to . . . I don't know . . . tell me to go to prom with Connor and make up with Portia and help me convince everyone else to do this dumb séance with me." Her voice cracked. She squeezed her eyes shut, swallowing. "I know I should know how to do all that stuff on my own, but I don't. So, wake up, okay? We need you out here."

She couldn't be sure, but she thought she felt a very light pressure around her fingers, the beginnings of Raven squeezing back. Her heart ached. She stared hard at Raven's face, looking for some other sign.

But there was nothing.

CHAPTER
21

MOONLIGHT DRIFTED IN THROUGH THE BASEMENT WINDOWS, painting Hendricks's closed lids silver. It was still late, and she was lying in Eddie's bed, her face tucked beneath his chin. His chest rose and fell beneath her cheek.

"You're not crazy," Eddie murmured, close to her ear. She could feel the soft scratch of his stubble against her forehead. There was a light pressure on the back of her head, his hands, touching her hair.

"How do you know?" she asked, her voice muffled by his T-shirt.

"I don't . . . I guess I just figure it you're crazy, then I must really be losing it." Eddie said this with a bit of a laugh, but Hendricks could hear the vulnerability beneath his words, the fear.

"We're both crazy, then," she said.

A pause and Eddie added, "Complete wack jobs."

"Total loons."

Eddie laughed, the sound a low rumble. Hendricks felt something inside her relax, a muscle she hadn't realized she'd been tensing. Right now, in this moment, she felt closer to Eddie than she'd ever felt to another human being in her life. She kept her eyes closed but smiled against his chest. If she concentrated, she could feel his heart beating against the corner of her lips.

She stopped smiling. Time slipped.

Hadn't this happened already?

For a moment she couldn't remember where she was.

You're in Eddie's room, she told herself. *You just ran away from Steele House, from the ghosts. Eddie's protecting you.*

But no, that wasn't right. Steele House had burned down.

And Eddie . . .

Fear shot through Hendricks's chest. She pulled away, her eyes searching Eddie's face. He was barely more than a silhouette in the dark, the line of a jaw, the curve of a nose.

"Where were you?" she asked, her voice cracking. "I've been looking for you."

"I'm okay, I promise," Eddie said. "But I need to tell you something." He looked serious all of a sudden, his brows low over his eyes, his expression drawn. Hendricks felt another beat of fear. "You have to let go."

"I can't," Hendricks said, her voice choked. "You have to come back. You *have* to."

Eddie's dark eyes seemed even darker than they had when he was alive. Hendricks couldn't stop staring into them. They seemed to be pulling her in, sucking her down . . .

And then, they started to burn.

Hendricks scrambled out of his bed, her heart leaping inside of her chest. Fire licked at the skin around Eddie's eye sockets and crawled up his face, making it bubble and melt. His eyebrows lit on fire. Hendricks tried not to scream.

"Let go," he said.

Hendricks couldn't breathe. She couldn't speak . . .

And then the bell rang.

Hendricks jerked awake, still screaming. She couldn't remember where she was, what time it was, what day. The lights blaring above her seemed so, so bright. They cast the room around her in intense, neon colors.

Hendricks blinked, and slowly the room came into clearer focus. She wasn't at home in her bed after all. She was sitting at her desk in history class, surrounded by other students, and she'd fallen asleep on her textbook.

She straightened, wiping the drool from her lips as snickers erupted around her. Her heart was beating fast inside of her chest. *It was a dream*, she told herself.

Of course, it was a dream.

It's just . . . it had felt so real. She could still remember how the nerves in the back of her head had flared as Eddie patted her hair, how his T-shirt had felt against her cheek. All warm and worn and cozy. A pang hit her right in the chest.

She thrust her arm into the air. "I—I'm not feeling well," she told her stunned teacher, already pushing away from her desk. She had to get out of here.

Her teacher said something, but she couldn't hear what it was. Her heart was beating hard and fast inside of her head, blocking out all other sound. She was finding it difficult to catch her breath. Her head was too full of Eddie's smile and Eddie's smell and Eddie's warning.

Let go.

She rushed into the hallway. The classroom door slammed shut behind her, and the sound echoed off the metal lockers so that she seemed to hear it again and again.

She buried her face in her hands, a second before the first sob escaped from her lips. It had seemed to claw up from some deep place inside of her. Tears blurred her eyes. It was the kind of crying she hadn't done since she was little. Her entire body felt like a closed fist, every muscle tight and aching. She couldn't breathe, couldn't see, couldn't do anything but let the sobs overtake her.

Her legs wobbled, and then she was crouching on the ground, shaking.

Let go.

How? she wanted to ask. It was the question that echoed through her head. *Please, Eddie, just tell me how.*

When she finally opened her eyes, Hendricks saw that the floor around her was covered in black rose petals.

Hendricks hovered outside of the front doors after school, bouncing on the tips of her toes. She watched the students stream out until finally Connor appeared. He was surrounded by some track guys that she still didn't know, as well as Finn and Blake, and he was talking and laughing.

Hendricks felt a sudden jolt of nerves. When she'd played this out in her head, Connor had been on his own.

Suck it up, Becker-O'Malley, she told herself.

"Hey, uh, Connor!" Hendricks called, waving. "Over here!"

Connor waved goodbye to his track friends and jogged up to her. "Hey, friend," he said, knocking her on the shoulder with his fist. "How are you?"

Terrible, Hendricks thought. But she couldn't say that.

"Swell," she said instead. She'd been trying to come off sounding laid back, but the word seemed weird the second it left her mouth.

"Swell, huh?" Connor said, grinning.

Hendricks swallowed. "I actually wanted to ask you something."

Connor raised his eyebrows. "Oh yeah?"

"Yeah," she said.

There was a beat of silence.

Connor laughed at her. "Okay, so now would be the time that you actually, you know, ask it."

"Right." Hendricks swallowed. *Here I go.* "So. How are you?"

What was wrong with her?

Connor laughed again, but this time it sounded a little strained. "Well, at least that's an easy enough question. I'm doing pretty great. We have a meet this weekend, and my times are better than ever. I heard you fell asleep in history."

"Oh right, that." Hendricks cringed, wishing that story had not made its way back to Connor. "That was embarrassing."

"I bet. It sounded like you were having a nightmare."

Shit. "What are people saying?"

Connor was trying very hard to keep a straight face. "The phrase 'screamed bloody murder' might have come up."

Hendricks groaned and lowered her head to her hands.

"Come on," Connor said, laughing. "It's not that bad."

"How?" Hendricks demanded. "*How* is it not that bad?"

Connor narrowed his eyes, like he was turning something over in his head, and then he leaned forward. "Okay, so you can't tell anyone this," he said, in a much lower voice. "But when I was in ninth grade, I fell asleep in English class." He paused, studying Hendricks. "Have you ever met Miss Lowell? The freshman English teacher?"

Hendricks shook her head. "I don't think so."

Connor blushed. "Oh. You would remember her. She's . . . let's just say that she isn't unattractive."

Hendricks laughed. "Okay . . ."

"And I was a freshman, remember. I had all these hormones. So, I fell asleep in her class one day, and uh . . ." He looked suddenly flustered, like he was wishing he hadn't started telling this story. "Well, I . . ."

"Wait," Hendricks said, stopping him. "This isn't going to be

196

gross, is it? I'm not sure I want to hear about some weird sex dream."

"No!" Connor blushed deeper. "God, it might have been better if it *was* a sex dream. This was even worse. I dreamed that we . . . got married. We had this big church wedding, she was in a white dress, and all my friends were there. It was the whole thing."

Hendricks pressed a hand to her mouth, snickering. "Oh my God . . ."

"That's not even the worst part," Connor continued. "Apparently, I was talking in my sleep the whole time, just saying *I do* over and over again. Blake *still* won't let me live that one down."

Just then, a car rumbled up to the curb, the window buzzing down.

"Hey, O'Malley," Blake called, his voice oddly stiff.

Hendricks lifted a hand in an awkward wave. "Hi, Blake," she said. "And my last name is hyphenated. *Becker*-O'Malley, not just O'Malley."

"Yeah, well, Becker-O'Malley's kind of a mouthful," Blake said. Finn was sitting in the passenger seat, but so far, he hadn't bothered looking at her.

"Connor, you coming?" Blake asked.

"Hold up a second!" Connor shouted, waving at him. Then, turning back to Hendricks, said, "Was that all you wanted?"

"No, actually." Hendricks wetted her lips. "I went to see Ileana last night, and she thinks we can get rid of the ghost that's been stalking Portia once and for all, but it means doing another séance. Tonight, during the full moon."

Hendricks hesitated, glancing back at Blake's car, before adding, "We'd all need to be there, though. The original seven."

Connor ran a hand back through his hair. "Ah . . . to be honest, I don't know whether they'll go for it. They're still . . ."

"Pissed at me?"

"Pretty much," Connor said apologetically. "And this whole situation has them really freaked out."

"I wouldn't ask if it wasn't important," Hendricks said. "I just want all this to be over with."

Connor nodded. "I can't make any promises, but I'll ask."

He waved goodbye and started walking toward the curb.

Do it, Hendricks told herself. She took a deep breath.

"Connor, wait!" she called, jogging after him. "There was just one more thing. I . . . I wanted to say that I think we should go to the prom together after all." She swallowed and then added quickly, "As friends."

Behind her, Blake laid on the horn, the sound causing every muscle in Hendricks's body to tense up at the same time.

"Let's *go*," he called, once the sound had died. "We're gonna miss it."

Hendricks noticed that the muscles in Connor's jaw had tightened, just a little. "The old Drearford drive-in theater is doing a marathon of all the Die Hard movies," he explained. "Blake wants to go early, to get a good spot."

"Oh," Hendricks said.

"Prom sounds cool," he said. And then, quickly, "As friends."

"Great . . . friend." She punched him in the shoulder, just like he'd punched her, but it somehow felt more awkward when she did it. Connor rubbed his arm where she'd touched him.

"Enjoy your movies," she said.

He laughed, "It's Die Hard, how could I not?"

As he started to jog back toward his friends, Hendricks couldn't help but hope that maybe she could still be the girl he wanted her to be.

Someday.

Ten minutes later, Hendricks was hovering outside of Portia's window, bringing her knuckles down hard against the cool glass.

There was a long pause, followed by a sound like shuffling foot-steps inside Portia's room.

A moment later, Portia pulled the curtain aside. "Hi," she said tentatively.

"Hey," Hendricks said, swallowing. "I just wanted to drop off my World History notes." She dug her notebook out of her backpack and handed the notes over.

"Oh, thanks." Portia flipped Hendricks's notebook open and scanned them. After a moment, she frowned slightly. "You just use one color pen for all your notes?"

Hendricks didn't even know how to begin to answer that question. "Why would anyone need more than one color of pen?"

"Well, typically, I use three. One color for important dates, an-other for important people, and a third for—"

"Never mind," Hendricks said, rubbing her eyes. "The notes aren't the only reason I'm here. I actually have some news—"

"Stop." Portia pinched the bridge her nose, cringing. "Hendricks, I love you. Your friendship means a lot to me, and I really don't want to fight, but I can't keep having this same argument over and over again—"

"This isn't about that," Hendricks rushed to say. "Look, I'm done trying to convince you that the ghost isn't Eddie, I swear. Right now, my only concern is getting rid of him."

Portia looked up at her, blinking. "Really?"

"Really. I saw Ileana yesterday, and she thinks she knows how to send him back where he came from," Hendricks continued. "We just need to gather the original seven and do another séance and . . . and close the portal at Steele House."

"Close the portal," Portia repeated. She ran a hand over her chin, and Hendricks thought Portia understood how much this was hurting her, how hard it had been for her to come to this decision. "You're sure that's what you want?"

"Yeah, well . . . I think it's the only way to fix things," Hendricks said, her voice cracking. She cleared her throat, telling herself to be strong. "We'd have to do it tonight, at midnight. I know you're not leaving your bedroom, but I was hoping, if it meant ending this thing, you might make an exception?"

But Portia was already nodding. "Midnight. I'll be there."

CHAPTER
22

MIST CRAWLED OVER THE GROUND AND DRIFTED UP THROUGH the air. It was like looking outside through clouded glass, everything hazy and blurred. Standing at the edge of the Steele House lot, Hendricks drew her jacket more tightly around her shoulders. She felt the cold through her coat, sinking into her. Her bones themselves seemed to shiver.

Beside her, Portia blew air out through her lips, teeth chattering. "Damn," she murmured, crossing her arms over her chest. "What's with the cold? Isn't it supposed to be spring?"

"I think it's just this place," Hendricks said. If she squinted, she could just make out the crack in the foundation through all the mist. It was like a sharp black gash, a gaping wound. Even though Hendricks had stood at the edge of the crack and peered down at the ground below, she couldn't shake the feeling that it led to some bottomless pit, that it was a cut through space and time. She cringed and looked away.

"You think the House is making it cold?" Portia asked. "Like, is it a . . . *mystical* cold?"

Hendricks glanced at her, frowning, and saw that Portia was biting back a smile. She groaned and rolled her eyes.

"Ha-ha," she said, deadpan. "Tell all the jokes you want now. In a few minutes they won't be so funny."

The smile dropped from Portia's face. "I know," she said quietly.

All three boys, Ileana, and Vi had already gathered around the crack, and now they seemed to be waiting for Portia and Hendricks to make their way up the hill. Hendricks felt her heart lift when she saw them standing up there. Everyone had come. No one was joking around or drinking beer or playing hacky sack this time. The mood was solemn, frightened. But they'd come.

Ileana cleared her throat as Hendricks and Portia silently joined the circle. "Very good, we've all made it back. Let's begin."

Hendricks caught a sudden movement from the corner of her eye and turned. There was a bag on the ground at Ileana's feet. It had gone still by the time Hendricks looked down at it, but she found that she couldn't pull her eyes away. There was something inside.

She stared for a beat longer, until . . .

There.

The thing moved.

Hendricks felt panic rise in her. "Ileana—" she started, but Ileana caught her eye and gave a sharp shake of her head.

To the rest of the circle, Ileana said, "The ritual to lay a spirit to rest is different from the one to call him forth. I'm going to need you all to kneel and place your right hand flat on the earth."

All six did as they were told. Hendricks shivered as her knees sunk into the cool, hard dirt. The mist seemed to cling tighter to her skin, to grow thicker around her. Somewhere above them, an owl hooted and then went abruptly silent. Hendricks didn't like the sound of that silence. It was as though something had gotten to the owl. She felt the hairs on the back of her neck lift straight up. Maybe whatever had gotten the owl was still there, lurking in the trees behind them.

"Good," said Ileana, when she was the only one left standing. "We don't use any candles or bread for this ritual. We don't want to remind the spirit of the comforts of the human world. We want to call him and bind him."

She hesitated, her eyes moving over the faces of everyone gathered. "It's a more . . . intense séance than the one we performed last time. It's important that everyone here is prepared for what's to come."

There was a beat of silence, and then, one by one, they all nodded. Ileana released a slow, heavy breath. Her eyes closed for a beat, like she was praying.

"Okay," she said, opening her eyes again. A tired look had fallen over her face, and Hendricks was suddenly very aware of the deep wrinkles around her eyes and mouth.

Ileana crouched on the ground and reached inside of the twitching bag, removing a rabbit.

"Oh God," Portia said, and Hendricks drew in a sharp breath. She felt her voice rise and get caught at the back of her mouth. The rabbit was very small, with matted brown fur and frightened black eyes that twitched anxiously around the circle. It wriggled in Ileana's hands, desperate to get away, but Ileana held it tight. She ran her long, thin fingers over the rabbit's back and leaned down to coo in its ear, comforting it.

The rabbit seemed to calm slightly. It stopped fighting, its ears flicked—

And then Ileana pulled a tiny knife from the inside of her sleeve and drew it across the rabbit's throat.

A shudder twisted its way up Hendricks's back. She wanted to scream, but all she could manage was a small whimpering sound.

Blood covered Ileana's pale hands. The rabbit twitched between her fingers, its muscles beginning to fail. Hendricks wanted it to die so that it wouldn't be in pain any longer. But the rabbit wouldn't go still. It wasn't dead but in the process of dying. Its glassy animal eyes were still moving, looking at them all, as though begging for help.

"No," Portia's voice was a choked sob. Across the circle, Finn said, "Holy shit," and Blake was slowly shaking his head, his eyes glazed over.

Hendricks couldn't move, couldn't breathe. She felt weak.

Ileana didn't meet any of their eyes but crawled forward and placed the dying animal at the center of the circle. Her hands, still red with blood, shook as she drew them away.

"In order to connect with the spirit world, we need a conduit," she said, in a soft voice. "Someone halfway between the living and the dead to act as a bridge. Without a human conduit, we must attempt to make the journey using an animal. It's less stable, but . . ." She shrugged, as though to say *what else can we do*, and her eyes flicked to Hendricks's. "We'll have to go fast, though. It won't be long before he bleeds out."

Hendricks somehow managed to find her voice. "What do we do now?"

"Keep your right hand pressed to the earth," Ileana said. "This will ground you. Now, take your left hand and grasp your neighbor's wrist, like so."

She demonstrated, pressing her right hand into the earth and reaching over with her left to grab Hendricks's right wrist. Her fingers were sticky with blood. The sensation made Hendricks's skin crawl, but she forced herself to stay still.

Ileana said, "This will complete the circle."

She waited as everyone followed her movements. Blake was the last. Once he grasped Vi's wrist, closing the circle, Hendricks felt something move through her, a sudden shock. She swallowed, that bad taste still clinging to her tongue and throat. It was like dissolving aspirin, bitter.

In the middle of the circle, the dying rabbit continued to twitch.

"Very good," Ileana took a deep breath, her eyes rolling up toward the sky. "I call upon light and earth to the north, air to the east, fire to the south, and water to the west. Draw a circle around those gathered here and keep us safe."

A scream ripped through the night close by. Hendricks would've sworn that it was human, but then the sound changed, becoming a sound like a bird diving after its prey.

A ripple of fear moved through the circle, all of them flinching at once. Seconds later the scream had died, and Hendricks couldn't have said what it was, or where it had come from.

"Don't break the circle," Ileana warned, her voice calm and easy. And then, in a louder, more authoritative voice, "Hail to the elementals at the four quarters. I stand between the worlds with love and power all around. Hear me."

Connor shifted beneath Hendricks's tight grip. She could feel his pulse beating steadily beneath her fingers, and she was suddenly grateful for him being there. It felt like he was keeping her in place, holding her steady.

"We are harboring a restless spirit," Ileana said. "He passed over to this side without permission, and now, we send him back."

Beneath them, the ground began to shake. At first it was just a slight tremble, like a train going past. Dirt and twigs rolled off to either side of the hill. Hendricks's hips knocked to either side.

A shape began to take form beneath the earth, a sort of mound, like there was something below them trying to crawl its way to the surface. It seemed to buck and jerk.

Hendricks tried as hard as she could to keep her hand pressed to the ground, the other tight around Connor's wrist. She was suddenly grateful she was kneeling. The strength had seemed to go out from her legs. She couldn't feel anything below her waist.

Ileana's strong, steady voice said, "He does not belong here. Take him back."

Across the circle, Hendricks heard Blake swearing. Finn wasn't saying anything, but his skin had very gone pale, and Hendricks could see a sheen of sweat on his forehead, shiny in the darkness. Both were staring hard at the trembling earth and trying, like her, to stay upright, to keep their hands pressed to the ground.

"Take … him … back …" A groan passed Ileana's lips. She swayed on her knees and then keeled forward. She kept her right hand pressed to the earth, and her left wrapped around Hendricks's wrist, so there was nothing to stop her from slamming face-first into the ground.

"Ileana!" Hendricks loosened her grip on Connor's wrist, intending to reach for her—

"Don't break the circle!" Ileana's voice sounded weaker than it had a moment ago. "If you … break the circle … I can't protect you."

She lifted herself off the ground, but it clearly took all of the energy she had left.

"Take … him … *back!*" Ileana forced the words through clenched teeth. Still shaking, she doubled over and started to choke. Tremors shuddered through her body, but for a while, nothing came out. She coughed and heaved …

Blood oozed from between her teeth. It was thick and black, almost the consistency of tar, and it poured over her lips and chin, soaking the front of her shirt. Hendricks recoiled. It didn't smell like blood was supposed to smell. This was putrid, like sewer water and feces and something else, something black and rotting. Ileana spat up another mouthful of blood, and then another, and then she collapsed again, her eyelids flickering. Her pupils had rolled back into her eye sockets so her eyes were mostly whites and bloodshot.

Hendricks's hand was weak around Ileana's wrist, but she didn't let go.

The mist began to churn. It circled the crack like water in a drain and then disappeared into the foundation. The screaming that could have been a human or a bird started up again, mingling with the howling wind. This time, it sounded much, much closer. It was just behind Hendricks's head, whispering into her ear.

And then it had moved past her, coming from below her feet, from the crack itself.

Hendricks's stomach turned over.

"Ileana," she said. The ground was still shaking. She could barely keep herself upright. She pressed her right hand more firmly into the ground and kept the other wrapped tight around Connor's wrist. "Ileana, what do we do?"

Ileana groaned but didn't lift her head from the dirt. Dried blood clung to her lips.

"We need to get the fuck out of here," Blake said. His eyes were wide and black with fear. He started to let go of Vi's wrist—

"Don't you dare break the circle!" Portia snapped back at him. "Didn't you hear her?"

"This shit is not funny anymore," Finn said. He was watching Ileana, and for the first time that Hendricks could remember, he didn't look remotely amused. He licked his lips. "Somebody needs to help her."

"Don't be a wuss," Connor yelled back at his brother. But his voice shook, and Hendricks knew it was only a matter of time before he was with them, wanting to leave, not sure how to handle the horror of what they were seeing.

"Take him back." Hendricks was practically whispering. She

cleared her throat and said again, louder, "Take him back."

Portia glanced at her. "Take him back," she said, too. "Take him back."

Vi joined, and then Connor. Eventually, Blake and even Finn added their voices to the chant, until they were all reciting the words as one.

"Take him back . . . Take him back . . . Take him back . . ."

The screaming rose to a fever pitch, echoing through Hendricks's ears. The otherworldly sound consumed her. Hendricks closed her eyes. She had a sudden flash of the future, how she would never be able to forget this moment, this anguish.

And then, all at once, it stopped. The night had been filled with noise. And now, suddenly, it was silent.

Hendricks opened her eyes. Her heart was thudding in her chest. She looked to all of the people gathered in the circle around her and saw the fear that she felt reflected in their faces.

"Is that . . . it?" Vi asked, in a very small voice.

Hendricks glanced at Ileana. She looked exhausted: her forehead was covered in sweat, and her hands were bloodied, but her eyes were open.

She let go of Hendricks's wrist, and, groaning, pushed herself back up to her hands and knees.

"Are you okay?" Finn asked, from the other side of the circle.

Ileana didn't answer him right away. Then, as though it pained her, she said, "It . . . it's done. We did it."

The gathered seven looked around at one another, their faces slowly breaking out into nervous smiles. Blake turned to Vi and gave her a high five. Finn hurried across the circle to kneel at Ileana's side. He helped her loop one arm around his shoulder so that she could stand again.

Hendricks, though, was looking past all of them, her eyes finding the spot on the concrete where, just a few minutes ago, there'd been a deep, jagged crack.

It was gone now. The crack was closed.

She let go of Connor's hand and approached, then knelt. She could see the place where the opening had once been. It was like a line through the concrete, like a long-healed scar. She ran a finger along the line, feeling a strange mixture of emotions as she examined it.

Relief, surely. Their ritual had worked. But just below that relief, there was something else, something just as strong. Regret. Sorrow. Pain.

If the portal to the other side was closed, then Eddie was gone forever.

She blinked, hard, chasing that thought away. The corners of her eyes were wet, but she tried hard to ignore the press of tears. The others wouldn't understand. This was a happy time, after all.

A hand dropped onto her shoulder, and then Connor was crouching beside her. "Hey," he said. "Are you okay?"

Hendricks swallowed. "Yeah, totally," she said in the most cheerful voice she could manage. Even she could hear how fake it sounded. She stood. "I'm going to walk home, I think. I—I'll see you tomorrow."

She ducked her head and headed into the woods, even as Connor called after her, "Hendricks, wait!"

The trees shed darkness over her as soon as she stepped beneath them, and the temperature dropped by several degrees. But Hendricks didn't shiver. Something in her chest released, and it felt good. It felt like solace.

As soon as she was far enough away from the others, she dropped to her knees and let the tears come.

CHAPTER
23

A WEEK HAD PASSED. HENDRICKS SAT ON THE FLOOR OF HER bedroom, staring down at the cardboard box. The words *old clothes* were still legible across the top flap. She stared at the books on the occult, blessed salts, crystals, the Ouija board, black candlesticks, and half-burned sage.

Sighing, she folded the top of the box closed and heaved it onto the top shelf of her closet, pushing it all the way to the back, where she wouldn't be tempted to look at it again.

It was time for a fresh start. She pushed her closet door closed.

There was a soft rap on the window behind her. Hendricks jerked around, her nerves on edge.

A second later, she heard Portia's voice. "Open up, girl, it's me."

Groaning, Hendricks crossed her room and unlatched the window. "You can use the front door like a normal person, you know."

"Where's the fun in that?" Portia held out her freshly manicured hand, her long pink nails like talons. "Help a girl out."

Hendricks grabbed Portia's hand and helped her crawl through the window. Portia was dressed more casually than Hendricks had ever seen her, in plain black leggings and a button-up shirt, but her makeup was flawless, and her curls had been piled on top of her head in an elaborate updo.

Hendricks saw a flash of Samantha Davidson, her hair done up in a similar style, but quickly pushed the thought away.

"You look amazing," she said, meaning it.

Portia beamed. Then, blushing she added, "Tell the truth, do you really think Vi will like it?"

"She's going to love it, you know that," Hendricks said.

"Good, I want everything to be perfect for tonight." Portia beamed. "Just *wait* till you see my dress. It's this unbelievable vintage gown. You're going to die."

Hendricks squeezed Portia's hand, grinning back at her. Prom was in just a few hours. She felt wistful, and a little nostalgic for this night, even though it hadn't happened yet.

Portia and Vi were going to have this perfect, romantic evening, and Hendricks couldn't help being a little jealous of that. But she was excited to go to the prom with Connor. It was going to be fun, at least, and fun was definitely something she could use a little more of in her life.

Portia's eyes flicked from Hendricks's damp hair to her sweat-pants and old Walter School T-shirt. "So you haven't even started getting ready."

"That's not true!" Hendricks said. "I took a shower."

Portia frowned. "For some reason that just makes me sadder."

Hendricks flushed. "Yeah, well not everyone needs three hours to get ready for a dance. I'm waiting to put my dress on until right before I leave so I don't stain it or anything." She nodded at the dress hanging off the back of her closet.

It wasn't quite right for prom. Hendricks had bought it for her friend Andie Rosenberg's bat mitzvah back in Philadelphia. It was short and black, with little glitter swirls all over it. She hadn't worn it since she was thirteen, but she'd tried it on this afternoon and it still fit. Sort of. The fabric was stretchy.

Hendricks had been perfectly fine with her dress until she saw how Portia was looking at it, her lip curled a little, like it smelled. Now she felt embarrassed. She pulled the dress off the back of her closet door and held it up to herself, trying to look more excited than she felt. "What do you think?"

Portia tilted her head to the side, her nose wrinkling. "It's . . . sad."

"Come on, no it's not."

Portia plucked at the hem. "Yes, it is, Hendricks. It wants to know why you hate yourself. And . . . isn't it a bit small? And . . . black?" Portia glanced back at Hendricks, one eyebrow arching. "This is prom. I wore something more cheerful to my aunt's funeral."

"Stop, it's the only dress I have," Hendricks said, irritated.

Portia chewed her lip. "Right. It's the only dress you have. Got it."

Something about her expression made Hendricks suspicious. "What did you do?" she asked.

"I didn't *do* anything, it's just . . ." Portia leaned out the window, and, with a grunt, pulled a black garment bag in from outside. "I had a feeling that you wouldn't be remotely prepared for the biggest social event of the year, so I brought my . . . backup dress."

Hendricks stared at the black bag. "Backup dress?"

"Yeah, I got two just in case my tailor didn't finish mine in time." Portia wouldn't meet Hendricks's eyes as she said this. "I was being pragmatic."

Hendricks let out a short laugh. She had no doubt that whatever vintage masterpiece Portia was wearing tonight had been finished for weeks. There was no way she would ever need a *backup* dress. Which meant . . .

"You bought me a dress," Hendricks said, dumbfounded.

Portia rolled her eyes. "Calm down. It's Rent the Runway. You can rent dresses for like forty bucks. I only rented this one in case my *real* dress looked completely ridiculous on me, which hey, it doesn't, so you can try this one. I think it's your size."

Hendricks eyed her friend skeptically. She and Portia were completely different sizes. Hendricks was tall and narrow, while Portia a good six inches shorter and curvy. There was no way she was fitting into one of Portia's dresses.

"You bought me a dress," she said again.

Portia thrust the garment back at her. "Ugh, will you just open it?"

Still frowning, Hendricks unzipped the garment bag, revealing silvery-blue fabric. Her breath caught in her throat as she pulled the dress out and held it up to examine it.

It was . . . breathtaking. Designed to skim close to the body, with a plunging V-neck line and a slit that would show her legs.

Hendricks gave Portia a look. The dress wasn't remotely Portia's size or style.

Portia groaned. "Fine, I bought you a dress. Or I rented it. Whatever. Want to try it on?"

Hendricks stepped out of her sweats and tossed off her T-shirt, pulling the slinky silvery dress over her hips. Somehow the fabric hugged her curves, making her seem like way less of a bean pole than she did normally. It fit perfectly, like it was made for her. She pulled her hair up off her neck as Portia zipped the back up.

"Would it be okay if I messed with your hair a little?" Portia asked slyly.

Hendricks chewed on her lower lip, eyeing Portia's elaborate curls. "I'm not sure . . ."

Portia pushed Hendricks into her desk chair. "Calm yourself. I just want to work with your natural messy-waves thing, okay?"

Deftly, she twisted Hendricks's loose waves into a low bun by her left ear, leaving soft tendrils around her forehead and ears. She pulled a small makeup bag from the garment bag that'd held Hendricks's gown and produced a handful of bobby pins, which she quickly stuck into Hendricks's hair, pinning the look in place. The result was a casually cool bun that left Hendricks's right ear and neck exposed.

"Voilà," she said, taking a step back. "What do you think?"

"Whoa," Hendricks said, impressed. "That looks great. Thank you."

"Just one more thing . . ." Portia pulled a single, diamond-studded cuff out of her makeup bag and clipped it onto Hendricks right ear. "There. Now you look like a rock star who pulled herself together for the Grammys."

Hendricks didn't know what to say. The look Portia had created for her was so completely different from Portia's own look, so entirely Hendricks.

She touched her diamond earing, her messy chic hair. "Thank you," she said.

Portia rolled her eyes. "Jesus, calm down. It's a dress and an earring, and I only brought them so that you didn't show up in that . . . well, whatever that thing is." She glanced at the dress still hanging from the back of Hendricks's closet, sniffing.

"Anyway, my mom wants pics of me and Vi before we head out, so I should probably go get dressed." She headed for the window again, but Hendricks caught her by the arm.

"No, no window," she said, steering her toward her bedroom door. "You'll use the front door like a normal person, okay?"

"I suppose that makes sense," Portia said. She stopped at Hendricks's door, suddenly serious. "We're all getting to the school around eight."

"Got it," Hendricks said, nodding. "I'll be there."

"You better be," Portia said. Then, with one last glance at Hendricks's gown, she said, "I seriously can't wait to see Connor go nonverbal over you. Tonight is going to be amazing!"

CHAPTER
24

HENDRICKS'S DAD DROPPED HER OFF IN FRONT OF THE HIGH school, his voice a little choked as he told her to have fun.

Hendricks waved goodbye and hurried to join the group of teenagers dressed in all colors of the rainbow, looking like confetti as they milled around the school's main entrance.

She paused, just for a moment, to take in the spectacle. She had to admit, she and the rest of the prom committee had done an amazing job. The school hardly looked like a school anymore. There was a red carpet draped over the front steps, and a giant red-and-white-striped life raft made out of balloons floated around the front doors. SS DREARFORD, a sign read. Couples were stopping beneath the balloons, grinning and snapping photographs with their phones. Portia had been right, they seemed way happier taking selfies than they would've been with a professional photographer.

Hendricks straightened and started moving through the crowd. She could already hear the music from the gym. The heavy bass vibrated through the floor, making her high heels tremble. She actually felt a jitter of anticipation as she hurried inside. This was the most normal she'd felt in a long time.

Tonight was going to be *fun*. She'd make sure of it.

The gym was packed. There was a DJ booth in one corner, a giant, light-up anchor draped with fish netting set up in front of it. Strings of lights dripped from the ceiling, and a cardboard cruise ship took up one entire wall. The light was all blue-tinted, making everything seem like it was underwater. All the shadows in the room were darker and strangely fluid.

Hendricks rose to her toes, peering over the heads of her classmates. The music changed, a new song started blaring through the speakers. All around Hendricks, people burst into cheers. They started jumping, pumping their fists into the air, and singing along. The blue lights flashed on and off, on and off.

There was Blake, dancing with some girl she didn't recognize, and farther away, Finn was staring down at his phone, his now-familiar twisted smile illuminated in the glow. Hendricks tried to wave at him, but he didn't look up. She dropped down from her toes.

She scanned the room and finally found Connor, sitting on the bleachers in the corner of the gym in a tux and bowtie. Hendricks broke into a smile. Taking a deep breath, she made her way through the crowd.

He looked up as she approached and grinned. "Hey, you," he said, and stood up, like this was one of those old movies where it was considered rude to sit when a lady was standing. Heat rose in Hendricks's cheeks as Connor eyes moved over her dress. He ran a hand through his hair, messing it up. "Wow. You look . . . I mean . . . that dress is great."

Hendricks swallowed. "Thanks. You look good, too."

Connor laughed. "So," he said, a little awkwardly. "What do you want to do? Dance? Grab some punch?"

Hendricks let her eyes close for a fraction of a second. She thought this part might feel weird, but it didn't. She wanted to dance with him. They were friends, after all, and they were here together. Prom was all about dancing. A slow song came on.

"Let's dance," she said, and took Connor's hand.

Connor's expression changed immediately. His cheeks reddened, and his lips twitched. He reached for her, but instead of taking her hand, his hands slid around her waist.

"Is this okay?"

"Oh . . . uh, yeah." Hendricks swallowed her nerves, as he pulled her in a little closer.

"I'm really glad you're here," Connor said.

"Why's that?"

Connor blew air out through his teeth, his eyes going wide. "Where do I even start? Portia and Vi are already all over each other, no surprise there. And Blake . . . well, he's here with Brandi Nelson? And I guess he never really talked to Brandi before, he only asked her out because he thought she was really cute. Turns out, she's this born-again chick, and she spent the whole walk over here talking to him about Jesus, while Vi and Portia tried to grill her about the church's stance on the LBGTQA-plus community."

"Oh my God." Hendricks choked out. "That sounds intense."

"That's not even the worst part." Connor leaned in a little closer. "You'll never guess who Finn's into."

Hendricks had no idea. "Who?"

"*Ileana.*"

"What?" Hendricks's stomach flipped. "*My* Ileana?"

"Oh yeah. He's practically ready to propose. I think maybe it was her badass car? Anyway, he spent all night asking me if I thought he was her type and if she ever went for younger dudes." Connor shook his head. "It's been, like, intense. I'm just glad you're here now to save me from all that."

The music changed, switching from a slow dance number to a song with a heavy bass. They wouldn't be able to hear each other unless they shouted over it.

Hendricks moved away from Connor, releasing a laugh that sounded a touch brittle to her own ears. Connor didn't seem to notice. He was still smiling his megawatt smile. It made Hendricks ache. She really loved that smile. And she loved *this*, when things were easy between them, just chill and friendly, the two of them gossiping about everyone else, making each other laugh.

"Come on," Connor said, smile growing wider still. He nudged her shoulder with his fist. "You're glad you came, too, right? This is fun."

Hendricks swallowed. Nodded. Connor was staring at her lips now, and she cringed, realizing she knew what he was thinking.

He wanted to kiss her.

She should've known that it would be impossible for Connor to see her simply as a friend. It wasn't even that the idea of kissing Connor was so terrible. It's just that she couldn't think about kissing him without remembering . . .

She was a monster.

She could feel Connor watching her, trying to gauge her reaction, and so she forced her lips into a wobbly smile. Suddenly, her face felt hot. The space around her was too stuffy, the people too close.

"I'm gonna find the bathroom!" she shouted, so loudly that a few people around them turned and snickered. Hendricks slipped through the crowd and headed for the hall before she could do something else humiliating.

By the time Hendricks reached the bathroom, she was breathing easy again. Other than the almost kiss, things were going well so far. They were dancing and talking and, for the most part, things were good. And after her reaction, she doubted Connor would attempt another almost kiss for the rest of the night. So that was a relief.

She leaned over the bathroom sink, peering into her mirror to double-check that her hair was still in place. Somehow it looked even better than when Portia first put it up. The bun was kind of messy, and the curls were all loose and rocker chic. She felt a pang, thinking of how much she wished Eddie could see her like this, all glammed up—

She gave her head a hard shake. *No.* No more Eddie.

Eddie was gone.

Sucking in a deep breath, she pulled out her purse and started rooting around inside for the lipstick she'd brought. Reapplying lipstick was the sort of thing that nice, normal girls who weren't hung up on their dead ex-boyfriends did at prom.

She uncapped it and leaned over the sink, puckering up.

The lipstick slipped from her grasp and clattered into the sink.

Hendricks hesitated, frowning slightly.

She reached for it—

The lipstick skated out from under her fingers. Then, it lifted very gently into the air and flew past Hendricks's face before coming to rest on top of her purse.

Hendricks stood very still. She wasn't alone. Her fear response was instant. Every hair on her body stood straight up. Her heart started to race. She glanced at the bathroom door.

Could she get there before he got to her?

She had to try.

She inched to the side, scanning the shadows of the bathroom for movement. There was nothing. Hendricks held her breath, her knees shaking. Her gown pooled around her feet, making it hard to move easily.

She couldn't figure out why Justin was invisible this time. She could always see him before. She was nearly to the door. She reached out and grabbed it.

The lights flickered. *On. Off. On.*

And then the air around her seemed to shift. It grew cool, and then a familiar scent washed over her.

Cigarette smoke and baby shampoo.

Hendricks breathed it in, feeling her eyes well up.

Eddie.

Something brushed against her face. It was the soft press of fingertips against skin. Hendricks's breath hitched. She moved her hand through the air for the fingers that had just touched her.

"Eddie," she breathed. "Eddie, what—"

Lips pressed against hers. It was a strange sensation, at once real, physical, but faint and freezing cold. Cold shivered through her, but she didn't move. She'd been dreaming about this moment for so long. Her eyes closed.

Arms encircled her waist. She lifted her hands and felt the soft, worn fabric of Eddie's T-shirt and, beneath, the shape of his body. He was cold, so cold. Keeping her eyes tightly closed, she lowered her head to his chest and snaked her arms up around his neck. Her eyes were sticky with tears, but they were good tears, *happy* tears. Eddie was here.

Distantly, Hendricks realized that she could still hear the music from the gym. She'd been so focused on Eddie, that she'd barely even noticed the music filling the room. Now, a slow song came on. It was "The Way You Look Tonight," which was totally cheesy and retro, but Hendricks loved it anyway because her parents had played it for their first dance when they got married.

Hendricks felt pressure on the small of her back, like Eddie's hand was pressed there. They swayed in time with the music, her feet drifting across the floor, her heart soaring. This, *this* was all she'd wanted tonight. Just the chance to dance with Eddie again. It seemed impossible that it was actually happening.

But it was.

When the song had ended, she lifted her head, blinking. There was still no one there. At least, not that she could see.

"I want to see you," she said, her voice cracking. "Please, let me see you."

No one answered. Hendricks felt something stir in the pit of her stomach, an ache. This was almost worse than not getting to see him at all. He was there and not there. Close enough to feel, to touch, but not to see.

And then he pulled away. Hendricks wrapped her arms around herself, feeling suddenly lost.

"Where are you going?" she asked, her voice taking on a note of desperation. She wasn't ready to say goodbye yet.

The lipstick from the sink lifted in the air and hovered in front of the mirror.

Eddie started to write,

I love you. You have to close the seal. He's comi—

CHAPTER
25

THE LIPSTICK HALTED MIDAIR—

And then the tube went flying across the room. It hit the wall and shattered, making Hendricks yelp and leaving a smudge of deep, crimson red that looked disturbingly like blood.

Hendricks pressed both hands over her mouth. Sweat broke out along her brow, and her heart was beating hard and fast. She was too afraid to move, to breathe.

Finally, she lowered her hands and whispered, her throat tight, "Eddie?"

But there was no answer, there was no change in the air, no soft scent of Eddie's familiar smell or cool brush of his hand against her back. Eddie was gone.

Her eyes crept back to the warning he'd left on the mirror.

He's comi—

Cold seeped through her. Eddie had meant to write *he's coming*, but he never finished.

Which meant *he* was already here.

Hendricks gathered the bottom of her gown in her fist and darted back into the gym. She didn't touch the bathroom door, but she heard it slam shut behind her, the sound a sudden crash of wood that made the walls tremble. The low rumble of laughter followed her down the hallway.

She yelped, but she didn't dare turn back around. *This can't be happening*, shouted a voice inside of her head. *You're imagining things, you're paranoid, you're—*

Hunted, said a second voice, overwhelming the first. If the séance didn't work, if Justin really was still here, then she needed to find the seven. Now.

Hendricks stumbled back into the gym and started pushing her way through the crowd of people. Music throbbed in her ears. The crowd raged. There were so many bodies, elbows jabbing into Hendricks's ribs and shoulders bumping into her, sending her tripping back a few feet, high-heeled shoes and wingtips stepping on her toes. Hendricks could barely move. Lights flickered, a dizzying array of blues and purples swirling and flashing all around her. They'd seemed so fun, earlier, but now they were menacing. They made the shadows seem darker.

"Portia!" Hendricks shouted, but her voice was immediately lost in the music and the cheering and the voices of other kids singing along. "Vi!"

She spotted Vi dancing in the middle of the room, which meant that Portia had to be close by. Relief flooded through her.

"Excuse me," she said, and started making her way through the throng of people. "This is an emergency—"

Vi wore a tuxedo jacket paired with a long black skirt with a slit that showed off her legs. Her hair was slicked away from her face. She was dancing with Portia. They were behind a small cluster of students, swaying to the music. Hendricks barreled through the group, muttering an apology. But when she finally saw Portia, her heart nearly stopped.

Hendricks's skin went cold. She stopped pushing through the

crowd, her arms and legs suddenly frozen. She forgot to move. She forgot to breathe.

That dress.

It was a white prom dress with a three-tiered skirt and a sweetheart neckline, and Hendricks would've recognized it anywhere. It had been altered. The puffy sleeves were gone, and some of the tiers had been removed from the skirt so that it was sleeker than it had been. But it was the same dress, Hendricks was sure of it. Samantha Davidson had been wearing that dress on the night she'd been abducted and mutilated.

Hendricks lifted her eyes to the girl's face, and, for one long moment, she thought that it actually was Samantha Davidson staring back at her.

She blinked and it was Portia again, laughing as Vi grinned and spun her in a circle, making her flowy skirt twirl around her.

"Portia," Hendricks called, cupping her hands around her mouth. She pushed toward her.

Portia frowned, hearing her voice, and scanned the crowd. When her eyes fell on Hendricks, her smile grew even wider. She took Vi by the hand, and the two of them headed over to her.

"You look gorgeous!" Portia said. "Did you find Connor?"

"Yeah, I did," Hendricks said, her eyes flicking back to Portia's dress. "What are you wearing—"

"Isn't it amazing?" Portia asked. "It's vintage. It used to belong to my aunt Sam."

"Your aunt Sam?" Hendricks repeated, numb. She felt a lump form in her throat.

"I told you about her, remember? She was supposed to plan her school prom back in the eighties, but she had a nervous breakdown and had to be taken away. She died earlier this year."

Hendricks's mouth felt dry. She barely remembered that conversation. Portia must've mentioned it back when she'd first joined prom committee, but Hendricks hadn't thought anything of it.

Now, of course, Hendricks couldn't believe she hadn't put it together before: Samantha Davidson had been abducted on prom night. That's why she'd been wearing this gown, why she kept hearing that stupid Prince song. She felt suddenly ill.

Portia shrugged. "Anyway," she said, with a flip of her hand, turning back to Vi. "I found this dress in her things. Stunning, right? It cost a fortune to get it cleaned, but I knew absolutely no one else would have one like it, so I had it altered and tailored to fit me. It was all beat up when I found it. Apparently, Aunt Sam did not take very good care of it."

Hendricks had a sudden memory of Samantha Davidson lying on her side in the clearing behind Steele House, her face covered in blood and dirt, sobbing. Justin dropped his knife, and she lunged for it, her eyes going wide as her fingers curled around the hilt. *I'll be back for you—*"

Hendricks blinked and, just like that, the image was gone. She stared at Portia's face. She'd always thought she looked like Samantha. Now she knew why.

"Portia," Hendricks said, her voice shaking. "*Samantha's* the one the ghost was after. That's why he's been stalking you, you look like her—or at least you look like how he remembered her." Hendricks grabbed Portia's wrists, holding tight. "I never told you because you didn't want to talk about it, but the ghost, it was never Eddie. It was this kid named Justin, he was obsessed with your aunt, and on prom night back in 1986—"

Portia pulled her hand away from Hendricks's and took a step backward, shaking her head. "What are you doing?"

"The ghost—"

"No." Her voice came down hard, like an ax. She wasn't smiling anymore. In fact, her entire face had closed up, her eyes flashing. "That's over, Hendricks, remember? We did a séance. We got rid of him."

Hendricks thought of the message Eddie had left for her in the bathroom. *He's comi*— "It's not over. The ghost is back. He—"

"Stop it!" Portia's expression turned to stone. "Look around, Hendricks. This is *prom*. It might not matter to you, but it matters to me. It matters *a lot*. While you've been moping about over your ex, I've been thinking about this and planning and trying to make everything perfect. And not just for me, for all of us. For you."

She took Vi by the hand and started heading deeper into the crowd.

"Portia, wait!" Hendricks called. She felt a lump form in her throat. "Please," she tried, fighting through the other students. "This is really important. Eddie—"

"Eddie?" Portia released a short, bitter laugh. "*Big* surprise, this is about Eddie again. Well, guess what? I don't care about your messed-up obsession anymore. Go be with Eddie. Enjoy your time together." Portia kept moving, heading deeper into the crowd. Hendricks was about to follow her when Vi stepped in front of her.

"I don't really want to get in the middle of this, but I think you should leave her alone." Vi sounded slightly apologetic.

"I get that she's pissed with me right now, but this is really important. I don't think she's safe."

Vi chewed on her lower lip, thinking this over. And then, shrugging, she said, "Is anyone ever really safe in this town?"

She turned, and the crowd swallowed her, just at it had swallowed Portia.

Hendricks tried to follow them, but the people were packed in too tight; she couldn't even make it a few feet. She felt her heart go still inside of her chest. She scanned the crowd for Portia, or Vi, but she couldn't see either of them.

Her mind spun. She didn't know what to do next, she didn't know where they would go, or how to make them listen—

A strangled scream ripped through the gym.

CHAPTER
26

IT WAS THE SAME SCREAM HENDRICKS HAD HEARD THE night of the séance. Human at first, and then animal, and then a sound that was nothing like any living creature had ever uttered.

Hendricks felt her stomach flip.

The light in the gymnasium had changed. It was no longer blue and strobing but was now a deep purple and red.

Below the bloody lights she saw her prom, the way it was supposed to be.

And then the lights flashed and she saw another prom woven in with images of her own like scenes from a movie. The room felt like it was closing in on her. Her feet felt unsteady. Her vision was blurred.

She pressed a trembling hand to her mouth, sobs welling up inside of her. She had only a few seconds to observe that *other* prom before the lights flashed back to blue, taking Hendricks to the present again. But she'd seen that it was unnatural. *Cursed.*

Oh God, she thought, turning in a slow circle. *Oh God, oh God, oh God . . .*

A few people had stopped dancing and were looking around to see where the scream had come from. But almost everyone else was still singing along with the music, smiling, unbothered. They seemed delighted by the changing lights. They threw their hands over their heads and cheered.

As Hendricks stood there, wondering what to do, the low, gravelly sound of someone laughing rumbled up from below the sound of music. A few more students lowered their hands, confusion flashing across their faces as the laughter echoed off the walls.

Hendricks felt sick. Justin's laughter disappeared as music filled the gym again. But now almost every student in the gym looked nervous. They seemed to understand that this wasn't normal, and they all glanced around at one another, confused. Hendricks thought she heard someone mutter, "Some sort of dumb prank . . ."

Her pulse thudded deep in her throat. The lights in the gym began to flash again, on and off, on and off, quickly, faster than before.

In one bright flash of red light, Hendricks saw students she knew looking around and whispering, fear etched on their features.

And in another, she saw the students from 1986, dancing and swinging in their pastel gowns and tuxes, smiles refreshingly bright. Only, their faces—

Oh God.

Hendricks's mouth went dry. Her breathing grew shallow.

Their faces.

Their skin was rotting, gray, and garish and pulled tight over their bones of their faces. The whites of their eyes weren't white at all, but a deep, bloody red. Their lips were scabbed, and hair clung in chunks to their chapped scalps. Blood oozed from their faces.

Hendricks felt the strength drain out of her legs. She wanted to run, but there was nowhere to go. Those bloody, rotten skeletons were dancing all around her, grabbing one another, laughing with their heads thrown back, green sludge oozing between their yellowing teeth. She could *smell* them. They were putrid, like things that were long dead. When they brushed against her, her skin crawled . . .

There was a sudden slam. Everyone went still.

Hendricks turned and saw Samantha Davidson standing in the gym doorway, dark curls hacked away from a bleeding scalp, her face mangled, her dress drenched in blood. She was still holding Justin's knife in one trembling hand—

All around her, people started to scream.

But Samantha locked eyes with Hendricks. She looked at her for a long moment, her face slowly rotting away. "He's coming for you."

Finally, Hendricks understood. Justin wanted the medium's power. He wasn't after Portia—not really. Whether he knew it or not, the person he was really after was Hendricks.

The lights flickered, once, twice.

And then they were gone. All of them. Hendricks was back at *her* prom, surrounded by people she knew.

She looked back toward the door, but Samantha was gone.

The music had died and now a strained silence filled the gym, punctuated only by unnerved whispers as they all looked around at one another, wondering what was going on.

Hendricks hugged her arms around her chest. She couldn't believe that she was still cursed, after all the pain she'd endured and Eddie's sacrifice. Would she never be free?

Almost like an answer, every single window in the gym shattered.

The sound of breaking glass was like a battle cry, and Hendricks threw her hands over her ears. Glass cut into her cheeks and arms and the back of her neck, teeny little nicks that felt like biting insects.

All around her, people crouched and covered their faces, screaming as the air around them filled with tiny, glittering shards.

The sudden silence that followed was like a whispered sigh. Hendricks couldn't quite manage to inhale. The silence was somehow worse than the sound of screaming and breaking glass. It was heavy, ominous. She felt the people around her shuffle anxiously, wondering whether it was safe enough to run.

Hendricks had been doubled over, staring at the floor, and so she saw the exact moment the first wasp appeared.

It crept up through the floorboards, wings first, body twitching. Hendricks choked down a scream and danced backward, but there was another one, perched on her foot and another clinging to a girl's leg. She saw one disappear into a girl's hair, and another buzzing around the sleeve of a boy's tux.

And then they were everywhere. They seemed to appear out of the air itself. As Hendricks watched, horrified, the insects multiplied, becoming dozens and then hundreds and then too many to count, a buzzing swarm that gathered thickly around people's hair and faces, clinging to their arms and the bottoms of their dresses, tissue-thin wings fluttering.

All around her, people raced for the gym doors, but there were too many of them. They'd become a stampede. People crashed to the ground, screaming, and—still—the crowd surged onward. Hendricks tried to break away, but she couldn't help being pulled along with them.

"Hendricks, wait!" Connor was suddenly behind her, grabbing her arm. As the crowd moved toward the door, he fought his way over to the far wall, breathing hard. "I—I think Vi and Portia disappeared through there."

He pointed to the side of the gym, where there was a door leading out into a hall.

Staring at the doors, Hendricks remembered the conversation she'd had with Portia the night she'd slept over.

Vi and I talked about, maybe, taking things to the next level after prom.

Hendricks thought of all the different ways Justin could hurt

Portia and began to feel sick. She started pushing harder, no longer worried about being polite. Eventually, they made it across the gym and out into the hall, letting the door to the gym fall shut behind them. The door muffled the sound of screaming voices and pounding footsteps, but the vibration still shuddered in Hendricks's ears, making it impossible for her to think.

"There's no one out here," Connor said. Hendricks nodded, scanning the hallway. A few plastic cups from the snack table had rolled up against the walls, and most of the balloons and streamers the prom committee had put up had already fallen from the ceiling and scattered across the floor.

Hendricks swallowed, her breathing starting to steady. "Do you know where else they'd go?" she asked Connor. "Back to Portia's house?"

Connor shook his head. "They took Portia's car, but her parents are supposed to be home all night, so I really don't think they'd go there."

"What about Vi's place?"

Connor frowned. "Her parents are pretty strict. I don't think they'd risk getting caught."

Hendricks was starting to feel desperate now. "Is there anywhere else they'd go? An after-party? Or maybe there's a spot around here where people park."

Connor chewed his lip. "There are a couple of places we could check out," he said, starting down the hall. "But I'm not—"

They rounded the corner and there she was.

Vi was curled in a fetal position on the floor, her skin pale and moist, the skin under her eyes bruised. She wasn't moving.

The window above her had been broken. A streamer hanging over it fluttered lightly in the breeze.

"Oh my God." Connor ran down the hall and dropped to Vi's side. He took her head off the floor and lightly patted her cheeks. "Vi? Vi, come on, wake up. Vi?"

Hendricks stood above them, horrified. It was just like it had been last time. She had a sudden flash of Raven, looking so still and pale in her hospital bed, of Eddie lying unmoving in the dirt.

Her heart gave a violent lurch. She didn't think she'd be able to stand losing anyone else.

Please don't be dead, she thought. She balled her hands at her mouth, holding her breath.

Vi's eyelashes fluttered. Her lip twitched.

And then she moaned. "Portia?"

Connor exhaled, his shoulders sagging in relief. "You're awake," he said. "Thank God."

But Vi was shaking her head now, trying to sit up. "Portia?" she said. When she saw that Portia wasn't there, she said again, more insistently, "Portia?"

"What happened to Portia?" Connor asked her. "Do you remember?"

Vi lifted a hand to her head, cringing when her fingers met her scalp. When she pulled it away, Hendricks could see the red stain of blood on her skin.

"W—we were walking down the hall. Portia was going to drive us someplace, so we could be alone. She was upset, because—" Vi glanced up at Hendricks, then swallowed and looked away. "She was upset," she said.

Hendricks felt an overwhelming wave of guilt crash over her. Portia was upset because of *her*, that's what Vi had been about to say. She was the reason Portia left the dance early.

"What happened next?" she asked, her voice raw.

"Some—some*thing* appeared outside the window. I didn't see what it was—it was dark. But then the glass broke and . . . and Portia screamed." Vi's face crumpled. "I—I tried to fight it off, but it was too big. It hit me. And then it dragged Portia out the window. And I—I . . ."

Vi couldn't seem to go on anymore. A sob escaped her lips, and she lowered her face to her hands. "I'm sorry."

"You did everything you could," Connor said, pulling his phone out of his pocket. To Hendricks, he said, "I'm going to text the others. We have to find her before . . ."

He swallowed and averted his eyes, leaving his sentence unfinished.

He didn't have to finish it. Hendricks already knew what he was going to say.

We have to find her before he kills her, Hendricks thought, and fear roared up inside of her, making her feel dizzy. Her knees knocked together, and she had to press a hand against the wall to steady herself.

Justin was back. Their séance hadn't worked.

She leaned out the broken window and peered into the pitch-black night. There was nothing out there, not a single stray student or chaperone standing on the streets, no witnesses.

Hendricks breathed deeply. If she searched her heart of hearts, she knew where the ghost was taking Portia. Steele House was the center of everything. There, Justin Morrelly was going to sacrifice Portia, just like he'd tried to sacrifice Samantha.

Footsteps pounded down the hallway behind her, and Hendricks turned just as Finn and Blake rounded the corner. Connor quickly explained what happened.

"I don't understand," Blake said. "We put him back, didn't we? That crack, or whatever it was, it closed. Isn't this supposed to be over?"

Hendricks flinched. Out of nowhere, Eddie's message came back to her:

Close the seal.

"It didn't work," she said, turning to face them. "Our séance wasn't strong enough."

"The séance where Ileana vomited blood and killed a freaking *rabbit* wasn't strong enough?" Finn said, his eyes flashing. "How is that possible? What more could we do?"

"We could use a conduit," Hendricks said. All at once the truth of what they had to do crashed over them.

Connor looked confused. "I don't understand. We already used a conduit, didn't we?" he said. "The rabbit—"

"The rabbit wasn't enough," Hendricks answered. "We need a human. We need . . . we need Raven."

CHAPTER 27

NONE OF THE LIGHTS WERE ON INSIDE OF RAVEN'S HOUSE, but they circled the block anyway and pulled to a stop up the street. They'd taken Connor's car. He drove, and Hendricks had the passenger seat, while Vi, Blake, and Finn were squeezed into the back.

Connor cut the engine, and for a long moment, none of them spoke. Hendricks knew they were all thinking about the horrible thing they were about to do, and whether they could really go through with it.

Finally, Hendricks cleared her throat. "What are we going to do about her mom?" she asked.

"I can distract her," Connor said.

Hendricks cut her eyes at him. "How?"

Connor scratched his chin. "Moms really like me."

"That's true," Finn said. He leaned forward, his head between the two front seats. "The rest of us can focus on getting Raven out, but how are we going to get inside?"

"Break a window?" Blake offered.

Connor shook his head. "You won't have to do that. They leave a key under the plastic turtle by the back door. I've seen Raven use it before, when she's gotten locked out. Hendricks, you go with Finn and Blake. Vi, do you think you could stay out front? Text me when they've gotten her out, so I know it's all clear?"

Vi nodded, her eyes distant. "Yeah," she said. "I can do that."

"Okay." Connor exhaled. "Let's go."

Hendricks, Finn, and Blake crept around to the back of the house. Blake reached the corner first and hesitated, one hand up to tell them to stop while he peered into the darkness. Hendricks froze, her skin pricking with nerves.

After a few minutes that seemed to stretch, he waved them forward. The little stone turtle was right where Connor had said it would be, on the ground next to the back stairs. Hendricks flipped it over and found the key nestled in the dirt.

She stood, slid it into the lock, and turned.

The door creaked inward, revealing a dark hallway.

Hendricks hardly dared to breathe. She crept into the hallway, the bottom of her gown clenched in her fist, Finn and Blake crowded close behind her. She'd removed her shoes back in the car, worried that the high heels would be too loud. It was the right move. Her bare feet made almost no noise in the hall.

A light flipped on at the front of the house, and Hendricks froze, her heart beating fast in her ears. A moment later, Connor's voice drifted toward them from the front door.

". . . just wanted to stop by to see how you were doing . . ." he was saying.

"That's so sweet of you, Connor," Raven's mom responded. And then, more hesitantly, "Are you . . . in a tux?"

Hendricks didn't wait to hear Connor's response. She swallowed and nodded at the others to keep going.

Raven's bedroom was the third door on the right. Blake and Finn slipped inside, their black tuxes nearly indistinguishable from the darkness. Hendricks hovered at the door, thinking.

How were they going to do this? Raven had an oxygen tube in

her nose, and an IV connected to her arm, the needle piercing the skin just below the crook of her elbow. They couldn't disconnect her.

"We'll have to take the oxygen and the IV with us," she whispered, her eyes moving over the equipment. Luckily, the oxygen tank was a small, portable version. She could carry that. She wasn't sure what was in the IV drip connected to Raven's arm—morphine, maybe? Or something else to manage her pain?

She began packing up the oxygen tank and the IV pouch while Blake eased Raven out of her bed. He carried her like a baby, her head resting against his silk tuxedo jacket, her bare feet dangling over his arm. Hendricks slipped the IV pouch into her clutch, making sure to stay close enough to Raven and Blake that she wouldn't accidentally pull the tubes from her arm. She leaned over to grab the oxygen tank.

"I got it," Finn told her, and hoisted it off the floor, grunting slightly. "Check the hall."

Hendricks nodded. Leaving her clutch with Blake, she crept across the room and poked her head into the hall. There was no one there, but she could see shadows stretching from the living room, and she could hear Raven's mother and Connor talking.

". . . how are your brothers doing?" Hendricks heard Raven's mom ask.

"Good," Connor said. "Patrick is liking school."

Hendricks closed her eyes for a beat, her chest tightening. It seemed criminal to sneak Raven out of her home. But what else were they supposed to do? If the roles were reversed, she knew that Portia would let herself be used as a conduit if it meant saving a friend. She could only hope that Raven felt the same way.

"Coast is clear," Hendricks whispered, nodding at the boys to go. "Come on."

. . .

Mist hung low over the Steele House grounds, obscuring the foundation and the grass in a milky-white cloud. It was thick as smoke, and it stretched beyond the boundaries of the grounds, rolling into the street and drifting through the trees.

"Whoa," murmured Blake, from the back seat. "That mist is intense."

"Where's Portia?" asked Vi.

That was a good question. Hendricks leaned forward in her seat, squinting through the windshield to try to make out some shape in the fog. She thought she saw movement, something deep within the mist stirring, but it was too thick for her to see anything else.

Connor slowed to a stop at the curb and cut the engine. One by one, they climbed out and made their way across the grounds.

The crack had reappeared in the foundation. It was bigger than it had been before. It was now wide enough for Hendricks to stand inside, arms outstretched, and not be able to touch either wall.

Portia lay beside it, curled on her side, her cheek pressed against the foundation. Tears and snot streamed down her face, streaking her makeup. Thick ropes bound her wrists and ankles, leaving deep red welts in her skin. She had a dirty rag stuffed in her mouth, but she tried to talk through it when she saw them, her eyes widening.

"Oh my God!" Vi had both hands pressed to her mouth, her eyes wide with horror. She took a stumbling step toward Portia, but Hendricks jerked out a hand, stopping her.

"Where's Justin?" Hendricks hissed, looking around. As far as she could see, Portia was here alone.

"You can't see him?" Connor asked. Hendricks shook her head.

His eyes flicked back to Portia. He must be using her as bait, expecting Hendricks to run up to her and make sure she was okay.

"We need to do the ritual now," Hendricks said. "Before he figures out what we're doing."

Vi looked at her like she was insane. "He's going to kill her!"

"Not if we get him first," Hendricks said. To the others, she said, "Come on. We have to hurry."

Finn and Blake carried Raven and her medical equipment up to the edge of the foundation.

"Get her as close as you can to the crack," Hendricks said. Blake nodded and gingerly placed Raven onto the cement, taking a moment to brush the hair away from her face. Finn set her oxygen tank and held the IV above her.

Hendricks nodded. This was good. "Okay, now we form the circle."

"What about Ileana?" asked Finn, frowning.

"There isn't time to get her," Hendricks said. "Raven will have to be our seventh."

And I'm a medium, she thought. *There has to be some part of me that knows how to do this.*

They knelt. Vi helped Portia press one hand into the ground and took the other while Blake did the same for Raven. The rest of them followed: one hand on the ground, one hand grasping their neighbor's wrist. Just like before, Hendricks felt a pulse move through her once the circle was completed. Some invisible power, protecting them.

She closed her eyes, trying to remember what Ileana had done next.

"I—I call upon light and earth to the north," she said hesitantly. As soon as the words were out of her mouth a flash of lightning broke across the sky, making her flinch. The ground began to rumble.

Her chest hitched. She didn't know what was happening, didn't understand the forces she was calling. She had a sudden memory of Ileana doubled over, blood spilling from her mouth as pain tore through her body. Oh God . . . what was she doing?

She wet her lips and forced herself to keep going. "Air to the east, fire to the south, and water to the west."

Wind rustled the trees above them. Thunder growled somewhere in the distance. It began to rain.

At first, there were only scattered drops, pricking at Hendricks's shoulders and hair. Then it changed, coming suddenly faster. The sound of water tapping against the packed earth was like hurried footsteps, followed by a heavy torrent that instantly drenched them all.

Hendricks gasped, her hair wet and heavy against her skin. She felt like she was drowning. She could barely breathe. Her fingers were slick around Connor's wrist.

"Draw a circle around those gathered here and keep us safe," she demanded.

Wind howled past them, kicking up heavy clumps of wet dirt, ripping the leaves from the trees. Lightning struck a low-hanging branch, which fell to the earth in a sudden crash, flames licking at the bark.

Hendricks felt the air around her go cold. It wasn't just the rain and the wind. She was sure that Justin was here, that her call for protection hadn't worked at all. *He* was doing this to them.

She blinked rapidly, searching the circle for his familiar leather jacket and dark hair, but it was too dark, and the rain was thick. It left everything hazy and unfocused. She could barely see two feet in front of her.

"Whatever you do, don't let go of the circle," she said, remembering Ileana's warning from the last séance. "He can't hurt us unless we break the circle."

"You sure about that?" said a voice directly into her ear.

Hendricks jerked her head around and found herself staring into Justin's dead black eyes. He grinned at her.

"Boo," he spat.

Hendricks forced herself to hold his gaze. Her nostrils filled with the bitter scent of him, rotting meat and decaying flesh. The taste of bile rose up in her throat, but she choked it down.

She wouldn't look away. She wouldn't be afraid.

"W—we are harboring a restless spirit," she said, speaking directly to Justin now. Though her voice felt hoarse and small, she could feel confidence building. "Take him back."

"Take him back," the others recited with her. Hendricks was heartened to hear how strong their voices were, how sure they seemed of her. Portia squeezed her wrist. She thought she saw something in Justin's face tighten. Fear, she thought, clenching her teeth together.

Good.

"Go back where you came from," Hendricks told him.

There it was again, that twitch of fear. It tightened the muscles in his jaw and narrowed his eyes. But he only smiled wider.

"I'm taking Sam with me," Justin said. "I need her."

Tell him now, Hendricks thought. If she told Justin that she was the medium, not Portia, then he might leave her alone.

But when she opened her mouth, she saw Samantha's mutilated face, her blood-covered dress. She felt her voice die in her throat.

Justin grabbed Hendricks by the shoulders and wrenched her out of the circle before she could say another word. Hendricks barely had time to catch her breath before he'd lifted her into the air above his head. The ground swam below her distantly, barely visible through the driving rain. She thought she heard her friends calling her name, but the sounds of thunder and wind drowned them out.

She felt like she was flying for a fraction of a second before the wet concrete rose up and slammed into her face. Dull, stinging pain tore across her cheek and chin. And then she was rolling, tumbling across the Steele House foundation. She threw out a hand on instinct. Pain rocketed up her wrist, but she managed to stop herself before she tumbled into the chasm. Everything was slick and muddy.

Lifting her head, she saw that the circle had devolved into chaos. Blake had dropped to the ground next to Raven and seemed to be trying to check that she was still breathing. Squinting through the rain, Hendricks realized that something had happened to her; Raven was convulsing, her arms and legs jerking against the ground. Her eyes had opened, but her pupils had rolled way back into her skull.

Oh God, she thought. The pain in her face seemed to diminish a little, or maybe it was just her panic, forcing her up. She crawled for Raven, arms trembling. Her wrist felt like it might be broken.

Justin moved through the circle with unearthly speed. Finn was in front of him, but Justin brushed him aside with an easy sweep of his hand. The six-foot-tall teenager went skidding across the ground like a stone across a still pond. When he lifted his head, Hendricks saw that it was badly scratched and red with blood.

Blake ran toward Finn, but a backhand to the jaw sent him spinning to the ground. Hendricks heard the dull thump of Blake's head meeting concrete and Blake's mouth fell open, the color drained from his face.

Vi was cowering away from the circle, but Justin found her. He picked her up as easily as if she were a doll and threw her, like he'd thrown Hendricks. Hendricks watched in horror as Vi went flying past them and hit the cement with a hard slap. She didn't move again.

Hendricks lunged forward, but she was too late. Justin had reached Portia first. He hoisted her over one shoulder and looked down at Hendricks, baring his teeth in a gruesome approximation of a smile.

He didn't resemble a boy anymore. His eyes were a pure, flat black, and blood oozed from around the sockets, trailing down his cheeks in thick tears. Skin slid away from his skull like old paint, revealing a yellowed skull and tender pink muscle tissue beneath.

He had the face of someone long dead.

"She's mine," he said. And then he stepped into the chasm and was gone.

"No!" Hendricks shouted. She pushed herself to her feet, ignoring the pain coursing up and down the side of her body. She glanced over her shoulder at the others.

Raven was still shaking on the ground. Her skin had gone deathly pale, and her eyelids were fluttering. Connor and Blake were helping Finn back to his feet, but Vi still hadn't moved.

Hendricks went cold with fear.

She had to do something. She had to stop this.

"Reform the circle," she shouted to the others. "Do the séance."

And then she jumped into the chasm herself.

CHAPTER
28

HENDRICKS HIT THE GROUND WITH A THUD. SHE GROANED
and slid her hands under her shoulders to push herself up to all
fours. Pain moved up her body. Her chest ached, and her knees
trembled as she steadied herself. She blinked, trying to make out
anything in the black.

The darkness down here was all-encompassing. The smell of
damp dirt filled her nostrils. She couldn't see them, but she had a sense
that the walls were very close around her. She held out a hand and
touched something moist.

She drew her hand back, recoiling. Whatever she'd felt had
seemed . . . *alive*. Horror moved through her. She didn't want to stay
down here long.

She looked up, blinking at the darkness above her, trying to make
out the top of the opening she'd just fallen through.

Rain beat down on her, clouding her view.

"Hendricks?"

Hendricks turned. She could just make out the silhouette of
Portia lying on her side on the ground a few feet away. The gag had
fallen out of her mouth.

"Oh my God, you're okay." Hendricks crawled over to Portia and
tried to undo the bindings at her wrist. "I thought—"

Someone grabbed her from behind and then she was flying. She slammed against the sides of the chasm, and it seemed to press into her, almost like it was reaching for her. She rolled to the ground, shaking. When she lifted her head, she saw the shadowy shape of Justin standing above her.

Demon. The word sprang to her mind, unbidden. Black-and-orange flames flickered around his eye sockets, and his skin seemed to be melting away. It slid from his skull in thick, fiery clumps. Staring at Hendricks, he snapped his teeth together with a sharp click, a warning.

A bit of his skin dropped off of his face, hitting the ground just inches from where Hendricks lay. It smoldered in the dirt.

Horrified, Hendricks crawled backward. She was shuddering all over, her muscles jerking. She drew a long, sobbing breath, and said, "What do you want?"

Justin was suddenly in front of her, crouching so that his face was only inches from hers. He grabbed her by the shoulders and shoved her into the side of the chasm.

"I want her," he said, and his burning eyes flicked to where Portia was still lying in the dirt. "I want her power."

Hendricks squirmed under his grip. Once again, she had the sensation that the dirt pressed against her skin was reaching for her, caressing her. Eddie's voice filled her head.

This town is rotten.

"You don't," Hendricks said, trying to fill her voice with confidence she didn't feel. "That's not Sam. She doesn't have any power. She's not the medium."

Justin looked confused for a fraction of a second. And then, he began to laugh. Still holding her in place with one hand, he reached into his pocket with the other and pulled out a knife, which he opened with a flick of his wrist. "*Liar.*"

All of a sudden, Hendricks heard a scratching sound.

It seemed to be coming from behind her.

Fear tightened her throat.

Oh God, what is that?

The dirt walls of the chasm were *writhing*. A wasp broke through the wall an inch away from her shoulder. Its wings pushed through the earth first, and then the rest of its wriggling body followed. It skittered over the wall before, wings twitching, it took to the air.

From her spot lying on the ground a few feet away, Portia began to scream. Hendricks opened and closed her mouth, but no sound came out.

Another wasp wriggled through the earth beside her ankle. Another followed, and another, another.

Hendricks was pounding against the dirt wall now, the heels of her feet kicking clumps of earth to the ground. Justin, laughing, only held her more firmly in place.

Wasps poured from the walls, their bodies swarming Hendricks, wings twitching at her skin. She opened her mouth to scream. But Justin's hand closed around her throat, and there was no air in her lungs. Darkness flickered at the corners of her eyes. She groped around against the dirt wall for something to hold on to, and a stinger dug into the flesh between her thumb and forefinger. She pulled her hand away as sharp prick told her that a wasp had stung her.

Portia, still curled on her side, her ankles and wrists bound, tried to scoot away from the sea of insects as they crept closer to her face.

Blood oozed from Justin's eye sockets. As Hendricks watched, the fire spread. Now it was crawling over his face and down his chin, moving to his neck and shoulders, quickly turning his black clothes to ash.

Hendricks tried to twist away from him, the flames were so hot.

Justin only held her more tightly, his fingers digging into her neck, making it hard for her to breathe.

Smoke filled Hendricks's nose as Justin lifted his knife to her cheek. Hendricks tried not to scream. She didn't want to give him the satisfaction.

Portia had managed to roll herself onto her knees. She leaned back against the opposite wall of the chasm, trying to use it as leverage as she pulled her feet beneath her.

The wasps had surrounded Hendricks now. They climbed up her legs, tangled in her hair, burrowed into her ears and nostrils. Portia sobbed quietly as she tried again to stand.

Justin pressed the sharp edge of his knife into Hendricks's cheek. She felt a burning in her face, and then the warm ooze of blood moving down her cheek. She used the last of her strength to flail wildly in his arms, but it was no use. The world around her began to flicker. The pain in her face grew—

Something cold swept over her. There was a thin, cracking sound, and from the corner of her eye Hendricks saw a layer of ice begin to creep across the walls of the chasm.

A wasp dropped out of her hair and landed on the dirt floor beside her feet. Dead.

And then, one by one, the rest of the wasps began to drop to the ground. The chasm itself seemed to go still.

Justin flinched and moved his knife away from Hendricks's face. "What's—"

"Eddie," Hendricks choked out. She knew without a doubt that it was true. She remembered the dead flower in her locker, the dead grass that had surrounded her the first time she'd seen Justin in the cemetery. Ileana said those things could be signs that someone was trying to reach her from beyond the void.

Which meant that Eddie had been with her all along, trying to keep her safe, just like always.

On the other side of the chasm, Portia had finally managed to crawl to her feet. Releasing a guttural scream, she lowered her head and charged forward—

Head-slamming right into Justin.

Justin's fingers sprang away from Hendricks's throat. She dropped to the ground, moaning. There was a sound like metal clanging against ice and then the dull thump of Justin's body. The flames that had been crawling up his face had gone out.

Hendricks didn't fool herself. She knew he wasn't really gone. She rolled onto her stomach, gulping down breath after breath. The air was thin with cold, the ice stretching. Her throat burned.

"Did I get him?" asked Portia, gasping.

"Yeah." Knees shaking, Hendricks pushed herself to a stand. It was getting harder to move. Hendricks didn't know how long they had before the entire chasm froze over. "We have to get out of here before he comes to. Give me your hands."

Portia turned her bound wrists to Hendricks, and Hendricks quickly dug her thumbs into the ropes and worked them free. Portia knelt and got to work on her ankles.

There was a moaning sound that made Hendricks freeze.

Justin was starting to move.

Hurry. Hendricks's hands trembled as she pulled at the bindings on Portia's ankles. The ropes were thick beneath her clumsy fingers. With one final tug, she pulled the last of the ropes free.

"Go!" she shouted, and Portia leapt for the chasm wall, using the twisting, frozen roots to pull herself up toward the surface.

Hendricks scrambled after her. It might have been her imagination, but the ice seemed to be creating little footholds into the dirt wall, making it easier to climb.

Thank you, she thought.

Portia scrambled over the side of the chasm above her. Her head reappeared a moment later. She reached down a hand.

"Come on!" Portia called.

Hendricks let go of the wall, grasping for Portia's hand. Her fingers grazed Portia's—

Something grabbed her from behind, yanking her back. Hendricks's fingers slipped.

"Hendricks!" Portia screamed, but it was too late, Hendricks was already falling. The back of her head slammed into the icy dirt. She groaned, her eyes closing.

When she opened them, again, Justin was towering over her, his face blackened and rotting. He was staring deep into Hendricks's face, as though seeing her for the first time. Understanding flickered in his eyes.

"I see," he said, grinning a terrible grin. "She's not the medium. *You* are."

CHAPTER
29

JUSTIN WRAPPED HIS BONY, GNARLED HANDS AROUND Hendricks's shoulders and dragged her to her feet, shoving her against the side of the wall.

She was trapped. She wouldn't be able to get past him.

As Hendricks watched, the fire began to spread from Justin's face to the chasm around them, melting ice as it jumped from the earthen floor to the walls, flickering, growing. A flame snaked toward her.

Hendricks released a cry as the heat drew closer. She looked around for a weapon, but there was nothing. Just melting ice and dead insects, the bloody stump of a rat's tail.

Something sour churned in her stomach.

Eddie, help, she thought. But she didn't feel Eddie's presence down here with her anymore.

"You're not going anywhere," Justin said, his lips twisting into a gleeful sneer. Hendricks saw that his teeth were all broken and blackened and half-rotted from his mouth. His gums were bloody. He brought his fist against the side of the chasm, knocking a clump of dirt to the floor. "Not ever, not now that I have you."

He punched the chasm wall again and again. The dirt shuddered and moved, crumbling around them.

Hendricks looked up. The sliver of sky had grown narrower. It was as though the walls were creeping inward, the crack knitting back together.

The portal was closing.

"Justin, you have to stop," she said.

But the thing holding her was no longer Justin. That boy, she realized, was gone forever. In his place was this skeletal, burning monster. Maggots crawled out of his black eyes, and, wriggling, dropped to the ground. Flames licked at his lips. Strands of black hair still clung to his scalp but it was dank and matted, plastered to his skeletal features with sweat.

"You're mine," he said, his voice a hoarse croak.

Hendricks wracked her brain, trying to think of what to do. A dark thought came to her. But once she thought it, she couldn't let it go.

Maybe I should let the portal close with me inside.

What was left for her up there in Drearford? She was a medium, like Samantha. Ghosts like Justin would follow her for the rest of her life. Everywhere she went, she'd see flickers of the dead. Whenever she met someone new, she'd wonder whether they were really there.

Maybe it was time for her to die. Let someone else be called.

And, if she stayed down here, she could be with Eddie forever.

No.

The voice inside of Hendricks's head was small but insistent.

No, she wouldn't give up. *No,* this couldn't be the end.

No, no, no.

She was a fighter. Now was the time to fight, not just for her life, but for things in her life that mattered. Things like prom and graduating and college. Things like her friends. Connor and Portia and Raven and, well, Finn and Blake, and Ileana now, too.

She curled her fingers into the dirt wall behind her. She loved Eddie. She would always love Eddie. But Eddie was dead and she wasn't.

Not yet.

It was time to let him go.

She wanted to live.

Gathering what remained of her strength, she threw an elbow into Justin's face. A jolt of pain shuddered up her arm as her skin broke against the last of his rotten teeth. Justin sputtered and stumbled backward, slamming into the opposite wall.

Hendricks didn't waste time. She grabbed again for the lowest root and pulled herself off the dirt floor. Pain flared through the muscles in her arms. Her shoulders burned.

Up one foot off the ground. Two. Her toes kicked at the rocks and dirt of the wall, sending it tumbling to the ground. Twice, she nearly slipped and went tumbling back to the ground, but both times, she seemed to grasp hold of a tree root at the exact moment before her balance tipped backward.

She twisted her hand around the root and pulled herself higher.

There was a shuffling sound below, and then Justin was on her, tearing at her ankles—

"You belong with me!" he was shouting in his hoarse, inhuman voice. "You're mine. You can't get away—"

Hendricks held fast. The root rubbed the skin on her palms raw. She cried out in pain, but she didn't let go.

Gritting her teeth, she yanked her foot out of his grip—

And then slammed it back into his face.

She felt the impact shudder through her and heard the shuffling sound of Justin stumbling backward. Hendricks pulled herself higher.

One foot closer, and she could hear her friends' voices echoing through the night. Her arms trembled. She grit her teeth and climbed farther.

Up and up.

Now she could tell that they were chanting. Their voices layered over each other, sounding stronger than she'd ever heard them before.

"Take him back! Take him back!"

Warmth spread through her. They hadn't given up. They were still fighting for her.

Hendricks glanced back down into the chasm and saw that the ritual was working. Justin was fading. He looked thinner than before, so insubstantial that Hendricks could practically see straight through him. Bits of him were drifting away, disappearing into the wind like ashes. He tried to gather himself, tried to pull his legs beneath his body and stand, but he couldn't seem to find the strength.

Yes, Hendricks thought. But when she turned back toward the surface, her heart stuttered. The crack was closing. There wasn't any more time. She had to reach the surface now if she didn't want to be trapped down here forever.

Somehow, she was able to find some lingering strength and pull herself up the last few feet, exhaling in relief when she felt solid concrete below her fingers and the cool brush of wind on her cheeks.

She'd made it.

She pulled herself up, collapsing on the foundation of Steele House, seconds before the portal slammed closed behind her. Hendricks thought she smelled a waft of cigarettes and baby shampoo. *Goodbye*, she thought. And then everything went black.

Seconds or hours later, Hendricks came to.

Slowly, slowly, the darkness around her faded. Pain replaced it.

It wasn't there one moment and, the next, it was in every part of her body—her legs, her arms, her *face*. She wished, for a sliver of a moment, that she was unconscious again, if only to have a few more moments relief.

She eased her eyes open. The world swam for a moment and then settled. She saw gray concrete splattered with dirt and blood. *Her* blood. She groaned and for a long moment she just lay there, breathing. She doubted she'd be able to move.

She was suddenly aware that she was alone. No one was leaning over her, poking her, wondering if she was okay.

Fear moved through her.

Where were her friends?

"Guys?" she moaned. Gingerly, she rose. In the darkness, it took her a few moments before she was able to make out a huddled mass at the corner of the foundation and hear the whispered sound of nervous voices.

They were looking at something.

Hendricks stared at them for a fraction of a second, trying to figure out what had them so transfixed. And then understanding washed over her and she felt a pang deep in her chest.

Raven.

All at once her pain was forgotten. She pushed herself to her feet, her legs shaking as she stumbled across the foundation.

Raven couldn't be dead. She couldn't be.

"Hendricks." Connor turned, seeing her approach. "You won't—"

"Is she okay?" Hendricks shoved past him and dropped to the ground next to Raven. Her heart was beating hard inside her chest, and it took her a moment to understand what she was seeing.

Raven was sitting. She was actually *sitting*. Her eyes were open, and she had one hand pressed to her head, like she was recovering from a headache instead of three months in a coma.

Slowly, she lifted her eyes to Hendricks's face, a hesitant smile flickering over her lips.

"Hendricks," Raven said in a deep, croak of a voice. She smiled weakly. "What'd I miss?"

CHAPTER
30

HENDRICKS SAW THE FLASHING RED-AND-BLUE LIGHTS AS
soon as they turned the corner.

"Shit," Raven muttered, from the front seat. "This is going to be
fun to explain to my mom."

"You think she'll be mad?" asked Hendricks. She'd insisted that
Raven take the front seat, so she was squeezed in the back of Connor's
car, along with Blake and Finn. Vi and Portia had set off on foot, need-
ing a few moments alone.

"Do I think she'll be mad?" Raven pursed her lips, pretending to
think. "I think she will have many emotions, one of which will most
definitely be anger. Especially since I can't exactly explain *why* I had to
sneak out."

"We needed you to help us stop an evil spirit from sacrificing
Portia to the void separating the living from the dead," Finn said, deadpan. "I don't see what's so hard to explain about that."

Raven laughed but it sounded feeble. Hendricks could only
imagine how weak she must have felt.

"Maybe just focus on the part where you're awake," Connor said,
pulling up to the curb in front of Raven's house. "That's the most
important thing."

Raven exhaled through her lips, nodding. "Yup. Let's hope
that'll be enough."

Cheryl stood on her front porch, talking animatedly to a young man in uniform. She glanced up at the sight of Connor's car, frowning slightly. Then, seeing Raven sitting in the passenger seat, her face crumpled.

"Raven!" she shouted and began to race across the yard.

Connor and Blake climbed out of the car to help Raven get out. She hadn't used her legs in over three months, so she was a little unsteady on her feet. The boys each slipped one of her arms around their shoulders and helped bring her to her mother. Finn and Hendricks stayed put in the back seat.

Cheryl threw her arms around her daughter's neck, causing all three teenagers to stumble backward a little. She was sobbing. Hendricks felt a sudden twist of guilt. She couldn't imagine how terrifying it must've been for her to go into Raven's room and find her hospital bed empty.

"My baby," Cheryl cried. "Oh my God, my baby! My baby!"

Raven answered, "Mom, it's okay, I'm fine."

Finn was suddenly leaning across Hendricks's lap to peer out the car window. He frowned and then turned to her. "Do you think Raven's mom totally hates you now?"

"Why would she hate me?" Hendricks asked.

"Well, Raven nearly died at a party at your house. And then her unconscious body disappeared in the middle of the night, and when she turned up again, she was with you." Finn shrugged. "If it were me, I'd start thinking that you weren't the best influence."

Hendricks hunched farther down in her seat, ducking her head and hoping that Cheryl hadn't spotted her yet.

Several long minutes later, the car door swung open. Hendricks peeked up from her crossed arms to see Connor leaning into the car.

"Hey," he said. "It's cool, she's calling off the cops."

"What did you tell her?" Hendricks asked.

Connor glanced up—probably checking to see that Cheryl was too far to overhear him—and then he leaned back down and said, in an undertone, "Raven claimed she was sleepwalking. She said Blake and I found her a couple of blocks away, and that's when she woke up. It was freaking *genius*." Connor shook his head, impressed. "Her mom's not letting her out of her sight for the rest of the night obviously, but we're all meeting Portia and Vi over at Tony's. You in?"

Hendricks wrapped her arms around her chest, shivering a little. She was still wearing her prom dress and, even though prom was over, she thought she deserved a little celebration.

And there was something else, too. A warmth in the air, the smell of fresh grass and flowers, *something*. She felt a lift of a hope in her chest.

New beginnings, she thought. The portal was closed, and Raven was awake.

Maybe, just maybe, things were going to get better.

"Yeah," she said, nodding. She threw open her car door and stepped outside, a breeze rustling her dress. "Tony's sounds perfect. I'll have to meet you there though. There's something I want to do first."

Hendricks stood outside of Drearford High, rolling her lower lip between her teeth. The school's windows were dark. She had Eddie's lighter in one hand. She flicked it open, watching the tiny blue flame shiver between her fingers, and then she flicked it shut again.

"Okay," she said, under her breath. She headed inside.

Up the school's front steps and through the balloon arch. Down dark hallways strewn with streamers. Into the empty gym. Hendricks looked around at the detritus around her and then walked to the center of the room, her torn prom dress dragging against the floor. She knelt before the school's mascot logo, a printed image of a lion leaping through the letter *D*.

"Eddie," she said, out loud, flicking the lighter open and closed. "I will always miss you. But I've been thinking about that tarot card I pulled for you, the Two of Swords. You have a decision to make. You can choose to go on to whatever comes after death, to be with your little sister and Kyle and . . . I don't know, hang out with David Bowie and Alan Rickman and stuff. Or you can stay here with me." Hendricks sniffed, laughing a little. "Seems like a pretty obvious choice, huh? I don't know . . . if you'd asked me before what happened tonight, I would've have said that you should stay. I wouldn't have cared that you weren't all here, just that there was some part of you still in my life. But now"—she looked around the room and tears welled in her eyes—"I realize how selfish that is. You should go, be with your brother and sister. Rest."

Her voice choked a little on that last word. She clamped a hand over her mouth, put the lighter in the middle of the logo, and stood.

It was time to move on.

EPILOGUE

DREARFORD HIGH WAS EMPTY, DARK. STICKY SOLO CUPS LAY strewn across the floor, mingling with crumbled napkins. Streamers had dropped down from the ceiling and come to coil amid the debris like snakes. Dead cockroaches lay on their backs, their legs still twitching.

A few of the younger students had propped the back door open with a brick, so they could sneak joints and warm vodka during the slow songs. They'd forgotten to remove the brick before heading to the after-party, though, and a breeze swept in through the still open door, blowing a paper plate down the hall like a tumbleweed and rattling a locker that hadn't been closed properly. No one would be back to clean the mess until the next morning. That's when they would first discover the streaks of blood in the hall just outside the gymnasium, the broken window, the floor littered with glass. Now, though, everything was silent.

And so, no one heard the creak as the back door swung open wider. No one saw the leather boot kick the brick aside, and step into the hall. The door slammed shut in its frame, the sound reverberating through the empty building.

Footsteps echoed off the walls. Their movement down the hall was slow, steady. There was no rush. The gym door swung open and closed with a soft *thwump*, and the boots walked to the center of the gymnasium, stopping just outside the Drearford High logo.

The scuffed silver lighter lay at the center of the logo, partially covering the lion's only visible eye. Though there was no light on inside of the gym, some outside glow seemed to catch on the silver so that it almost looked like the lighter itself was illuminated.

Eddie Ruiz leaned over and picked the lighter up. He opened it, allowing the twitching blue flame to illuminate the soft outlines of his face and reflect in his dark eyes. He flicked it closed again, and with a sigh, he slid it into the pocket of his jeans, where it settled easily into the worn grooves of denim.

He'd missed this thing.

ACKNOWLEDGMENTS

As always, thank you to my wonderful Alloy family—specifically Laura Barbiea and Josh Bank—for supporting me from the prologue to the final pages. I'm so incredibly lucky to have access to such brilliant minds!

Also, a huge thank-you to my team at Razorbill. This series has benefited immensely from Jessica Harriton's brilliant notes, as well as the support of Casey McIntyre and Jennifer Klonsky. Additional thanks go to Bri Lockhart, Felicity Vallence, Elyse Marshall, Kristin Boyle, and the rest of Razorbill's sales, marketing, and publicity teams. I'm continually blown away by how hard you work to help readers find my books.

In addition to the people named here, there are so many others working behind the scenes to make this book happen. I am grateful to all of you. I couldn't have done it without your support.

And finally, as always, thanks to my fabulous, encouraging family and friends, and specifically to Ron, who really believes in this one.

For more thrills and scares,
check out Danielle Vega's
THE MERCILESS series

and
*SURVIVE
THE
NIGHT*